LOST PROPHECY:
AWAKENING

Print Edition

KIMBERLY BERNARD

ACKNOWLEGEMENTS

With love and gratitude to my husband, and children, my inspirations. To all the amazing English and Literature teachers, who encouraged me to write since childhood. To my husband, who continued to push me and believe in my ability to create a literary work of art and also tolerated late nights of writing and PC problems. To my grandparents, who where there for me when no one else could be. Many thanks to my good friend and editor, Rebecca Duffield.

Lost Prophecy: Awakening
By: Kimberly Bernard
ISBN: 978-0-9972155-0-2
All rights reserved.
Copyright © 2014, Kimberly Bernard
Cover Art Copyright © 2015, Kimberly Bernard

~ To all the wanderers, dreamers, and those that imagine beyond what they are told.

"It is easier to perceive error than to find truth, for the former lies on the surface and is easily seen, while the latter lies in the depth, where few are willing to search for it." - Johann Wolfgang Von Goethe

CHAPTER ONE
November 1, 1996
Cozumel, Mexico

The cries were faint at first; so faint that Anthony dismissed them as the sounds of the wind. He could not have asked for a better night. The sea glistened under the full moon while the waves lazily lapped at the shore of the secluded beach. His wife, Vanessa, was more beautiful than ever, as she lay next to him in the moonlit sand. After five years of marriage, the passion and desire he felt for her were only intensifying. Her long, flowing, brunette hair fell perfectly, blown by the warm Mexican wind that caressed her bikini-clad figure. *Maybe tonight their union would be successful*, thought Anthony, as he initiated a passionate kiss. They tried to conceive for two years to no avail and Vanessa refused to see a fertility specialist. She called it, "messing with God's plan." She wanted to let nature take its course, for better or for worse. For their fifth wedding anniversary, Vanessa suggested a vacation in Cozumel. Anthony jumped at the idea! Though he had great success, he was eager to get a break from his demanding advertising business. His work had become all-consuming and borderline toxic. Equally, Vanessa desired to escape from the drama of the local hospital where she worked as a nurse.

The cries were more distinct now and Anthony wondered about their origin. Probably some animals mating or fighting, he thought, as he caressed his wife's body. From what he observed, no one else was on the beach, and the local residences were not within earshot.

Vanessa also noticed the sounds. "Do you hear that?" She asked, pulling away from him.

"Yeah. I thought it was the wind, but now I cannot ignore it," Anthony said.

"It sounds like a baby," Vanessa said, visually scanning the shoreline.

"A baby?" Anthony said, incredulously. "Who would bring their child to the beach at this hour?"

"I don't know." Vanessa replied. "Let's go check it out."

Before Anthony could object, Vanessa was up and skipping along the beach. Disappointed that their perfect mood was being disrupted by what was probably some idiot causing a raucous far down the beach, Anthony reluctantly got to his feet.

"Bet you can't catch me!" Vanessa teased, as she broke into a sprint.

"I'll take your bet and raise you one," Anthony joked, while chasing after her.

Vanessa's endless positivity and adventurous spirit were contagious! She never ran out of energy. She had an appetite for life that could never be quenched. It was her vivaciousness that turned his head from day one. What began as a high-school mission trip to construct houses for the impecunious people of Tijuana, Mexico turned into the love of a lifetime. Everyone doubted their love-at-first-sight story, but ten years later, they were still going strong. Watching her run down the beach, he could not help but grin at her effervescent personality.

Just as he was about to grab her, Vanessa abruptly stopped.

"Giving up already?" Anthony laughed, circling his arms around her.

"No. . . Look!" Vanessa gasped.

Following her gaze, Anthony saw what caused Vanessa to stop in her tracks. About fifty feet in front of them and only fifteen feet from the water, a baby lay on the beach, sleepily crying.

"What in the world!?" They both uttered at the same time.

Instinctively, Vanessa bolted to the baby and coddled him in her arms. The baby boy appeared to be only hours old. He was wrapped in a blanket of sea plants. He was naked, except for a thick strand of hemp around his neck. Dangling from the hemp was a stone comparable to the size of a slightly elongated chicken egg. The stone was jagged and looked like some type of quartz. Anthony watched in awe, as Vanessa's comforting embrace lulled the infant back to sleep.

"Where did he come from?!" Vanessa asked, bewilderedly.

"I don't know." Replied Anthony, equally confused.

Gazing at the sleeping child, Anthony noticed he gripped something tightly in his right fist. Careful not to wake the child, Anthony pried the object from the baby's grasp.

"What's that?" Vanessa asked.

"Looks like a note," Anthony said.

Anthony unrolled the delicate paper. He was astonished to find strings of small pictures and symbols, but no words. They reminded him of hieroglyphics, an ancient form of writing.

"What does it say?" Vanessa questioned, urgently.

"I have no idea. It looks like hieroglyphics or something." Anthony said, showing Vanessa the mysterious writings.

Vanessa's jaw dropped. She was rarely at a loss for words, but the perplexing message left her speechless. Unable to decipher the contents, Anthony rolled the paper back up and put it in his pocket. *This was ridiculous! How could someone leave a tiny baby on the beach? Especially at night! Where were his parents!?* In search of anyone who might be able to provide answers, Anthony began scanning the beach in circles. There wasn't a soul to be found.

"We need to find the parents. Let's call the police." Vanessa said.

"Right. Let's wait for the morning, though. This kid needs some sleep. If we involve the police at this hour, we will all be up the entire night. For everyone's well-being, I think we should take him back to the hotel for the night and start the search in the morning."

"In the meantime, what should we call him?" Vanessa asked.

"Well, at least I have an answer to for that!" Anthony replied.

"What do you mean?" Vanessa asked, turning to face him.

Anthony was staring down at the sand. Just beyond where they found the baby was an unusual display of patterned, black, beach pebbles. The moonlight's reflection illuminated the stones. They stared down, as the name, NACXIT, glowed in the night.

CHAPTER TWO
November 1, 2011
Acworth, Georgia, USA

Nick Murphy was preparing to enter the unknown. He was in enemy territory and it was up to him now. He was the only one left. He knew someone was tracking him, but speculated he was relatively well hidden. Swiftly, he shimmied behind a pillar and held his breath, so no motion was detected. Hoping his opponent would make the first move, he crouched low and peered around the huge column. *Goin' in for the kill*, he thought, deviously. He caught the enemy looking in the opposite direction. He took his shot. It was a direct hit.

"Damn!" The opponent screamed.

"Gotcha!" Nick triumphantly declared.

"Nice shot!" Jacob exclaimed, giving him a high five.

For his fifteenth birthday, Nick invited his friends to a paintball match. He loved the game and the strategy, but it was the adrenaline rush that made paintball his all-time favorite! He insisted on leading the team because he had a secret advantage that helped him strategize. Some people would describe him as cocky or arrogant, but Nick liked to think of himself as confident. Of course, if they knew about the voice, they might think he was crazy. His parents certainly thought he was.

Nick heard the voice for as long as he could remember. As a child, his parents attributed his one-sided conversations to an imaginary friend. When Nick turned twelve and the "friend" was still around, his parents became alarmed. They subjected him to a world of doctors and harsh medications. After three years, five doctors and more than ten different medications, Nick convinced his parents that he was finally cured. Meanwhile, he would secretly flush the pills. Frankly, he was tired of all the tests and awful side effects of the medications. More so, he liked the voice. It was not destructive or manipulative. It did not force Nick against his will. It had a motherly persona, giving Nick warnings

9

or encouraging him to think things through. Oddly, he never had to initiate. The voice came to him. He tried to decipher her pattern of initiation. Once, he purposely summoned the voice, but she did not respond. Her rules concerning the timing of her presence prevailed.

Nick's attention reverted back to the buzz of friends around him.

"Good game," said one of his worthy opponents.

"Thanks," Nick said, grinning, while he exited the paintball field.

Each of the five fields at the paintball venue were tagged with a different theme. The Castle was Nick's favorite. It required more strategic movement than Bunker Hill. That field was mostly trench warfare. Just beyond the fields, the concessions facility was located under a wooded area. He saw his mom sitting at a picnic table reading a book. Nick and his friends, Jacob and Colin, walked over to her.

"Hey guys! How did it go?" His mom asked.

"Awesome!" Jacob replied. "Nick dominated as always."

"Are you sure they didn't let him win because it's his birthday?" She teased.

"Not a chance!" Colin assured her. "They wish they had such an excuse for the way they played!"

Nick straddled the picnic table bench next to his mom and gulped down one of the drinks she purchased for them. Jacob and Colin grabbed their drinks and sat down on the opposite side. Being an only child, Nick relished every minute with his friends. Since kindergarten, the three of them were buddies. They grew up playing soccer together on various recreational teams. Currently, they were an indomitable trio on their high-school team. Nick never told them about the voice nor would he. He may be cocky on the field, but when it came to personal and emotional matters, Nick was still finding his confidence. He was fearful he would be labeled with a mental disorder and treated differently.

"Hey! When are you going to get your learner's permit?" Colin asked.

"Probably this Saturday. We are going to drive up to Cartersville. The lines are always shorter there." Nick replied.

"Don't forget the school attendance form and an original copy of your birth certificate. They won't accept a black and white copy." Colin reminded him.

In that moment, Nick could have sworn he saw a worried look flash across his mother's face, but he was too consumed with the idea of becoming a driver to give it much thought. He could not wait to start driving! His dad let him drive around the school parking lot a few times. Ever since that day, he studied his driver's manual from cover to cover. Other kids at school said the written test was easy, but the potential embarrassment and ridicule he could experience from failure was great motivation to study the driver's manual daily.

"You guys ready to go?" His mom asked abruptly. "It's getting late."

"Yep," Nick replied. "Can Jacob and Colin sleep over?"

"Not tonight. It's a school night. This Saturday, after your party, they can spend the night. Now, let's get going. I have to take Jacob and Colin home, then get started on dinner."

"All right. Come on. Let's go," Nick said as they all walked toward the car.

By the time they dropped off Jacob and Colin, it was dark. Vanessa pulled into the driveway of their two-story estate. Nick's family lived in an upscale, golf community just north of Atlanta. It was a delightful community with pristine landscaping and a crime rate so low that no gate was necessary. Nick's family lived in the first of three phases, where the majority of the houses where set on the golf course. There, the houses were more opulent and sybaritic, and they were closer to the clubhouse.

"I'm going to check the mail," Nick announced, exiting the car.

Usually, Nick glossed over the mail, except for the week of his birthday. Other than packages, Nick rarely received anything by mail. His father was a computer guru, so they used the internet for everything. Of course, his parents received the occasional bill or magazine, but for the most part, the mail was obsolete at the Murphy residence. He already received fifty dollars from his father's parents. He was hoping that the card from his mother's parents would be waiting for him.

Nick sauntered to the end of the driveway and reached into the mailbox to find a couple of items for his parents and the card he was expecting. In addition to his grandparents' card, there was another envelope with no return address or stamp. It simply read, "N. MURPHY" in the center. The envelope looked worn and slightly crimped, almost like it got wet. His intrigue compelled him to wait and open it in private. Nick gathered his cards along with the mail for his parents, and returned to the car to grab his backpack.

"Anything for me?" His mom asked.

"No, it's just the usual junk and two birthday cards for me." Nick replied.

"Who sent the cards?"

"One is from Nana and Grandpa, but the other one I'm not sure about. I'll have to open it to see. There was no return address."

They walked into the house together and were greeted by his dad. He was sitting at the kitchen counter working on his laptop. After standing to kiss his wife, he gave Nick a hug and quickly went back to typing on his computer.

"Hey birthday boy! How were school and your paintball war?" His dad asked from behind the laptop.

"School was okay. Paintball was awesome! We got to play on Castle. The other team had no strategy. They were just pointing and shooting at whatever moved."

"I'm glad you had fun. While I was out today, I bought you something. It is the first of a few things your mother and I got you for your birthday. Go check it out!"

Nick eagerly ran to the table and began wrestling with the wrapping paper. The shape of the present gave it away; *it was definitely a video game, but which one?* He ripped off the final pieces of wrapping paper to reveal the latest version of *Halo,*

Reach. Like many guys his age, Nick was a video game fanatic. Often, his incessant play left his mom begging him to expand his horizons, but beside soccer and paintball, Nick's interests were limited.

"No games until you finish your homework. Then it's all yours." His dad reminded him.

"Awe, man," Nick whined, wishing his dad would break the rules for once.

Nick's dad worked hard and was frequently stressed. He was high strung and never really took the time to slow down and relax. He started his own business at a young age and was immensely successful. Obtaining financial success in his career and providing financial security for his family were his driving forces. While he liked to splurge on things occasionally, he rarely acted in prodigality. Though he had a regular office, he was frequently able to work from home. Mainly, he was a one-man show with temporary employees because no one could meet his unrealistic expectations. If you want something done right, you have to do it yourself was his motto. As a result of this philosophy, he had little time for anything other than work. By all means, Nick's dad was great, but Nick felt like he competed with the computer for his father's attention. Anytime they went somewhere as a family, his dad was glued to his phone and dealing with business matters. Nick never questioned his father's love, but he longed for a true father-son connection. His dedicated efforts to provide for the family were appreciated, but Nick wished his dad would devote more time to taking interest in his life. Nick was sure his mother felt the same way.

Nearly opposite from his dad, Nick's mom was the epitome of a universal diplomat. She possessed a rare calm about her that could put anyone at ease in a matter of moments. First hand, Nick knew how well she could mediate or negotiate him and his buddies out of a quandary. If he had a personal problem, or became frustrated with schoolwork, he went straight to her. She was employed as a full-time nurse, but she made him feel like a priority. As an only child herself, she inherently understood and

13

encouraged his need for companionship and socialization. Of all people, Nick thought his mom would be the one to understand, or at least accept, the voice. He was crushed when he realized he was wrong. Instead, she was the one to initiate all of the psychiatric evaluations and the subsequent medications. Every time he brought up the voice, he could sense her fear and discontent. Her quest to make him "normal" infuriated him. Her goal was to suppress the voice. The result was the suppression of Nick's ability to trust her.

Because the voice was motherly toward Nick, giving him warnings or encouraging him to think, he framed it in his mind as female. He had not gone so far as to give her a name, so he referred to it as "She" or "Her." All of the therapists believed the female voice developed in response to realizing he was adopted. They theorized that it was his way of coping with repressed feelings of abandonment.

He certainly could not repress his eagerness to open his mail. Nick thanked his parents for the game and made his way upstairs to start on his homework. He entered his bedroom, tossed the video game onto his bed, and clunked his backpack on the floor next to his desk. He retrieved the birthday cards from the front pouch where he put them earlier. He opened the card from his grandparents first. It was the typical "Happy Birthday, Grandson" card with colorful graphics and a short poem about how he is "the best grandson ever." He took out the one hundred dollar bill and placed it in a safe place on his desk. Then, he eyed the mysterious card marked N. MURPHY and opened it. Inside, there was a single-sided postcard made from the same strange paper as the envelope. The card was filled with odd pictures. Nick thought they might be pictographs. Confused, he stuffed the card back in the envelope and dismissed it as a mistake. Clearly, it was not a birthday card and clearly, it was not for him. Other than the pictures, the only word on the card was written at the top: NACXIT. *"What's a Nacxit?"* He muttered to himself. He chuckled, *"If that's a name, they've got the wrong N. Murphy!"*

He threw the card in the trash. As he took out his school books, the word, "BELIEVE," began echoing in his head.

CHAPTER THREE

Vanessa Murphy was nervous. She did not want to tell him the truth. She avoided this day for fifteen years. It pained her to lie to her son; she just did not know how to explain herself to him. When she and Anthony returned from Cozumel all those years ago, they concealed the full story from everyone. Nick's grandparents did not even know the whole story. Neither she nor Anthony really understood exactly what happened on the beach the night they found Nick. Of course, she knew Nick would have questions when he found out he had a Consular Report of Birth rather than a standard birth certificate. The trouble was, instead of calmly discussing issues, Nick tended to be volatile. He argued for the sake of arguing sometimes, which was unnerving. He was expecting a birth certificate to take to the Department of Motor Vehicles for his learner's permit. Although the Consular Report of Birth would satisfy the DMV, Nick was sure to probe unrelentingly about his original birth certificate and the anomalies the report presented.

The contrived story they told Nick and the immediate family was that the Cozumel trip was not a vacation. Instead, it was a trip to finalize adoption paperwork and retrieve a baby from his birth mother. They suspected Nick's birth mother might reconsider the adoption, so their plans were clandestine. Of course, this was all fabrication. Only through greasing the Mexican officials' palms were they able to procure a Consular Report of Birth. After finding Nick, they extended their stay for two weeks. They visited multiple families in Cozumel, in search of the parents. Then, a local man, Roberto, apprised them of exposing the child to potential dangers. He hypothesized that spreading news of an abandoned baby might bring black market sharks with a taste for blood. He believed the baby was likely abandoned by a desperate mother and convinced them to take Nick home as their own. Anthony and Vanessa were torn. How could they take someone else's child? What if the birth mother made a mistake and wanted him back?

Ultimately, she and Anthony agreed with Roberto. They decided to take the baby back to the U.S. and become a family, which was easier said than done. Without a birth certificate, the U.S. Consulate would not issue the Consular Report of Birth, which would declare the baby as theirs and allow them to take him back to the U.S. as a citizen. They returned to Roberto and told him about their dilemma. Roberto claimed to be well connected with some people at the U.S. Consulate and assured them that, for a fee, their problem could be solved. He asked them how they would like their names to appear on the report in addition to one thousand dollars. Vanessa was not thrilled about the name they discovered on the beach, but Anthony insisted they keep it. He felt it was a way to honor whoever gave the baby his name. Because it was an unusual name and hard to pronounce, they agreed to use Nacxit for the legal name, but they would call him Nick. Within a few days of submitting the information, they had an authentic Consular Report of Birth. Neither Vanessa nor Anthony asked questions or told anyone exactly what happened. They boarded their flight, breezed through immigration, and never looked back . . .until now.

Vanessa's mind raced with scenarios that could arise once she presented the document to her son. When Nick was six, he asked them where he was born. At that time, they revealed that he was adopted. He accepted the news well and only asked them if he would ever have to go back to Mexico. Vanessa and Anthony explained to him that they were his only parents. They loved him unconditionally, and he would never have to go back to Mexico. Obviously, simple and cutesy answers would not suffice anymore.

"I'm worried about this whole birth certificate thing with Nick," Vanessa said to Anthony, as she prepared dinner.

"What's the big deal?" Anthony replied. "We've already told him he's adopted. What's there to worry about?"

"You and I both know very well that our adoption story is weak. He might demand to see his original birth certificate and probably inquire about his biological parents. Let's not forget his legal name. That'll be a real shocker! I'm also worried about the voice he claims to hear resurfacing due to the stress of it all. It took so long to cure him of that. I just hope that he can cope."

"Relax. All you have to tell him is that his birthmother requested that we name him Nacxit, but since it was kind of weird, we just decided to call him Nick. Lots of kids go by a nickname and never use their legal names."

"And what happens when he asks about his real parents? What if he says he wants to contact them?" Vanessa bit her fingernail.

"Just tell him WE are his real parents and you can give him my office number." Anthony cracked.

Vanessa was not the slightest bit amused. Anthony was not taking the situation seriously. This Saturday was going to be a nightmare and every motherly instinct she had told her so.

CHAPTER FOUR

The remainder of the week seemed to drag on as Nick eagerly awaited the arrival of Saturday. It was the usual agenda of humdrum classes, relentless homework assignments, soccer practice, and the high school football game on Friday night. Nick despised football but the purpose of going to the game on Fridays was never to actually watch it. Most people masqueraded behind the game to socialize. Nick hung out with the rest of his soccer teammates who generally stood around eating snacks and fantasying about the cheerleaders. Jacob and Colin were the only two guys that he considered close friends. All of the other guys were part of the popular crowd and, although everyone was equal on the soccer field, the social hierarchy in the high school hallways was much different. Todd was the team captain and the all-around "perfect" guy. He had the looks, athletic skills and, most importantly, the charm. He was nice enough but in a pretentious way. Academics seemed to be his only weakness. The other guys looked up to Todd and followed his lead. Colin and Jacob were the exception. Since Nick, Colin, and Jacob were friends for so long, they stuck together.

Nick did not look anything like the All-American Todd. Although his parents told him he was born in Mexico to a Mexican family, he did not seem to possess any of the traditional Mexican traits. He had a pale complexion with red hair and blue eyes and was tall for his age. He had interest in a lot of girls at school but had trouble approaching them. Why did girls socialize in groups? Though he was confident enough, the inevitable audience was understandably intimidating. Especially since girls that clearly liked him when they were alone usually acted differently in the company of others. His other concern was the voice. He never spoke about the voice with anyone besides his parents and he was uncertain how a girlfriend might react.

After most football games, Nick and his friends frequented the local Waffle House. However, Nick had to wake up early to get his permit. He decided to ask one of his older friends to drop him off on the way to Waffle House. When he walked through the front door, it was almost 8:00 P.M., and Vanessa and Anthony were in the living room watching television.

"Hey, I'm home," Nick announced, shutting the door behind him.

"You're home early. How was the game?" His dad asked.

"I think we won. The last time I looked at the scoreboard, we were ahead by fourteen. I decided to call it a night early because of the driving exam tomorrow morning."

Nick badgered his mom for over a week about his birth certificate. He had never actually seen the document. It never crossed his mind until recently. He knew he was adopted, so it would not be a big surprise to see different people listed as his parents. Again, he decided to mention it, since tomorrow was the big day.

"Do you have my birth certificate for tomorrow?" He asked his mom.

"Of course." She said. "You've been hounding me non-stop for a week. Did you think I would forget?"

"No, just making sure it's ready for tomorrow."

"I'm sorry. I've just been stressed out at work lately." She lied.

"It's ok, Mom. Now, can I see it?" He asked.

"Sure. It's over on the kitchen counter in a manila envelope."

Nick walked over to the kitchen and went to the refrigerator to grab a soda. He hopped on a bar stool at the counter and pulled the certificate out from the envelope. As he read the document line by line, confusion washed over him. Instead of it being a typical, birth certificate document, it was titled: Consular Report of Birth. He expected to see the names of his birth parents and the name of the hospital where he was born, but he did not. His birth statistics, such as his weight and time of birth, were also missing. The report solely stated that he was born in Cozumel, Mexico on November 1, 1996 to Anthony and Vanessa Murphy and he was a citizen of the

United States. Perhaps the most disturbing piece of information on the document was his name. His parents had always called him Nick. He assumed it was short for Nicholas, but the name glaring back at him was a name he only saw once before: Nacxit.

* * * *

Nervously, Vanessa began biting the nails on her right hand. The tension was mounting. She waited for the looming confrontation with Nick. She loved him unconditionally, but Nick's disputatious personality was exhausting; she braced herself. He was never belligerent or combative, but he could certainly hold his own in an argument. Anthony seemed unconcerned as he hid behind his computer while a re-run of Seinfeld played on the television. Vanessa tried to remain calm, as Nick walked back into the room.

"So, exactly what is this and where is my birth certificate?" Nick demanded.

"Don't worry honey. The only reason the DMV wants your birth certificate is for proof of citizenship. They will accept that document in lieu of a birth certificate," she replied, trying to dodge the question, in hopes of skirting the issue altogether.

Locking eyes with his mother, Nick repeated, "What is this? Where is my birth certificate?"

"Well, when a child is born abroad to U.S. citizens, the U.S. issues that document to prove citizenship. This way, the child is authorized to be brought back to the U.S. from the foreign country," Vanessa calmly explained.

"Ok, but where is my actual birth certificate? I thought I was adopted. This document lists you guys as my parents," Nick argued.

"Because your birth certificate is in Spanish, I didn't think it was necessary to bring it home from the safety deposit box," Vanessa lied. "That report is all you need for the DMV tomorrow. They certainly are not going to be able to read, let alone accept, a birth certificate from Mexico."

23

"Okay, fine. But why does this say Nacxit? Is that Spanish for Nicholas or something?"

"No, that is your legal name. Your biological mother requested that we name you Nacxit. Since it is an unusual name, we just decided to call you Nick," Vanessa replied.

Nick paused for a moment, as if trying to do a mental fact check. Vanessa held her breath, as she waited to see if her answers satisfied him. She was not prepared for the question that came next.

"Are you in contact with my biological mother or father?" He asked.

"Of course not. Why would you ask us that?" Vanessa said while she and Anthony quickly exchanged puzzled looks. The question caught his attention, as well. Abruptly, Nick left the room and ran up the stairs. Vanessa and Anthony sat on the couch in bewilderment, wondering if they should chase after him. He came down a few seconds later with another envelope in his hand.

"Well, someone is in contact with them," Nick said, slapping the card down on the coffee table.

Vanessa took the envelope from the table and noticed the N. MURPHY written across the front. There was something familiar about the paper of the envelope.

"What's this?" Vanessa questioned.

"Look at it," Nick ordered.

Vanessa opened the envelope and pulled out the card. Anthony looked on from beside her. Vanessa felt her stomach churn as she saw the string of pictographs neatly arranged on the card and the name, Nacxit, written across the top. She felt Anthony tense up and let out a muffled gasp.

"Where did you get this?" Vanessa asked, trying not to show her anxiety.

"It was in the mailbox on my birthday with the rest of the mail. I don't think the mail man delivered it because there was no stamp or return address." Nick replied, sounding calmer.

Vanessa was at a loss for words. Anthony seemed to be just as shocked and confused. Besides Anthony, herself, and the mystery birth parents, there were only two other people who knew about his name, Nacxit. Roberto and the Consular clerk who completed the paperwork were it. As far as she knew, neither of those two people knew where they lived. Just as Nick appeared out of nowhere fifteen years ago, it seemed this envelope did the same.

CHAPTER FIVE

The driving exam was one of the easiest exams Nick ever took. Out of the twenty questions, Nick only missed one. Once he passed the exam, he presented the required documents so he could obtain the permit. Considering all of the commotion from the previous night, he was surprised he did so well on the exam! After he showed his parents the mysterious birthday card he received, his parents evasively told him they would all sit down after his birthday celebration and discuss it. He did not know what to think of all of this, but he was angry and, for the first time in his life, the voice was getting on his nerves. Usually she only said a few words whenever Nick was having difficulty with something. Now, she was constantly echoing the word "BELIEVE," consistently enough to bother him.

Nick and his parents arrived home from the DMV around 11:00 A.M. Because his birthday fell on a Tuesday, they planned to celebrate with the family and have his friends spend the night on Saturday. Jacob and Colin were supposed to arrive at 1:00 P.M., so Nick went straight upstairs to clean his room. On his way upstairs, he noticed the card with the pictographs lying on the coffee table in the living room. His parents were still in the garage unloading the last of the groceries. He grabbed the card from the table and continued upstairs.

Nick's room was large compared to the average teenager's bedroom. He had enough room for a queen-sized bed, a set of bunk beds that doubled as a seating area, and a desk for schoolwork. He also had an en suite bathroom and walk-in closet. Like most teenagers, Nick's room was a total mess. Not in the mood to sort through the ocean of dirty laundry, school papers, books, video game equipment, and soccer gear that veiled the floor, he crammed everything into his closet. After about thirty minutes, Nick noticed the pictograph card he threw on his desk. Looking for an excuse to break from cleaning, Nick decided to do a little research.

27

He spun around in his desk chair and accessed the internet. Assuming the card was from his biological parents in Mexico, he searched the terms "Mexican pictographs." While filtering through the results, he concluded that pictographs were not used anywhere in modern Mexican society. They were associated with ancient history, primarily the Mayan civilization. Nick had studied and written papers on the Mayans for various history classes. As he recalled, they were a fairly advanced civilization for their time, acknowledged for their language and mathematics. *Why would my birth parents send me a card written in an ancient language?* Just as Nick was about to search for "Mayan pictographs," Jacob appeared in his bedroom doorway.

"Hey man! Whatcha doin'?" Jacob asked.

"Dude, you're early. I thought you weren't going to be here until one," Nick said.

"Yeah, well my mom had a spin class at the gym, so she dropped me off early," Jacob said, entering the room.

"Oh, okay. So, you wanna go shoot some hoops down by the clubhouse?" Nick asked.

"Sure. Hey, what's this?" Jacob asked, picking up the card.

"I wish I knew," Nick replied.

"What do you mean? Where did you get it?"

"It was in the mailbox on my birthday. I think it's from my biological parents. Anthony and Vanessa are being deceptive and expect me to oblige."

"Whoa! Your biological parents? Where are they from. . . Egypt? This writing looks like something out of a video game!" Jacob joked.

"It is Mayan, I think. I was just researching it before you got here." Nick quickly closed his internet browser.

"Mayan! Dude, didn't that civilization die out like a thousand years ago?" Jacob asked, incredulously.

"I'm just as confused as you. The whole thing is pretty outlandish. My parents are acting so weird. Last night, I asked my mom for my birth certificate, and she gave me some certificate from the consulate in Mexico that did not list my birth parents or any of my pertinent birth statistics. When I asked her for my actual birth certificate, she gave me some lame answer about how she left it at the safety-deposit box; she didn't think it was important. Then, I showed them the card and they freaked out and told me we would talk about it on Sunday afternoon. They are clearly being shady."

"Wow man! Sounds like some weird stuff going on. So, you ready to go play basketball?" Neither empathy nor attention to detail were Jacob's strong points.

"Yeah. Let me put my shoes on," Nick said, grabbing his shoes from under the bed. He sat down on the bed and laced up his shoes while Jacob dropped his bag on Nick's bed and waited by the door.

"By the way, who is Nacxit?" Jacob asked as they left the room.

Nick reached into his wallet, pulled out his freshly printed driver's license, and handed it to Jacob.

"Apparently, I am," Nick said, closing the door behind him.

* * * *

Vanessa and Anthony were eating lunch in the kitchen when Nick and Jacob came downstairs. Because of the way things transpired the night before, Vanessa knew that Nick was angry. Instead of his usual jovial attitude, he was brusque with them all morning. They rode in silence to and from the DMV, despite Vanessa's attempts to get Nick talking. She tried congratulating him on passing the driving exam, but he just thanked her and shrugged it off, acting like it was not a big deal.

"I made you a sandwich," Vanessa called, as Nick walked by the kitchen.

Nick was halfway out the door when he replied, "I'll eat it when we come back. We are going over to the basketball court."

As the front door shut behind him, Vanessa relaxed with a deep exhale. She knew they were going to have to tell Nick the whole story. Somehow, they were going to have to explain every last detail about the night on the beach and the two weeks that followed.

"So, how should we go about this?" Vanessa asked Anthony, as he finished eating his lunch.

"Do what?" Anthony asked.

"Tell Nick! What do you think I'm talking about?!"

"I don't know, okay Vanessa? I'm still concerned about the origins of that card. You realize it is strikingly similar to the paper we found him with that night." The tension wore on both of them.

"Of course, I realize that. That's why I think it has to be from the birth parents." She leaned exasperatedly on the kitchen counter.

"I'm having a hard time believing that. If the birth parents wanted to contact him, there are about ten thousand better ways to do it. Assuming they somehow know who found the baby and assuming they somehow found our address, why wouldn't they at least send a card in a language we could understand? Furthermore, if the card did not arrive by US mail, then, how did it end up in the mailbox?" Anthony ran his hands through his hair, giving it the slightest tug. Vanessa hastily offered an explanation, grasping at straws.

"It's not completely out of the question for someone to be out of touch with society and write in some outdated script. I've heard of numerous tribes in India and countries in Africa that speak and write in unknown languages. Maybe they got the address from Roberto. He knew our names and was very familiar with the hotel where we stayed. I'm sure it would not have been hard to look up the credit card records to get an address. Besides, Roberto and the biological parents are the only ones who know about the name Nacxit," Vanessa countered.

"How do we know it was the biological parents that left Nick on the beach?" Anthony argued. "I mean, how do we know that Nick wasn't kidnapped first, then left on the beach? Maybe the whole thing was some crazy, botched ransom attempt!"

"So what are you saying? Fifteen years later, these supposed kidnappers want Nick back and they feel the best way to go about it is to leave strange cards in the mailbox?" Vanessa asked.

Anthony thought for a moment. "Well, when you put it that way, I guess that doesn't make much sense. My point is that something way more complex is going on here; something more than just the simple 'give us our child back' scenario."

After talking with Anthony, Vanessa was certain of two ideas. Firstly, they were going to have to tell Nick the truth about everything, and secondly, there was no way in hell that Vanessa was giving up her son to anyone, biological connection or not!

CHAPTER SIX

"You are never going to win!" Colin proclaimed, triumphantly.

"Whatever! It's almost 4 o'clock in the morning! We've been playing video games for over six hours now. What do you expect?" Jacob conceded.

"Yeah, I'm becoming delirious," Nick concurred, turning off the game and collapsing into bed. From the mini paintball war they had in the backyard, to the new foosball table, to the new video games he received, Nick was exhausted. Almost the entire soccer team showed up to his birthday celebration but only Jacob and Colin slept over. When Nick's mom awoke them at 2:00 P.M., he felt like he just fell asleep.

After saying goodbyes to Jacob and Colin, Nick went to his room to resume the research on the pictograph card. He already came to the conclusion that the pictographs on the card were Mayan. He was looking for a way to translate them when his mom knocked on the door.

"Nick, can you come downstairs? We need to talk," she said.

"All right, I'm coming," Nick called as he turned off his computer and headed downstairs to the family room.

He placed the card on the table in front of them and took a seat in one of the recliners adjacent to his dad. His mom spoke first.

"Nick, what we are about to tell you may be difficult for you to understand. In fact, your father and I do not fully understand it. That is the reason we never told you the truth; because we do not have all the answers. The card that was in the mailbox just adds to the mystery of the events that we're going to describe. It all happened fifteen years ago."

Nick remained silent. Anthony spoke next.

"Please remember that we love you more than words can express. You are our son: biological or not. We only want you to be happy, healthy, and thriving. Please don't be scared to ask us questions. I can't guarantee that we will be able to answer right away, but I promise that we will work through it together."

Nick was thrown. He had never seen his parents like this. His dad was actually not behind a computer screen! Instead, he was completely focused on the conversation. Nick felt like they were about to tell him something horrible; like he came on a spaceship from outer space. Initially, he thought they were going to tell him that they adopted him illegally or something to that effect. Though, the confusion and concern that was on both his parents' faces told him the story was much more complicated than an illegal adoption. He took a deep breath and listened as his dad began to tell him the story.

"For our fifth wedding anniversary, your mom and I decided to take a vacation to Cozumel, Mexico. On the night of November 1, 1996 we went to a secluded beach to enjoy a romantic evening together. While relaxing on the beach, we were interrupted by a strange sound. I thought it was an animal at first, but your mom insisted in was a baby. Because it was rather late at night for a baby to be out at the beach, we went to investigate. That is when we saw you. You appeared to only be hours old. You were wrapped in some kind of plant just beyond the water. Your mom instinctively picked you up and soothed your cries." Vanessa let out a sniffle.

Anthony continued. "We searched the beach for whoever left you behind, but there was no one to be found. So, since it was so late, we took you to our hotel room for the night. The next day, we got up early to find your parents. We started knocking on doors and asking if anyone knew your parents' whereabouts or how you got there. After asking a myriad of people, we were about to contact the police when we met an interesting man, Roberto. Roberto warned us of the potential dangers, like human trafficking, we could be exposing you to. He suggested we raise you as our own. He theorized that your parents were not able to raise you for some reason, and we could give you a better life in the United States. Your mom and I didn't want to take you away

34

from your family, but we tried our best to locate them. We didn't want to put you in danger. Ultimately, we decided to bring you home with us. It was the best decision we ever made."

Nick pondered their story, while his parents sat with worrisome smiles. He still wanted them to clear up some things. He began his onslaught of questions.

"So, technically, I'm not adopted. I'm kidnapped." Nick stated with disapproval.

"I certainly wouldn't put it like that, but yes, you technically are not adopted. We tried to find your parents, but they just didn't want to be found." His dad responded.

"How did you get that consulate birth report?" Nick challenged.

"We had Roberto help us out with that. He knew some people at the U.S. Consulate, and he was able to acquire the paperwork. It was the only way we were able to bring you back. Otherwise, the Mexican government would have kept you in an orphanage, while they attempted to locate your parents."

"What about the name Nacxit? Was that story a lie, too?" Nick accused.

"Not entirely. We know your parents wanted to name you Nacxit because they told us."

"Told you how? You said you never met them." Nick questioned.

"They left your name spelled out in pebbles on the sand about five feet from where we found you."

With each additional detail that they relayed, the story came across more and more fabricated. Echoes of the word "BELIEVE" were beginning to make sense. Nick understood why his parents kept the truth from him for so long, but that did not validate their decision. His life, as he knew it, was a lie. *Don't I have the right to know? Why did it take some requirements of the DMV to initiate disclosure of the facts?* If he had not received the mysterious pictograph card in the mailbox, he would have dismissed the entire story as a practical joke. Remembering the card, he inquired about it.

"So what does the pictograph card have to do with anything?"

"That is where the story becomes convoluted. When we found you on the beach, you had two items with you. The first item was a tightly rolled piece of paper with a string of pictographs that was very similar to the card you found in the mailbox. The second item was a necklace. It was a thick strand of hemp with a fairly large piece of quartz dangling from the center. We think it was a keepsake, or family heirloom, from your parents. While we were waiting on the paperwork from Roberto, I asked people around the town if they knew what the paper said. No one could tell me anything. Roberto suggested that it might be Mayan, but he wasn't sure."

In anticipation of Nick's next question, Nick's mom pulled out a small box from underneath the coffee table and handed it to him. He took the box from her and opened it. Inside were the necklace and the roll of paper. Waves of emotion crashed over him, as he stared at the necklace in the box. He recognized the stone. The stone before him was the very same stone that appeared in his dreams countless times. The settings of the dreams were always different, but the stone was always the same.

The look of shock on his face must have been undeniable because his parents instantly started asking him if he was all right. Nick stared with a hypnotized glaze into the box. This was unreal.

"What is it? Are you okay?" He heard his mom asking.

"Yeah, I'm fine," he responded. "It's the stone. It reminds me of something I've seen.

"What?!" His parents both burst out loud.

"I'm not sure," Nick said. I think maybe it was in my dreams."

As his parents sat with bewildered countenances, Nick was consumed with wonder. *Where are my biological parents, and why did they leave me on the beach? Did something tragic happen to them or was it just a question of responsibility? Maybe I really was kidnapped and my real parents were desperately searching for me.* Suddenly, he felt isolated and alone. *Can I trust the two people sitting across the room from me?* His anger was mounting.

"You don't know what these pictographs say? Nick sternly asked, laying both papers side by side on the table.

"No. We inquired with several townsfolk and no one could tell us anything," Vanessa replied.

"Why didn't you find someone here in the states to translate them?" Nick asked, incredulously.

"After we went door to door in Cozumel and were repeatedly turned away, I guess we got discouraged. I'm sorry there is not more we can tell you. We just want to help you through this," Vanessa said, sheepishly.

"Yeah, just like you 'helped' me fifteen years ago." Nick shot back at her.

"That's uncalled for!" Anthony scolded him.

"Uncalled for?! I'll tell you what's uncalled for! You two conspired with some stranger to kidnap me!" Nick yelled. "How can I trust you guys anymore?! You both ignored the only clue to my existence!" Nick fumed, storming out of the room before his parents could respond. He went to his room, slammed the door, and blared his stereo. He wanted answers. Filled with rage toward his pseudo-parents, he realized his first priority was to determine the exact meaning of those pictographs.

CHAPTER SEVEN

Despite his anger, Nick decided to accept his adoptive parents' version of events. They had not been truthful with him but he lacked the evidence to pursue an argument. Nick hoped the pictograph translations would clarify the obscure circumstances surrounding his abandonment. Nick believed his biological parents were alive and wanted to contact him. His parents were not convinced, but their opinion was irrelevant. With the translations in hand, he would prove his real parents were alive and persuade Anthony and Vanessa to allow a meeting.

He desperately needed to get the pictographs translated. For ambiguous reasons, his biological parents decided to use the ancient language of the Mayans. His internet searches turned up very little, so he decided to take the pictographs to his history teacher. Hopefully, he would be able to steer Nick in the right direction.

On Monday morning, he arrived an hour early to meet with his history teacher, Mr. Ambrose. Mr. Ambrose was a short, fat man who was obsessed with Egypt. He had a gigantic mural and fake pillars erected in his classroom to complete the effect. There were rumors that he slept in a sarcophagus, but Nick thought it was just high school rhetoric. Nick found Mr. Ambrose in his classroom, rummaging through a box of papers.

"Hi Mr. Ambrose." Nick said, walking up behind him.

"Oh, hello there Nick." Mr. Ambrose said, regaining his composure. "What brings you to me so early? I'm going to tell you right now that I'm not offering any more extra credit assignments until after Christmas."

Nick was insulted. He probably held the highest grade in the class. "No, I don't need any extra credit. I'm here to ask you a question about some things that I found. I think they are Mayan. I was wondering if you could help me translate them." Nick handed him the rolled up paper and the card.

"Mayan? You certainly didn't find anything Mayan around here. Where did they come from?" He asked, unrolling the paper.

"Actually, a family member gave them to me. He found them in a souvenir store down in Mexico," Nick lied.

Mr. Ambrose took his time and looked at both pieces of paper meticulously. He went to his bookshelf behind his desk and pulled out a book called, *The Ancients of Mesoamerica.* He flipped through the pages with specific focus. When he found what he was looking for, he compared the papers to the picture in the book. After a few minutes of frenzied back and forth motion, he finally spoke.

"This souvenir you've got here is unparalleled. I've never seen something written in actual Mayan. Normally, the cheap souvenirs string random pictographs together, with no rhyme or reason. They never take the time to make them appear authentic because the majority of people have no idea what authentic Mayan pictographs look like. Interestingly, what you have here seems to be written as the ancient Mayas would have written it. The only legitimate writings we have left for comparison from the Mayans, are codices, or books, that have been partially translated by scholars. Here, have a look at the Dresden Codex." Mr. Ambrose spun the book around, so Nick could see it.

Nick looked back and forth between the book and the pieces of paper just as Mr. Ambrose had done. Mr. Ambrose was right. The pictographs on the paper were strikingly similar to pictographs from the Dresden Codex.

"So, you can translate these papers?" Nick asked excitedly.

"Unfortunately, no." Mr. Ambrose chuckled. "You are going to need an expert in Mayan language and culture for that. I know a professor in Florida that runs the Center for Mesoamerican Studies. If anyone can read your papers, it's him. I recognize some of the well-known symbols, but without knowing their context, the information is useless."

"Tell me what you can read." Nick prodded.

Mr. Ambrose took the rolled up paper first and began pointing to individual pictographs. "These few here represent

40

numbers. This symbol means 1 and this symbol means 5. The only other symbols I recognize are child, key, and fire." He took the card and picked it up. "Now on this one, the numbers 1 and 5 appear again, but other than those numbers, the only thing I recognize is a symbol that generally means savior, or salvation."

"That's it?" Nick said, deflated.

"Yes. I told you I wouldn't be able to tell you much." He took out a sticky note from his desk and wrote down a name and phone number. "Here is the information you will need to contact the expert. His name is Professor Elliot Shelton."

Nick zipped his two pictographs and the sticky not into the front of his backpack.

"Thanks for your help, Mr. Ambrose," Nick said, as he turned to leave."

"Not a problem," he replied. "Let me know what Professor Shelton says. You've got me curious now."

"Okay, I will," Nick said. He walked out of Mr. Ambrose's classroom and continued to his homeroom.

* * * *

Mr. Ambrose returned to his search for the Historical Society newsletter as Nick left the room. He searched for a few more minutes and let out a sigh of frustration. *Maybe I left it in my car*, he thought. He turned his attention to the open book still sitting on his desk. The pictographs that Nick Murphy had just shown him were no souvenir. When he asked about the papers' origins, he discerned Nick's hesitation. What was remarkable about the samples was that they were written recently. They were not something that was dug up thousands of years ago. Although there were still Mayan villages scattered through Central America, none of them communicated via pictograph anymore. Mr. Ambrose was intrigued. The authenticity of the pieces was truly stunning. Nick seemed exceptionally eager to get the papers translated. He told Nick everything he knew, except for one symbol. It was the symbol for island, which appeared right before the symbol for fire. He was far from an expert in Mayan

41

hieroglyphics, but he knew his Egyptian hieroglyphics well. In Egyptian, whenever there was talk of an island and fire, it always meant one thing, The Isle of Flame, which was better known to most as the lost island of Atlantis. With the symbol for key also in the pictograph, he was desperate to know more. Hopefully, Nick would call his longtime friend and colleague, Professor Elliot Shelton, soon. He was going to make it his prerogative to find out how Nick Murphy obtained those pictographs!

* * * *

The rest of the school day, Nick kept coming up with different theories for the translations from Mr. Ambrose, while the voice continued to echo, "BELIEVE." The child symbol was no surprise. However, the symbols for fire and key had his mind reeling. Maybe there was a devastating fire, which was the reason his biological parents had to abandon him. Maybe, his parents died in the fire, and someone else left him on the beach that night. That would explain why they could not be found when his current parents went looking for them. He was having trouble coming up with a theory for the key symbol. The symbol for salvation was baffling, as well. Who else could have sent the card? He reached in his pocket and felt the stone necklace between his fingers. He was still confused about it appearing in his dreams. He had never physically seen the stone, until his parents presented it to him last night. *How was it possible that I was dreaming about it all these years?* He speculated that the stone might help him find the truth. Nick thought that having some parts of the pictographs translated would have given him some answers, but his questions just led to more questions.

CHAPTER EIGHT

The hospital was busy for a Monday. Vanessa plopped down at the nurses' station next to her colleague, Gina, who was uploading patient data from the physicians' morning rounds.

"Finally catching your breath?" Gina questioned.

"I hope so." Vanessa replied. "Never a dull moment around here."

"Hectic mornings make me crazy." Gina confided. "You are welcome to sit down and help me finish these charts." Gina suggested, smiling mischievously.

"No way! I think I would rather attempt open-heart surgery than deal with all of that tedious data! Vanessa proclaimed.

Vanessa had been a nurse for over fifteen years, but still loved her field of work. There was always untrodden territory, so she was never bored. Today, despite her constant quest for knowledge, she was distracted. She was on pins and needles about Nick and how he was responding to his birth story. She feared that all the stress of finding out the truth about his birth would trigger the voice in his head to return. After three, long years of doctors and medicines, it seemed they finally cured Nick of his hallucinations. The doctors claimed that it was a rare, but mild, form of Schizophrenia. Nick did not exhibit any of the other classic symptoms associated with Schizophrenia such as abnormal motor behavior and depression. He had one and only one symptom: the voice. According to Nick, "she" was not demanding or hurtful. When Nick described the voice as motherly, Vanessa became uneasy. As crazy at it sounded, she could not erase the thought that maybe the voice was his mother. Vanessa always suspected that something tragic happened to Nick's real parents. Many people have claimed to see ghosts. Was it so far-fetched that someone could be hearing one?

Despite her angst over how Nick would handle this moving forward, divulging his birth story actually allayed the feelings that she had been carrying. Telling Nick the truth was gut wrenching, but if he could handle the truth without having a mental break down, then, it was better this way. However, the revelation of him dreaming about a stone he had never seen before was disturbing. It was improbable that the dreams were a coincidence, but they were scared to speculate how those dreams were actually occurring.

In his fit of rage, Nick challenged their reasoning for neglecting to translate the pictographs. She would never admit it to Nick, but she was terrified of what those pieces of paper might say. During the two weeks she and Anthony spent searching for Nick's parents, they all formed an incredible bond. Vanessa's motherly instincts kicked in immediately and she could not fathom handing Nick over to anyone. Especially someone who abandoned him on a beach! Nick's immediate quest to translate the pictographs scared her to death. She prayed that whatever the papers revealed, their message had become irrelevant.

Vanessa's only regret about telling Nick the truth was his desire to contact his biological parents. She could count many reasons why this was a bad idea. First of all, they were complete strangers. Second, the circumstances that led to Nick's abandonment fifteen years ago might still exist. Third, she could not bear the thought of Nick getting hurt. When his heart broke, so did hers. Fourth, if he could establish contact, his desire to meet them would be inevitable. She was not sure how to handle that. There are a lot of questions that need to be answered before there could be any meetings, she told herself.

"Vanessa. . . . Vanessa. . . ." She heard her colleague Gina, chirping.

"Oh sorry!" Vanessa said. "What were you saying?"

"Someone needs to give Mrs. Alvarez her bath. I did it yesterday, so it's your turn, champ," Gina teased with that same mischievous smile.

"What? Since when are we responsible for that? What happened to the nursing assistants?"

"One is out sick and the others are overloaded with two new patients that were just rushed into the ER. Yesterday, I washed her hair, so it shouldn't take long. Just do the basic rub-a-dub-dub," Gina giggled.

"All riiiiiight," Vanessa agreed, pretending like she did not see the humor in the situation.

Vanessa made her way around the rectangle perimeter of the nurses' station to the corner that led to the 300 hallway. She gathered some cleansing supplies, as she headed to room 304. Mrs. Alvarez was an elderly woman who recently suffered a stroke. The surgery went remarkably well, for her age, but Mrs. Alvarez had been in a coma for the past week. Doctors said she could wake up at any time, but there was no telling when. Mrs. Alvarez was motionless in the bed. Her vitals monitor beeped in the background. Vanessa organized her supplies on a tray next to the bed. She removed Mrs. Alvarez' blanket and untied the front of her hospital gown. Unfolding a washcloth, she dipped it into the basin of warm water and began wiping Mrs. Alvarez face. As gently as possible, she continued down her neck to the rest of her body. She turned her on her side, so she could wash her backside. Patients in comas were prone to bed sores, so the rotation would help to increase her circulation, also. When she finished bathing her, she re-tied Mrs. Alvarez's gown and put a fresh pair of no-slip hospital socks on her. Just as she was pulling the blanket back over her, Mrs. Alvarez grabbed her arm. Vanessa jumped and let out a yelp. Mrs. Alvarez's grip tightened.

"Mrs. Alvarez! Are you awake?" There was no response. "Mrs. Alvarez, can you hear me? You're in the hospital." Again, there was no response. As Vanessa tried to pry Mrs. Alvarez's hand from her arm, she started to speak.

"Listen. . . . ," Mrs. Alvarez whispered.

"Mrs. Alvarez, you are in the hospital. Can you hear me?"

"Listen . . . . . .Listen." She repeated.

"Yes, I can hear you, Mrs. Alvarez. Are you in any pain?"

Mrs. Alvarez eyes suddenly popped open, and her grip began to cut off the circulation in Vanessa's arm. Starring directly at Vanessa, Mrs. Alvarez spoke again, "Listen to him . . . He is the leader . . . Do not doubt him, he holds the key . . . Trust in him."

Just as suddenly as she grabbed Vanessa's arm, Mrs. Alvarez released her grip, closed her eyes, and went limp. Now free to move, Vanessa stumbled backwards and lunged toward the nurse's station pager.

"Nurse's station," Gina responded.

"Gina! Mrs. Alvarez is awake! Come quick!" Vanessa yelled.

About ten seconds later, Gina came bursting through the door. "What's the matter?" Gina asked.

"I don't know." Vanessa said, taking a deep breath. "It's just that Mrs. Alvarez is awake and she startled me. We should call one of her doctors."

"She's awake?" Gina questioned, skeptically, eyeing the motionless Mrs. Alvarez.

"Yes! She just grabbed my arm really hard and started talking!"

"Grabbed you hard? She's pushing eighty and hasn't moved in a week!" Gina said, gently shaking Mrs. Alvarez's shoulder and calling her name.

"Yeah well, look at my arm! You can see the red marks from where she grabbed me."

Getting no response, Gina went to the vitals monitor to check the activity log. "I don't know what exactly happened in here, but according to Mrs. Alvarez's monitors, her brain activity hasn't changed. She's still in a coma.

"That's impossible! She grabbed me, and she was talking! Her eyes were open, too!" Vanessa exclaimed.

"It was probably just muscle reflexes. That's common in coma patients." Gina explained.

"No way! I'm telling you she was awake! She spoke to me!" Vanessa insisted.

"What did she say to you?"

"It was kind of weird. At first, she was just whispering the word 'listen.' Then her volume increased, and she said 'listen to him,' and then something about trusting him because he has a key." Vanessa recounted.

46

"Who is the 'him' she was talking about?"

"I have no idea!" Vanessa squealed.

In all of her years as a nurse, Vanessa never experienced anything like that before. *Was Mrs. Alvarez speaking nonsense or was she actually talking to her? She must have been speaking nonsense*, Vanessa thought because Mrs. Alvarez had never met her. Maybe Mrs. Alvarez was in the middle of a dream and the warm water and movement caused her to verbalize what she was experiencing. Vanessa had no explanations, whatsoever! All she knew for sure was that she would not be giving any more sponge baths to Mrs. Alvarez!

CHAPTER NINE

The minute Nick arrived home from school, he went straight to the phone in the kitchen. On the way, he gave a half-hearted wave to his dad who was busy in his office. He went into the front pocket of his backpack and took out the sticky note from Mr. Ambrose that had Professor Shelton's number on it. Realizing that the number was a Florida area code, Nick decided to use his cell phone to avoid long-distance charges. He bounded up the stairs to his room to retrieve his cell phone. He dialed the number on the paper and listened for an answer. After many rings, he began to tap his right foot impatiently. Finally, someone answered.

"Thank you for calling the Center for Mesoamerican Studies. This is Renee speaking. How may I direct your call?" A female voice inquired.

"Hi, may I please speak to Professor Shelton?" Nick said.

"May I ask who's calling?" She asked.

"My name is Nick Murphy. I was given Professor Shelton's name and number from my high school history teacher, Mr. Walter Ambrose."

"Hold please," the receptionist replied, sweetly.

Nick waited on the line with anticipation. The hold music was unusual. A wordless, tribal rhythm repeated. It sounded like soft drums, a flute, and an intermittent tambourine. Nick realized he was pacing through his bedroom, so he sat down on the bed. The minor translations that Mr. Ambrose provided had him in a state of wonder all day. His already endless list of questions was growing by the minute! Assuming that Professor Shelton could translate the papers, Nick was already orchestrating a plan to convince his parents to go to Mexico. He was hoping that deciphering the papers would remove the ambiguity surrounding his abandonment. If he could convince his parents that his biological parents were good people and were victims of some unfortunate event, he was certain they would agree to a meeting.

Nick pulled out the stone necklace from his pocket and examined it. As an expert of Mesoamerica, maybe Professor Shelton could tell him if the stone held any special significance. Nick decided not to mention the stone with the professor until they discussed the papers. He wanted to feel him out before he shared too much information. Just as Nick was thinking about all the things he wanted to say, the receptionist came back on the line.

"Hello, Mr. Murphy?"

"Yes, I'm still here."

"I'm sorry, but Professor Shelton has left for the day. Can I take a message or can I transfer you to his voicemail?"

"No, that's okay. What time does he usually arrive in the morning?" Nick asked.

"He's usually here by 9 A.M."

"Okay, I'll try back in the morning."

Disappointed, Nick thanked the receptionist and hung up. He did not want to leave a message because Professor Shelton had no idea who he was, and he wanted to explain the situation in detail. As much as it irked him, he would just have to wait.

Trying to take his mind off of the pictographs, Nick decided to play a few rounds of *Halo* before dinner. He sifted through the mess on the floor for a controller. He turned up the television volume and was about to start the game when his cell phone rang.

"Hello?" Nick answered.

"Hello, is this Nick?" The voice on the other end asked.

"Yes, who's this?" Nick asked.

"Hi, Nick, this is Mr. Ambrose."

"Oh, hi," Nick replied, completely flabbergasted that his teacher was calling him directly.

"I just wanted to see if you were able to get in touch with Professor Shelton. He can get really busy at times, so I just didn't want you to get discouraged if you were not able to catch him the first few times." Mr. Ambrose explained.

"Actually, I just tried calling him a few minutes ago but his receptionist said he left for the day. I'm going to try him again in the morning."

"Okay, sounds good. I'll see you at school. Goodbye," Mr. Ambrose said and hung up the phone.

Nick did not know what to make of Mr. Ambrose's phone call. He did not realize how interested Mr. Ambrose was in the translations. Of course, he was a history buff, so it made sense that he would be excited about things like that. Mr. Ambrose had an obsessive nature evidenced by his extravagant Egyptian displays. Nick decided it was weird, but normal for a history teacher and went back to his *Halo* game.

After an hour of playing, Nick heard the garage door, indicating his mom had just arrived. He went downstairs to tell her about the progress he made with the pictographs.

Nick walked into the kitchen, as his mom was walking in from the garage. His dad had since transitioned from his office to the kitchen table with his laptop. His mom seemed distraught.

"Hey, how's it going? Everything okay?" Nick asked.

"Yeah. I'm fine," his mom said trying to crack a smile. I just had a rough day at work. Everyone thinks I'm crazy."

"Oh yeah, why's that?" Nick deliberately drew out his question to emphasize that he knew exactly how that felt.

"Well, one of our comatose patients decided to wake up and talk to me. Within moments, she went right back into the coma. Of course, I was the only one in the room, and her brain wave monitor showed she never woke up, so no one believes me."

"Nice," Nick said smiling, while sliding into a seat next to his dad. "What did comatose lady tell you? Did she give you the winning lottery numbers?" Nick questioned, jokingly.

"I wish. Then, I might have some evidence that it actually happened. She spouted some gibberish about listening and trusting some guy who has a key. Everyone at work is poking fun of me now," his mom said with a half-smile.

"I'd probably do the same," Nick's dad chimed in.

"Thanks, honey. I'll be sure to remember that," Nick's mom quipped, sarcastically.

Nick was slightly taken aback by what his mom had just said. What were the chances that two mysterious references to a key would come up in two different settings in the same day?

"She specifically said the word key?" Nick questioned.

"Yeah. She said 'he holds the key' and to 'trust him.' Why do you ask?"

Nick pulled out the pictographs from his pocket. "I'm sure it's just a coincidence. I took the pictographs to my history teacher, Mr. Ambrose, today. His specialty is Egypt, so he couldn't tell me much. However, one of the symbols that he was able to translate was one that means 'key.'

Nick's parents looked at each other and then at him. "Well, 'key' is a very common word with a ton of different meanings. As you said, I'm sure it's a coincidence. Tell us more about your history teacher and what he was able to translate," his dad said, closing his laptop and turning his attention to Nick.

"He's weird. He's fanatical about Egypt. His whole classroom is a shrine to anything and everything Egypt. Despite Egypt being his specialty, he was able to tell me that the pictographs are Mayan and he gave me the number of a professor in Florida that is an expert in Mayan language and culture. Also, he told me that the rolled up paper you guys found on the beach has the numbers 1 and 5 and the symbols for child, key, and fire. The card I received in the mailbox also has the numbers 1 and 5 along with the symbol for savior or salvation. The symbol for child makes sense, but I can't really come up with an explanation for the rest. I tried calling the professor, but he had already left his office for the day. I'm going to try him again in the morning."

"Wow, you're not wasting any time, are you?" His dad commented.

"No. I think translating the pictographs is important. Enough time has been wasted already," Nick said, glaring at them.

"Let us know what you discover. We are eager to find out the truth. Child, key, and fire? There definitely wasn't any fire or key where we found you." His dad said, ignoring Nick's implied accusation.

"And the numbers? Can you think of any explanation for those?" Nick questioned.

"Nothing in particular. The possibilities with numbers are endless," Anthony said. They could be anything from a date to a time to an address or a phone number.

"Great. I guess I'll just have to wait and see what the professor says." Nick said.

"So, what do you want for dinner? Spaghetti or tacos?" His mom asked, deliberately changing the subject.

"Spaghetti works. We had tacos at school."

"Okay. Dinner will be ready in thirty minutes. Have you started on your homework?" His mom asked.

"Not yet. I was going to start after dinner," Nick replied.

"Okay, so go ahead and set the table and then bring your laundry downstairs, please."

While his mom started dinner, Nick ruminated over the pictographs. He was becoming engrossed in what already seemed like a relentless pursuit. From him being abandoned on a beach, to strange pictographs, to a random comatose patient, he contemplated how they all could be related. Surely, the professor would be able to provide some of the missing pieces. The anxiety of the unknown engulfed his every thought. He was on the verge of something. He just knew it!

CHAPTER TEN

The next morning, Nick arose early to call the professor. He showered, dressed, and packed up his homework. Most mornings, Nick's dad took him to school because he did not have to go to the office. Even though the hospital where his mom worked was only ten miles away, traffic could get bad on the main roads, so she had to leave early to avoid the inevitable traffic. After packing up his backpack, Nick went downstairs to make his lunch. The school cafeteria was not the most reliable for a quality meal. Half of the time, the meals were unpalatable. He packed his lunch every day and if the cafeteria food was up to par, he would eat both or share with his friends.

After everything was packed and ready to go, Nick ventured to the living room, scrolling through his previously dialed call log. He selected the Florida area code number. Again, he listened as the phone rang and rang. The same receptionist from the day before answered with the same pleasant greeting. Nick requested to speak to the professor and was put on hold with the tribal music playing softly in the background. He visualized a desolate village in South America with a local medicine man chanting hymns of healing the tribe. This led him to wonder if his birth parents were part of such a tribe. His imagery was abruptly shattered by the professor's voice on the line.

"Professor Shelton," he answered.

"Hi, Profesor Shelton. My name is Nick Murphy. My history teacher, Mr. Ambrose, referred me to you. I hear you are an expert in Mayan language and culture.

"Hi, Nick. Yes, I know Mr. Ambrose well. I spoke to him late last night, and he told me to expect your call. He said you have some Mayan pictographs that need to be translated?"

"Yes. A relative of mine got them at a souvenir store down in Mexico, and I was curious about what they say."

"Of course. I'm delighted to assist you, but I will need the originals. Translating ancient text can be difficult to do by copy because some minute detail might get overlooked. Could you mail them to me?"

"I have a really nice, high-end scanner. I would prefer to send them by email, so they do not get lost or stolen in the mail," Nick said resolutely.

"If I'm going to take the time to translate the pictographs, I want to be sure that what I'm examining is authentic. From the colors used to the position of the subjects, every detail of ancient pictographs has significance. Even a high-end scanner can sometimes distort colors and shapes. I have to insist on reviewing the originals."

"I'm sorry, but I'm not comfortable mailing the originals. If you can't accept a high-resolution scan, then, I'll have to find someone else. I'm sorry to have wasted your time."

"Well, in that case, I guess I'll have to accept the scan. I just hope I will be able to provide you with an accurate translation," the professor conceded.

"Excellent! Where should I send them?" Nick asked.

"My office email address will be fine. You can find it on our website. Can I assist you with anything else?" Professor Shelton asked, clearly annoyed.

"Actually, I wanted to ask you about something else my family member found in Mexico. I'm not sure if it has any significance in the Mayan culture or not. It's a large piece of quartz, I think."

"A piece of quartz?"

"Yeah. I mean it could be another type of mineral, but it looks like quartz."

"How big is it?"

"It's about the size of an egg, but it's elongated and jagged."

"What color is it?"

"It has a pale green color to it."

"Quartz does have significant meaning in the Mayan culture. Ancient Mayan's believed it held considerable healing properties. Of course, if it was purchased in a souvenir shop, it may not even be quartz. I would have to see it in person to be sure."

"Oh, well, thanks anyway."

"Not a problem. I'll keep a look-out for your pictographs."

Nick noticed his dad waiting on him in the car. He grabbed his backpack and ran out to the driveway. He was not sure what to think about Professor Shelton. His request to have the originals seemed genuine, but Nick did not want to take the chance of losing the only pieces of evidence he had that could lead him to his biological parents.

"Running late this morning?" His dad said as Nick shut the car door.

"I had to call that Mayan professor. That's what held me up. Sorry."

"Oh, what did he say? Will he translate the pictographs for you?"

"Yeah, he said he was looking forward to it. He wanted the originals. He didn't want to accept a scan or copy. I didn't really feel comfortable sending them off like that. I told him to either accept the scan or I was going to find someone else to translate them."

"You weren't rude were you?" His dad accused. "You know, sometimes your stubborn nature can be misconstrued as being impolite.

"No! I just told him the facts." Nick replied, agitated.

"Ok, then. I'm just giving you some worthy advice. I guess it's just hard for me to realize how mature and responsible you've become. I will always cherish the memories of your first few weeks with us. You were the answer to our prayers." Nick's dad said, trying to stop the tears from welling in his eyes.

Instantly, Nick felt remorse for snapping at him. His dad's sudden display of emotion was uncharacteristic and left him speechless. They backed out of the driveway and headed out of the neighborhood toward Nick's school in silence. As each minute crept by, the awkwardness intensified. Although it seemed like an eternity, finally, the car came to a stop in front of the high school after a mere ten minutes.

"No matter where the pictographs lead, I just want you to know that your mom and I love you and have always done our best for you," his dad said as Nick threw open the car door.

"I know," Nick assured him, getting out of the car.

"Hey!" His dad shouted, as Nick was shutting the door.

"Yeah?" Nick responded.

"Have a terrific day at school. I love you and I'm praying for you," his dad said, encouragingly.

"Love you, too," Nick called back. It was one thing for his dad to pray, but Nick was far from praying for others or for himself. He didn't see the point. He slammed the door and hurried into school, trying to shake the conversation.

By the time he walked into homeroom, he was in turmoil. His dad told him he loved him at drop-off every morning, but it was always as a casual good-bye. Where did he think the pictographs would lead that caused such an emotional outburst? Nick was elated about getting the pictographs translated, but his dad's demeanor distressed him. For better or for worse, Nick was going to email the images the minute he got home.

CHAPTER ELEVEN

After talking with Nick, Elliot sat at his desk, reflecting on the conversation. Walter Ambrose had told him that the kid had some intriguing Mayan pictographs. Nick claimed that the writings came from a souvenir shop in Mexico, but Walter swore that the pictographs were definitely not spurious trinkets. Walter explained that the writings certainly were not thousands of years old, but written as an ancient Mayan would have written them thousands of years ago. Outside of the scholarly community, not many people knew how to achieve that. Walter mentioned that he was able to translate parts of the pictographs and was extremely excited about what he believed to be a reference to The Isle of Flame. Elliot was skeptical. Walter reminded him of his second wife who was loquacious and always exaggerating things for attention. Walter was eccentric. Elliot shared his love of history, but Walter took it to another level. Walter courted history like a tantalizing mistress and ancient Egyptian culture was his erotica. The mention of The Isle of Flame must have sent him spinning into euphoria.

The Isle of Flame, or Aalu, is described as an island in the Atlantic Ocean where the founders of ancient Egypt claim they sought refuge after a tremendous flood. The description of the island, which included concentric circles of water and land, volcanoes, fertile grounds, and an illustrious city, is strikingly similar to the lost city of Atlantis as described by Plato in Critias. Interestingly, the ancient Mayans told a similar story about their ancestors arriving in the Yucatan after a flood had destroyed their homeland. Some historians believe that the two stories are one in the same. They speculated that Atlantis was not a myth, but a real place that reached its peak of civilization between 1500 – 1200 B.C. Sometime around 1200 B.C. there was a cataclysmic event that caused a devastating flood and the magnificent city was lost forever. Some theories suggest that Atlantis survivors colonized the Nile River Valley, the Yucatan, Ireland, Greece and Rome, which gave rise to the greatest civilizations mankind has ever seen. In theory, the Mayans could possibly be descendants of Atlanteans. Of course, this is viewed as pure speculation. No one knows for sure, but sometimes, truth is stranger than fiction.

If Walter was correct in his tentative translations, the mention of The Isle of Flame in authentic Mayan pictographs would be remarkable. However, considering they are recent pictographs and not ancient, the historical value is suspicious. Elliot's real motive for requesting the originals from Nick was so he could track down the origin. Examining the type of paper on which the pictographs appear is the only hope of achieving that. Neither he nor Walter wanted Nick to know the potential value of what he had. Unfortunately, Nick was too smart and refused to send him the originals. Elliot wondered why Walter had not mentioned the piece of quartz. He was more engrossed with the stone than the pictographs. Nick seemed hesitant to divulge information. Possibly, Walter did not know about the stone. Operating on that assumption, Elliot decided he would keep it that way. In the event that the stone held some sort of value, he wanted it for himself. Walter did not need to know everything. Elliot leaned back, kicked up his feet on his desk, and took a deep, satisfying breath. He had a feeling that the Nick Murphy saga was about to get very interesting.

* * * *

The school day was anything but normal. About twenty minutes after Nick was dropped off, a school bus ran into one of the "portable classrooms," as the administration called the trailers that lined the school's bus port. Apparently, the bus driver fainted and lost control of the bus, as she was pulling into the bus loop. The local news showed up faster than the ambulance! The cameras rolled, and the crowd watched, as they separated the bus from the trailer. Thankfully, the foreign language teacher, who taught in the trailer, was not inside when the bus crashed. The driver and passengers only suffered minor bruises. Of course, all the kids were threatening that their parents were going to sue, but

60

the lack of injuries made that implausible. Surprisingly, this was not the first time that one of the trailers had suffered damage. Earlier in the school year, some delinquents set fire to one in the early morning. When everyone arrived to school that morning, they were greeted by the fire department and what was left of the trailer. Again, no one was hurt, but the running joke throughout the school was that comprehensive health insurance was a prerequisite to a trailer class.

After the school bus incident, there was a series of unexpected fire alarms. The first time the alarms sounded, Nick was taking a math test. His teacher made everyone hand in their exams as they exited the classroom in order to prevent cheating. Unfortunately, while everyone was waiting outside, Nick heard numerous conversations about answers to certain questions. Nick had no need to participate. He thought the test was easy.

About an hour later, Nick heard the annoying buzzing of the fire alarm a second time. This time, Nick's outdoor gym class was uninterrupted as he watched the student body flood the parking lot. The third time, Nick was the first to the door in literature class. The school intercom system crackled to life and the Vice Principal instructed everyone to ignore the false alarm and anymore throughout the day. She apologized and announced that the fire alarm system was malfunctioning. The malfunction must have been repaired because the alarm did not sound for the rest of the day.

Nick's last class of the day was world history with Mr. Ambrose. They were studying the Middle Ages. Nick did not particularly like history; it was a subject that did not fundamentally change from year to year. Nick longed for learning subjects on the cutting edge of education, and there was nothing new about History. The same could be said about math, but mathematic equations are, at least, interactive. With its endless facts to memorize, Nick was bored out of his mind in History!

All of a sudden, Mr. Ambrose seemed to be paying extra-special attention to Nick. Prior to their pictograph meeting, Mr. Ambrose hardly acknowledged him. The only time they ever interacted was on the rare occasion that Mr. Ambrose called on him when they were going over homework answers. Today, Nick was Mr. Ambrose's star student. He greeted him when he walked in the classroom and asked if he had gotten in touch with Professor Shelton. Nick confirmed that he had spoken with the professor and did not elaborate on much else. Mr. Ambrose did not seem satisfied with his answer, but he let it go because he had to start class. The duration of the class, Mr. Ambrose appeared to be surveilling Nick's every move. Nick could feel his gaze staring him down from across the room. *What's gotten into him?* Nick thought to himself. *Is he freaking out over the pictographs?* Nick shook his head and resolved to bolt for the door as soon as the bell rang. However, he could not escape before Mr. Ambrose called him to his desk. Annoyed, Nick grabbed his backpack and walked up to the desk.

"So Nick! What did Professor Shelton say about the pictographs? I'm fascinated!"

"He asked for the originals but I wouldn't send them to him. So he took a scanned copy." Nick told him.

"Oh, don't worry! Professor Shelton is a preeminent scholar you know. He will take excellent care of the pictographs. I can assure you."

Nick wondered why Mr. Ambrose pushed the point after he already refused. "I know. I just want to be safe," Nick defended.

"Okay. At least you will get the translations quicker."

"Yeah. That will be nice." There was an uncomfortable pause as Nick surveyed the almost hungry look on Mr. Ambrose's face. "Um, so . . . I've gotta go. My ride is waiting. If there's nothing else. . ." Nick inched toward the door, trying to escape more questions.

"No, that's it. I'll see you tomorrow." Mr. Ambrose looked visibly disappointed.

Nick could not escape the room fast enough. *Creepy much?* Nick thought, glancing back in case Mr. Ambrose decided to follow him. Suddenly, Colin was by his side. Nick let out a loud gasp.

"Hey, man. You look like you've seen a ghost and you spook like a girl!" Colin teased.

"Ha! No, just Mr. Ambrose." Nick said, a little startled.

"Dude, that's worst then a ghost!" Colin chuckled.

"Yeah, no kidding. That guy is weird."

"So, where you going?" Colin asked.

"To the parking lot to go home. Isn't your mom picking us up?" Nick said, confused.

"Yeah, in like two hours. We have soccer practice." Colin looked at Nick sideways.

In his rush to get away from Mr. Ambrose, Nick had forgotten all about soccer practice. "Oh yeah! Duh!" Nick admitted. He turned around and followed Colin back to the locker room. While changing into his soccer gear, Nick wondered why Mr. Ambrose was so intrigued by the pictographs. Something did not feel right. Nick just could not put his finger on it. He jogged out onto the soccer field. Between his dad's bizarre emotional moment and Mr. Ambrose breathing down his neck, the pictographs were wreaking havoc on everyone. Nick could only imagine the repercussions that awaited him after they were translated.

CHAPTER TWELVE

Soccer practice ran twenty minutes longer than usual because of the coach's lecture on accruing penalties. Nick was the worst offender! As with most things in his life, he was aggressive. He did not deliberately set out to break the rules; he was just determined to win and the rules sometimes got in the way. In professional soccer, the referees would never give a yellow card for slide tackling someone. On the contrary, in high school soccer, many times the referees saw it as too aggressive and Nick would get carded. The coach understood that Nick was just playing the game, but he also warned him that he needed to control himself better for the sake of the team. Their team was a strong contender for the state finals this year and Nick did not want to blow it. The coach wrapped up the topic of sportsmanship and released them.

Nick, Colin, and Jacob all made their way to the parking lot to find Mrs. Stetson, Colin's mom. All their parents took turns driving the boys to and from school and various activities because they all lived within a few miles of each other. Mrs. Stetson greeted them and they began the short drive home.

"So, what did your parents end up saying about your birth certificate? Did you get your learner permit?" Jacob asked.

"Yeah, I got it." Nick said. "They explained the birth certificate thing. Everything is okay, now." Nick did not want to go through the whole story with his friends because so much of it did not make sense. If he had trouble understanding it, how could they?

"Is your name really Nacxit?" Jacob laughed.

"Unfortunately, yeah. My biological parents insisted on it." Nick replied with a smile.

"Nacxit?!" Colin exclaimed. "What kind of name is Nacxit? You must have some fascinating biological parents."

"Well, at this point I really couldn't tell you. Soon, I hope," Nick wished.

"What do you mean? Did you identify them? Are you going to meet them or something?" Jacob asked.

"Not yet. Once I find out who they are, I'm going to convince my parents to let me meet them," Nick said, assuredly.

"Wait, don't your real parents live in Mexico?" Colin questioned.

"Yep. I think it will be a nice trip!" Nick smiled again.

"I guess so." Colin replied.

For the remainder of the ride, they discussed the soccer team and the possibility of going to state finals. Mrs. Stetson pulled into Nick's driveway. Nick thanked her as he shut the car door and walked up to the house.

He opened the front door and was immediately greeted by the savory aroma of his mom's scrumptious roast. He walked into the kitchen and found his mom slicing up carrots. His dad was sitting at the kitchen counter, hunched over his laptop. They asked him about his day and informed him that dinner would be ready in another twenty minutes. That was just enough time to email the scanned pictographs to Professor Shelton and take a shower.

He went directly to his computer, took the pictographs from his pocket and put them into the scanner. Since Mr. Ambrose gave him the partial translations, Nick felt the need to keep the pictographs and the stone necklace with him at all times. He felt a connection to them and wanted to guard them closely. He reviewed the image, as it appeared on the screen. Because both papers were fairly small, they were both able to fit into one scan. Satisfied with the image, Nick saved the file to his computer and opened his email. He wrote a short message to Professor Shelton, reminding him of their previous conversation. He attached the image of the pictographs, requested confirmation of receipt, and sent the email. One more time, he examined the pictographs at his desk. The prospect of the pending translation and authentication was simultaneously exciting and terrifying.

CHAPTER THIRTEEN

It took three weeks for Professor Shelton to get back to Nick. Nick emailed him every few days to ask if there were any updates. When he did not get a response, he left him a voicemail stating that if he did not get back to him with an update in the next few days, Nick was going to find someone else to do the translations. Mr. Ambrose had been hounding him at school, too. Nick told him he was not getting any updates from the professor and was unsure what to do. Mr. Ambrose told him to just be patient because translating ancient text could take a lot of time.

Nick was tired of waiting. If Professor Shelton was so scholarly, why was it taking him so long? He was contemplating looking for someone else. Finally, he got an email from the professor on the last Tuesday of November, just before the Thanksgiving holidays. In the email, the professor apologized for the delay and lack of communication. He claimed that he had a family emergency and was not able to start translating the pictographs until a week ago. He said he finished translating the pictographs but he had a couple questions for Nick, so he would call him tomorrow afternoon. Nick was annoyed that Professor Shelton did not include the translations in the email.

Wednesday was early dismissal at school. Nick was thankful for the short day because he was unable to concentrate. For weeks all he thought about was those pictographs! Finally, today was the day the meaning would be revealed! Oddly, Mr. Ambrose left him alone for the past week. Nick almost grew accustomed to daily inquiries from him. When he got to history class on Monday of the previous week, Mr. Ambrose resumed ignoring him. Mr. Ambrose did not call on him the entire week. Nick was not sure what caused this sudden lack of interest, but he was happy that Mr. Ambrose was off of his back.

As he and his dad arrived home from school, his cell phone rang. He saw the Florida area code on the caller ID and felt an overwhelming surge of anxiety. *This is it!* He thought, racing to the privacy of his room.

"Hello?" Nick answered.

"Hi, Nick. This is Professor Shelton. I'm sorry it's taken me so long to get back to you. I've been busy with some family issues."

"That's okay. I'm glad you were able to finally translate the pictographs. I'm anxious to know what they say." Nick responded.

"Well, I must say, the translations are quite unusual. They're certainly enigmatic."

"Really? How so?"

"You said that a family member bought them from a souvenir shop down in Mexico. Are you sure about that? The translations are not something you would find on a souvenir."

"Honestly, I'm not sure of their exact origin. The rolled up paper was found by a family member on a beach in Mexico back in 1996, and the card was hand delivered to me almost four weeks ago. I am sorry that I wasn't completely honest with you before, but I didn't think it mattered," Nick said.

"I see," said the professor. "Was the beach in Mexico in the Yucatan?" The professor questioned.

"Yeah, it was a beach in Cozumel. How did you know?" Nick asked.

"What about the card? Who delivered it to you?" Professor Shelton asked, ignoring his question.

"I don't know. I found it in my mailbox with my name on it," Nick replied.

"Your name? But the image you sent me says Nacxit," the professor argued.

"Yeah, that's my given name," Nick explained.

"Your given name is Nacxit? The professor asked, incredulously.

"Yes. Why? Does it mean something?" Nick asked.

The professor paused a minute before he answered. "It's just Nacxit is an ancient Mayan name. Are your parents of Mayan ancestry?"

"They could be. I'm adopted. I've never met my biological parents," Nick admitted.

Nick waited for what seemed like forever for a response. He wondered if the line had been disconnected. "Hello? Are you still there?" Nick asked.

"Yes, I'm still here. I was just making some notations," the professor replied. His tone had completely transformed. "I'm going to email you a complete report of everything I translated but while I have you on the phone, I'm going to go ahead and read you what the pictographs say. Now, keep in mind that these translations are not exact because Mayan pictographs do not translate directly into English words. There is a surfeit of ambiguity. One picture could represent a hundred different things, so I've done my best based on the context of the other pictographs in the sequence. Do you understand?"

"Yeah, please go ahead," Nick replied, his heart pounding.

"Alright, the roll of paper that you say came from the beach says:

Savior Child of Ixchel. Leader at the end of time brings first key of salvation. Great altar brings isle of flame for peace.
And the card pictograph says:

Time is ending. Union of five at great altar will give rise to salvation.

"Does any of that mean anything to you?" The professor asked.

Nick tried to process everything the professor just said. He was completely caught off guard. He expected the pictographs to contain information about his biological parents, such as an address or phone number. He thought there would be an

69

explanation for his abandonment. What the professor just told him had him more confused than ever.

"No, I'm totally confused. What does it all mean?" Nick questioned.

"I was hoping you could tell me," the professor said. "I guess the only way to find out is to ask the author or authors."

"The author? I have no idea who wrote these!" Nick exclaimed, revealing his exasperation.

"In that case, there is nothing more I can tell you. I will email you the report in a few minutes. Take care. Goodbye," the professor said, hanging up.

Before he could muster a goodbye, the line clicked. The phone slipped out of his hand and hit the floor with a thud. He was disheartened and dumbfounded. He was so excited at the possibility of gaining clarity, but that quickly faded. The words that the professor just spoke to him might as well have been in Greek. Just as he took out the pictographs from his pocket, the voice started echoing "BELIEVE" again. Nick thought the pictographs would reveal the solution; instead, they were adding more obscurity to an already complex puzzle. Despite the increasing mystery, Nick's determination would not falter. One way or another, he was going to get some answers!

* * * *

Elliot was in a hurry to get off the phone with Nick Murphy. *Why tell the boy more than was necessary?* He sat at his desk looking at the pictograph translation report. He studied the pictographs over a hundred times, but he still could not believe what he was seeing. He emailed the report to Nick and smiled to himself. The poor kid was clueless. Elliot was elated. From what he gathered, Nick was telling the truth about how he acquired the pictographs. He suspected any pictograph that mentioned Ixchel would be from Cozumel or somewhere nearby.

Historically, various groups of Mayans populated Central America. Ixchel and her husband, Itzamna, were considered to be the founders of the ancient Yucatec Mayans. Depicted as gods,

Mayan writings and surviving myths describe them as Caucasians arriving to the Yucatan from a flooded eastern land. Temples were erected in honor of Ixchel and Itzamna on the eastern shores of Cozumel. To most scholars, Ixchel was considered the Mayan goddess of medicine and fertility. However, she was referenced in multiple remaining codices in various settings. In the Dresden Codex, Ixchel is depicted with a serpent on her head and an overturned vase in her hands the symbolism of which is much debated. Some claim the vase represents the womb, and the inversion of the vase is symbolic of childbirth. Others claim that the emptying of the vase represents the beginning of the rainy season, thus confirming Ixchel as a rain goddess. An unpopular theory associates Ixchel with the moon and psychic powers in addition to her status as a physician and midwife. This particular theory was of a certain interest to Elliot.

The fact that Nick was named Nacxit was even more captivating! The Quiche Maya, from the Guatemalan region, immortalizes an important warrior named Nacxit that possessed a powerful crystal. He arrived in the Yucatan after a catastrophic flood destroyed the ancient homeland of Patulan-Pa-Civan, located in the Eastern Alantic Ocean. The myth states that Nacxit gave the sacred stone to Balam Qitze, the leader of Patulan-Pa-Civan, before the voyage across the Atlantic to Mexico. Surprisingly, the description of Balam-Qitze is strikingly similar to Itzamna, Ixchel's husband. It would not be farfetched to consider them one in the same.

The "end of time" is a well-known date on any Mayan calendar. The Mayans were impressive astronomers. The development of their calendar is one of their most praised accomplishments. Their renowned calendar ends on the winter solstice of 2012, on December 21st. The winter solstice of 2012 was significant because the Sun would be precisely aligned with the galactic equator. Some scholars claimed that the Mayans anticipated this rare celestial event and believe it marked the end of the world. Scholars have debated extensively what this ending would bring about, whether it be the actual apocalypse or something metaphorical.

Finding a Yucatec and Quiche Mayan reference in one document was absolutely remarkable! It almost certainly meant that the author was either familiar with both dialects or the author was versed in dialect from which they both originated. Probably the most remarkable discovery was the mention of The Isle of Flame. Walter's translation was correct and could certainly be a reference to the mythical kingdom of Atlantis. As a scholar, Elliot knew that many civilizations acknowledged a devastating flood and an Atlantic homeland, but it was a stretch to assume they were all speaking of Atlantis. Of course, most ancient historical accounts are no more than theories.

Elliot salivated at the possibilities! *This kid could be holding evidence that Atlantis existed!* Furthermore, if his evidence led to the discovery of the ancient kingdom, he was not going to stand by and watch a naïve child take credit for the largest historical find of all time. Every account of Atlantis included boundless riches. *That would be an added bonus,* Elliot thought.

He had emailed the translation report to Walter last week. Walter pestered him for days about his theories. Elliot felt ambivalent about what information to relay to Walter. At the moment, Walter did not know about the piece of quartz that Nick had or the fact that Nick's given name was Nacxit. He considered cutting Walter out altogether but he still needed him to extract as much information as he could from Nick. *That kid had answers and Walter was going to get them!* Nacxit and the unveiling of his enigmatic, biological parents, was going to bring Elliot fame, fortune, and surely, a reason for early retirement.

CHAPTER FOURTEEN

Nick spent the rest of the evening studying the translation report that the professor emailed to him. He was intrigued by all the symbols and their meanings. The professor included alternate meanings for each symbol so Nick could understand that the translations were not likely exact. Nick painstakingly researched the different terms from the translations on the internet. He found an online encyclopedia article about Ixchel. Apparently, Ixchel was an ancient Mayan goddess that represented medicine and fertility. He could not decide whether the pictograph was referring to the actual goddess, someone named after her, or what she represented. A "savior child of Ixchel" might mean a surviving child of a doctor or maybe a child that was saved by a doctor. *Maybe my mother died in childbirth*, Nick thought. Perhaps, he had brothers or sisters and one of them abandoned him on the beach after their parents died. Nick searched the term "isle of flame" and was disappointed that there were no results. He wondered if the island it was referring to was Cozumel. After two hours of research, Nick heard his mom calling him from downstairs. He shut down his computer and went downstairs.

"So?!" His parents both said to him as he entered the kitchen. "Did the professor give you the translations?"

"Yeah, and they are not what I expected," Nick said. "The messages are weird. They are like a riddle."

"Okay. So, what do they say?" His mom pressured him while his dad appeared to be listening from behind his laptop.

"See for yourself," Nick said, placing the report on the kitchen table.

The three of them hovered at the professor's report. After five minutes of intense review, his dad stood upright.

"You're right. This is weird," his dad said.

"I concur. Whoever wrote these messages has me baffled. What is an Ixchel?" Nick chuckled, as his mom botched the pronunciation.

"It's pronounced ee-SHEL and I'm not sure what it means. I looked up the term online. The only result I found was about an ancient Mayan fertility goddess who was also a doctor. I'm not sure if this refers to the goddess or someone who bears her name. It could also just be a concept. The professor told me that the symbols can have multiple meanings, so nothing is exact."

"I'm surprised that the professor was not able to answer your questions. Isn't he supposed to be the Mayan expert?" His dad asked, doubtingly.

"He probably can. Unfortunately, he seemed like he was in a hurry. He gave me the translations and hung up the phone before I had a chance to say anything. I'm going to come up with a list of questions and call him back tomorrow," Nick said.

"So, how do you feel about all this, Nick?" Vanessa asked.

"Honestly, I think my biological parents are dead. It's really the only logical explanation. I think the pictographs are trying to tell me that my parents died in some tragic event and I may have other family members looking for me. Do you see where it says 'one of five?' I think I have brothers and sisters that are trying to contact me. I think they are the ones that sent the card and possibly left me on the beach that night." Nick speculated.

"That's quite a supposition. You shouldn't be so negative, though. They could still be alive." Anthony reassured him.

"I doubt it. I really thought the pictographs would give me a definitive answer. I wish we knew who wrote them," Nick yearned.

"Well, we may be able to get you one step closer," Vanessa said smiling at him.

"What? How?" Nick asked, excitedly.

"Like you, we expected the pictographs to reveal more information. We assumed there would be a reference to Cozumel, since that's where we found you. So, we've been planning a family vacation to Cozumel over Christmas break. What do you think?"

"Really?!" Nick exclaimed. "That sounds awesome! Since you told me the story, I've been dying to go! The pictograph mentions an 'isle of flame,' so I was thinking that it was referring to Cozumel."

"Our plan is to find Roberto, the local guy that helped us with your documents. We are hoping that he will know something about the card you received in the mailbox. He is really the only one that knows your given name," Anthony said.

"Maybe, he will be able to make sense of the other pictograph now that we have it translated." Nick said, positively.

"Yeah. That's an excellent idea!" Anthony said.

"When do we leave?" Nick asked.

"Because of the holidays, flights are filling up. We thought the best time to go would be the day after Christmas. We will leave on December 26th and return on January 2nd. That will give us a week to explore and enjoy ourselves," Anthony said.

"That's perfect!" Nick cheered. "The next few weeks of school are going to be torture!"

"You'll make it," Vanessa said, smiling at him. "Now, you guys have to decide where you want to go for dinner because I don't feel like cooking tonight."

"Ironically, I'm in the mood for Mexican," Nick said.

"Ha!" Anthony laughed. "I could go for some Mexican, too."

"Okay, then. Mexican it is," Vanessa said.

While his parents freshened up for dinner, Nick took the report back up to his room. He was so thrilled about the Mexico trip that he called Colin and Jacob to tell them the exciting news. He could not help but smile to himself, as he realized that in a few short weeks, while his friends were bundled up in front of a fire, he would be in his bathing suit on a warm, Mexican beach!

* * * *

Walter Ambrose sat on his couch demolishing a microwavable, frozen dinner. Although the name suggested it was a man-sized portion, Walter was always hungry afterwards. Sometimes, he would make two of the meals to fill him up, but tonight, he was going to fill up on some blueberry pie his mother had made fresh that day. At forty-one, Walter did not mind living with his mother. She cooked for him, kept the house clean, and mostly kept to herself. Occasionally, she would ask him to fix something or go to the grocery store and Walter would gladly oblige. After all, he was pretty much getting a free ride. He did not have to pay rent, cook, or clean! Tonight, his mother had Bingo at her church, so Walter had to make his own dinner. She would always invite him and encourage him to find a nice Christian girl, but Walter refused every time.

Walter had become complacent in the single lifestyle. His mother asked him if there were any pretty teachers at his school. He told her that there were, but they were all happily married, which was not far from the truth. There were a few unmarried, attractive teachers, but most of them were either too young or too stupid. Walter wanted a woman who shared his intense passion for history. Highly opinionated women were a turn-off for him. He held a strong disdain for know-it-alls. He desired a woman that was voluble, but eloquent.

A few months ago, he tried one of the online dating sites. He went on three dates and called it quits. His initial impressions of two of the women were pleasant, but when he asked them out for a second date, they made up excuses not to meet again. The third woman had completely misrepresented herself in her profile. Walter felt sick after going to dinner with her. He suspected she may have had a sex change because all her mannerisms were masculine. He decided it was better to spend his energy seeking knowledge rather than dumb love.

As he finished up his meal and prepared a slice of succulent, blueberry pie, he thought about the pictograph report that Elliot sent over almost a week ago. He was ecstatic to learn that his initial translations were correct! The pictograph did mention the "isle of flame." Walter had tried to reach Elliot numerous times to discuss exactly what everything meant, though he had yet to reply. He also kept a close eye on Nick, lately. Two days ago, he overheard Nick complaining to a friend about not having received the report. Walter wondered why Elliot held the information back from Nick as long as he did.

Walter and Elliot met in college at the University of Georgia. Unlike himself, Elliot was a womanizer. Walter was not sure how many times he had been married, but he knew of at least three women who where unfortunate enough to marry Elliot. Elliot had a son with one of them but Walter did not think they had much of a bond. Both history majors, Elliot and Walter collaborated on numerous projects together in college. Elliot was drawn to Mesoamerica while Walter fell in love with Egypt. After he got his Bachelor's degree, Walter began working to reduce his exorbitant student loan debit. Elliot, on the other hand, came from an affluent family and continued on to earn his Doctorate. Walter aspired to earn his Doctorate as well, but instead decided to save for a year in Egypt. Recently, he applied for a position as a guest researcher at an Egyptian university so he could explore the pyramids and possibly assist in some excavations. Unfortunately, he did not receive a response back, yet.

Walter stuffed the last morsel of pie in his mouth. He was already reaching for the entire rest of pie, when the phone rang. He struggled to quickly chew and swallow before answering the phone.

"Hello?" Walter choked.

"Walter? This is Elliot. I need to talk to you about the pictographs. Do you have a minute?"

"Of course! I've been waiting for your call," Walter said.

"My apologizes. I've been busy. I spoke to Nick Murphy today and emailed him the report. He gave me some interesting information. He is adopted, and his given name is Nacxit. I think his biological parents are of Mayan descent," Elliot conjectured.

"Really? I wonder why he never mentioned that to me. What do you make of the mention of Ixchel? I'm also curious about the key. Whatever it is, do you think Nick has it? Walter asked.

"I'm not really sure at this point. Look Walter. I need you to keep a close eye on this kid. I think he's going to indirectly tell us everything we need to know. He has no idea how deep this research runs. I'm going to avoid his calls so I expect him to become frustrated and possibly reach out to you. You need to extract whatever you can from him. Something that may seem insignificant, now, could be important later. Can you handle that?"

"Absolutely, but do you have any theories? Do you think 'the isle of flame" is Atlantis?" Walter asked.

"Again, I'm not sure. I need more information. Until I have evidence, I do not want to continue speculating. Your job is to gather as much evidence from Nick as you can. Remember to be as vague as possible. We don't want him to uncover the true value of his discovery." Elliot warned.

"Not a problem." Walter said. "I'll try to keep quiet and let Nick do all the talking."

"Exactly." Elliot said. "Now, I have some work to finish up. I'll speak to you later. Goodbye."

"Okay, but-- " Walter could not finish his question before he heard the line click on the other end. He knew Elliot was busy but he did not have to be insolent. Walter hung up the phone and turned on the television. He flipped through the channels until he found a Star Trek marathon. He viewed two-and-a-half episodes and headed off to bed. He changed into his footed, sphinx-print pajamas, set his alarm clock, and climbed into his sarcophagus-shaped bed to dream about The Isle of Flame.

CHAPTER FIFTEEN

During the Thanksgiving holidays and the subsequent weeks that followed, Nick's conscious and subconscious thoughts were consumed by the pictographs. School, soccer, and life in general became a blur. His dreams became increasingly abstruse. Prior to the arrival of the pictograph, Nick always dismissed his dreams as meaningless images. He never bothered to relate them to real life or ponder them once he awoke. In light of this new information, he started to pay more attention. Every time he had a dream about the necklace or anything that could relate to the pictographs, he found himself analyzing every aspect of the vision. The necklace was a common theme as it always had been. The pictographs were occasionally present, but recently, there were brief appearances of an elderly woman in distinct settings. Sometimes, she was just a figure in the background; and at other times she was mouthing inaudible words. Nick started to believe that this woman was the personification of the voice he heard all his life.

The frequency in which he heard the voice had changed, as well. Instead of the occasional guidance, she incessantly reiterated, "BELIEVE." When he had accepted his birth story, he expected the voice to cease. She still continued!

This had never happened before, and Nick was increasingly puzzled by it. The stakes seemed higher, and lately, every decision he faced seemed pivotal. Nick battled a momentary lapse in self-confidence. *Am I just a mental patient with a vivid imagination?* He shook himself out of his self-deprecating mode. The voice had never been wrong. He chose to accept that she was still trying to help him "BELIEVE" something.

* * * *

December 16th was the last day of school before the Christmas holiday. Walter was just as antsy as the students to begin the holiday break. For the last day of class, Walter played a movie during each period. He knew that most of the class would be absent and no one would pay attention to a lecture.

Nick was under his scrutiny for about two weeks. Just as Elliot predicted, Nick became frustrated when he was unable to reach the professor, forcing him to seek aid from Walter. Regrettably, after Walter encouraged Nick to be patient because the professor is busy man, Nick never broached the subject. Walter assayed to directly solicit information from him in the form of seemingly, harmless questions. To his chagrin, Nick was uncooperative and only responded with tenebrous answers. The scarce bit of information that Walter obtained was by snooping.

A week earlier, he overheard Nick talking to his friends, Colin and Jacob. They were challenging him to a re-match at the paintball arena after Christmas. Nick teased that he would love to put them to shame again, but he would be out of town. Colin and Jacob jabbed back about him sitting on a beach, while they would be stuck with their boring families. A few days later, Walter noticed Nick diligently working on something, during an important history lecture. Abruptly, he stopped lecturing, marched over to Nick, and demanded that Nick hand it over to him. Walter snatched the paper, placed it on his desk, and told Nick he could retrieve it after class. Nick seemed too embarrassed to protest. After he finished his lecture, Walter gave the class a jumpstart on their homework. While the class was reading, Walter sat down at his desk and reviewed the paper he confiscated from Nick. It was a series of notes and questions Nick wrote next to certain symbols that Walter recognized from the pictograph report. After reading everything that Nick wrote, Walter deduced that Nick believed either his biological parents, or someone acting on their behalf, created the pictographs. Furthermore, Nick surmised that he may have other siblings, and his biological parents may be deceased. When the dismissal bell rang, Nick shot straight up to Mr. Ambrose's desk to retrieve his "secret" notes. Little did he know that Walter had already committed the material parts to memory.

It was not until yesterday that Walter stumbled upon the last piece of the puzzle. Nick walked across the parking lot after school on his way to soccer practice. By sheer luck, Walter was getting in his car, going home for the day. A female acquaintance came running out of the building and shouted Nick's name. Nick caught site of her and shouted a friendly, "Hey!" With her ponytail bouncing, the girl squealed, "Have fun in Cozumel! Make sure you bring me something back!" Nick smiled and assured her that he would. *Cozumel*, Walter thought. *That could not be a coincidence.*

Walter packed up and exited his classroom almost as quickly as his students. *Let Christmas break begin!* He made his way to his car and called Elliot. The professor picked up on the fourth ring.

"Walter, how's it going?"

"Wonderful! I have some information for you about Nick!" Walter gushed, trying to catch his breath from the near sprint to the car.

"Splendid! Go ahead. I'm listening."

"Since we last spoke, I've been doing my best to glean lots of private information. Nick came to me a few days after you ignored his calls. He was frustrated, but he did not confide in me. I attempted to ask him subtle questions but he remained vague. I overheard Nick talking to some friends, and I confiscated some notes he was making in class. I found out that he and his family have plans to visit Cozumel over the Christmas break. He thinks that the author of the pictographs is either his biological parents or someone acting on their behalf, like a sibling or other relative. He's going to Cozumel to attempt to find the author, I'm sure of it. I think he believes The Isle of Flame is Cozumel, but I don't really have any proof."

"Interesting," Elliot said. "Did he mention anything about a stone?"

"A stone? No. Why?" This is the first Walter heard of the idea.

"No reason, just curious."

"So, what do you think? Is this whole thing worth pursing or do you think we should leave it alone?" Walter questioned.

"I think you should pack your bags."

"Pack my bags? To go where?" Walter asked.

"Looks like we are going to Mexico," Elliot said. Then, Walter heard a click on the other end of the line. Walter knew one thing. He would never get accustomed to Elliot's phone etiquette!

CHAPTER SIXTEEN

The Murphys departed from Atlanta bound for Cozumel on Monday, December 26th. The flight to Cozumel lasted three hours, landing them at the Cozumel International Airport around 2:00 P.M. They collected their luggage from baggage claim and proceeded to the rental car counter.

After an insufferable, hour-long wait, Anthony was agitated. Normally, he would have demanded an upgrade for the poor service, but he reminded himself they were in Mexico. From his first visit, he learned that complaints fell on deaf ears. The rental agent processed their reservation at a snail's pace and eventually handed him the keys to a foreign model Nissan sedan, with few upgrades. Anthony, Vanessa, and Nick walked to the designated parking space, loaded their luggage, and began the short jaunt to the hotel.

The island of Cozumel was approximately thirty-miles long and nine-miles wide, making everything easily accessible. They rental car probably was not necessary but Anthony was not keen on utilizing public transportation. Rumor had it that it was exceedingly slow and unreliable.

In order to help piece things together, they had decided to return to the Seaside Reef Hotel and Resort. The hotel was situated directly on the northwestern shoreline and it was walking distance from the city of San Miguel. Other than a different exterior color and some updated décor, the hotel appeared the same. After check-in, they rode the elevator to the sixth floor and proceeded to room 612.

The room was a standard hotel room with a king size bed, pullout sofa, and bathroom. Anthony valued the finer things in life, but admittedly, he was cheap. Anticipating they would not be hanging out in the room much, he could not justify the indulgence. It was not a bad room; it just had a view of the parking. Nick was the first to comment on the room.

"Well, it's not the Ritz Carlton, but it will work," Nick joked.

"What do you know about the Ritz Carlton?" Anthony questioned.

"Enough to know that this room certainly wouldn't meet their standards."

"Yeah, well, if you want to foot the bill for a week, they have a nice ocean-view suite available. Shall I call the front desk and have us transferred?" Anthony teased.

"Uh. . .On second thought, this room is stupendous," Nick smiled.

"That's what I thought," Anthony said, returning the grin.

"It's only for a week. We're going to be exploring and adventuring, anyway." Vanessa added.

"True. So what's for dinner?" Nick asked

"Are you hungry already? It's only 4:00 P.M.," Vanessa said.

"I was thinking about trying out the hotel restaurant tonight. That way we can plan out our day for tomorrow and go to bed early," Anthony suggested.

"Good thinking, honey," Vanessa said while Nick nodded in agreement.

For the next few hours, Anthony and Vanessa gave Nick the grand tour of the hotel. There was an impressive gym and spa area, along with a beautiful, new, infinity pool that overlooked the gorgeous, emerald sea. Cozumel was known for its world-class scuba diving. Vanessa had tried to talk him into going on their last trip, but Anthony belligerently refused. Anthony could not understand why anyone would elect to be submerged for long periods of time with a limited oxygen supply. Instead, they went snorkeling off of the hotel shore. Due to the rocky shoreline, there was no natural beach. The hotel had compensated for this by creating their beach at the top of the rocky shore by boxing it in and filling it with sand. It was the fact that this beach was neither authentic nor private that drove Anthony and Vanessa to the place they discovered Nick.

After exploring the hotel, they congregated in a cozy, shaded cabana and ordered drinks from the tiki bar. Anthony and Vanessa were not heavy drinkers, only indulging on occasion. Anthony looked at the drink menu and decided on a virgin piña colada. Vanessa agreed that a piña colada sounded delicious, so they decided to share it. Nick ordered a virgin strawberry daiquiri, topped with whipped cream and a cherry.

Anthony closed his eyes and breathed in the salty air. He did not realize how much he needed a vacation. He felt the same conviction he had fifteen years earlier. He was still a workaholic. He still could not let loose and enjoy the fruits of his labor. He still struggled with balance, prioritization, and initiating family time. In less than six months, Nick would be able to drive on his own. Soon, he would be off to college. Anthony truly coveted the time he spent with his family. Fully recognizing his neglect, he internally pledged to God and himself to make lasting changes once and for all.

"So, Dad, what are the plans for the week?" Nick asked.

"Well, first, it makes sense to locate Roberto. Other than whoever actually filled out your Consular Report, Roberto is the sole person who knows about your real name and how we found you. He knew where Vanessa and I were staying, so I don't think it would be too hard to get our mailing address from the hotel," Anthony said.

"You think he mailed the other pictograph?" Nick asked.

"Honestly, I don't know what to think, but I do know that, if someone was trying to get in touch with us, Roberto would surely try to help. I think that finding him is our best shot at getting some answers. Did you ever get back in touch with the professor?" Anthony asked.

"No. I tried calling him numerous times but he was never in the office. It's like he gave me the translations and never returned to work," Nick said.

After hearing the translations of the pictographs, Anthony and Vanessa were bewildered. They expected some sort of explanation or apology, not the cabalistic message that Nick presented to them. Anthony found it a little odd that the professor suddenly cut off contact with Nick. The pictographs were determined to be authentic, and Anthony expected the professor to be ecstatic. Instead, he disappeared. This irked Anthony to no avail.

They spent about half an hour talking and enjoying their drinks before heading to the restaurant for dinner. The hotel restaurant was not the usual American Mexican restaurant. The menu and atmosphere were similar to an upscale, American steakhouse. In addition to the indoor formal seating, the restaurant offered a breathtaking view of the Caribbean Sea from the terrace. They could not get enough of the sunset dinner and the melt-in-your-mouth piece of chocolate cake that followed.

After dessert, they returned to their room. As Anthony opened the door, a pungent smell rushed to his nose. It was not a bad smell, but it was not particularly aromatic, either. It smelled like cheap musk. He entered the room with Vanessa and Nick at his heels. They all stopped in their tracks, as the door slammed behind them. The room was not at all how they left it. All three of their suitcases were opened and in a state of disarray. Drawers were wide open as was the sliding, glass door to the balcony.

"Oh, no! We've been robbed!" Vanessa exclaimed.

"I'm going to call the police! Nick, go down to the front desk! Tell them what happened!" Anthony instructed.

Immediately, Nick bolted out of the room, and Anthony raced to the phone. Upon dialing, he was greeted by a male, Spanish-speaking voice. Anthony spoke to him in English. Luckily, the man seemed to understand. In broken English, he asked Anthony his location and said he would send an officer. After he hung up, Anthony assessed the situation for possible stolen items. He glanced over to the desk. To his surprise, his laptop was there, untouched.

"Vanessa, are you missing anything?" Anthony asked.

"I had my purse and wallet with me, so the only valuable thing left in the room was my tablet. Thankfully, it's right there."

She motioned to the nightstand. "It doesn't look like anything has been stolen," she said with relief.

Anthony's mind was reeling. *What kind of thieves went to the trouble of breaking into a hotel room without taking anything? The laptop and the tablet would have sold for two hundred dollars or more! The items were in plain sight. Why would they leave them behind?* By the time Nick walked back into the hotel room with the hotel manager, Anthony had scoured through their suitcases.

"Dad, this is Mr. Rodriguez. He wants to know what happened," Nick said.

"Hello, Mr. Rodriguez. We came back from dinner and found the room like this. At the moment, it doesn't look like anything was stolen, but we are still checking. Nick, check and see if you are missing anything," Anthony directed.

"Mr. Murphy, I am very sorry about all this. We have never had anything like this happen! Please allow me to upgrade you and your family to one of our luxury suites, free of charge," Mr. Rodriguez said in a heavily-accented, apologetic tone.

"Thank you very much for your understanding. I assume the police will want to investigate the room, and we would like to get some sleep. So, we'll gladly accept the upgrade," Anthony replied.

"You called the police?" Mr. Rodriguez asked with a look of concern on his face.

"Yes, of course. Is something wrong?" Anthony questioned.

"It's okay, but, in Mexico, sometimes the police can cause problems rather than solve them. Don't worry. I will take care of them. Shall I get an employee to help you move to your suite?"

"No, that won't be necessary," Anthony said.

"Very well. When you are ready, the new key card will be at the front desk. Please let me know if you need anything else," Mr. Rodriguez said as he smiled and exited the room.

"All my stuff is here," Nick said, closing his suitcase.

Anthony was beyond confused. It appeared that the thief or thieves came in and out from the sliding glass door on the balcony. The room was on the sixth floor, which meant that coming and going would not be easy. *Maybe that was why they did not take the laptop; it would have been too bulky to carry,* Anthony thought. Also, it meant that this was not a crime of opportunity. A break-in on the sixth floor required time and planning. *Did someone specifically target us?* No one besides immediate family and friends knew they were in Mexico. Anthony was starting to fret. Every instinct he had screamed at him to pack up their things and return to Atlanta in the morning. Despite this, he knew Nick needed answers and Mexico was the only place they were going to find them. Reluctantly, he helped Vanessa and Nick pack up and move the rest of their belongings to their new suite. He sent Nick back to the front desk to retrieve the new room key. Anthony was uneasy, and nothing was going to change that, until they returned safe and sound to Atlanta.

CHAPTER SEVENTEEN

The next morning, Nick woke up to the sound of his parent's muffled voices. It sounded like they were arguing in the next room. Nick rolled out of bed and groggily opened the bedroom door. He had his own room, now in the Starfish Suite. He found his parents sitting on the couch in the living room. Abruptly, they stopped arguing and greeted him with forced, good-morning smiles.

"So, how did you sleep?" Anthony asked.

"It was great, until your arguing woke me. What's going on with you guys?" Nick asked.

"We are just concerned about the break-in last night. I went downstairs this morning to speak with the hotel manager about the police. I was wondering why we were not interviewed last night. Apparently, an officer showed up, and the manager told him it was a rogue housekeeper and that the hotel would handle the situation. Since nothing was actually taken, the officer accepted that explanation and left without question. I told the manager that I still wanted to file a police report, and he told me that the police here are worse than the criminals. He told me to just be thankful that nothing was taken and enjoy the rest of our vacation," Anthony said.

"So, what's wrong with that?" Nick asked.

"Someone broke into our room and was looking for something. I don't know what, but no one goes to all that trouble and just leaves empty-handed. For all we know, the hotel could be running some sort of scam. Maybe the employees are in on it. How do we know it won't happen again? I don't know. I just think the police should be involved," Anthony said.

"We were only checked in for a few hours. Maybe whoever broke in got our room mixed up with someone else's. Maybe they were expecting the people that were in the room before us," Vanessa suggested in an effort to allay Anthony's worry.

"I considered that scenario, but I would assume that most people know the standard check-in and check-out times of hotels. Even a common criminal would not make that kind of mistake." Anthony declared.

After a brief silence, Anthony spoke again. "Maybe you're right. Maybe it was just a case of mistaken identity. How about we get breakfast and see if we can track down Roberto?" Anthony said to Vanessa, abandoning the argument.

"I'll get dressed." Nick said, going back into the bedroom.

He knew his dad was too upset to just change the subject like that. He could tell he was trying not to ruin the vacation. He appreciated his dad's gesture. Secretly, he was uneasy about the break-in, too; however, he was desperate to get answers, and Roberto seemed like an ideal start. He threw on cargo shorts and a wrinkled t-shirt. He put on deodorant and ran a comb through his hair before meeting his parents back in the living room.

"That was record time!" His mom observed.

"Yep. So, do you guys know where Roberto lives?" Nick asked.

"We know where he lived fifteen years ago. Hopefully, he still lives in the same house, or the current resident can tell us where he's moved," his dad replied.

"And if they can't?" Nick questioned.

"Then, we will have to come up with a different game plan." Anthony declared as he gathered the car keys and walked toward the door.

"Great," Nick said sarcastically, following his parents to the door.

They left the suite, making sure they brought all their valuables with them. The hotel offered a complimentary continental breakfast in the restaurant every morning. After enjoying their quick breakfast, they exited the hotel and made their way to the rental car. When they reached the parking lot, they all simultaneously donned their sunglasses. It was a brilliant day. As they were walking to the car, Anthony turned and scrutinized the hotel building.

"That's how they did it!" Anthony exclaimed, pointing at the window-washing platform strung down the side of the building.

Nick and Vanessa followed his gaze.

"Wow!" Vanessa said. "That's pretty smart. No one would think anything of a couple guys on a window-washing platform and that platform could give them access to all the rooms on the east side of the building."

"Exactly. I told you! This break-in was premeditated. I don't think the hotel is in on it. It would have been much easier for them to just use a duplicate key card from housekeeping," Anthony said.

"So, it was random? How do we know others were not robbed? That's not something the hotel manager is going to admit. It could have been a mass robbery, and we were just one of many," Nick added.

"Yeah, that's plausible. When we get back tonight, I'm going to see if I can find any other guests that were robbed. I'd feel much better knowing that we weren't the only ones." Anthony said while they all climbed into the rental car.

Anthony cranked up the car, and a Mariachi band played on the radio.

"This is my favorite song!" Vanessa joked.

"Whatever," Nick said, grinning at her.

As the Mexican music played in the background, they pulled out of the hotel parking lot onto the main road. Nick was amazed at how different his dad was when he was away from work. He was attentive, compassionate, talkative, considerate, and most of all, he had a sense of humor. Altogether, he was like a different person. Nick found it both bizarre and encouraging.

Initially, they drove toward San Miguel but Anthony suddenly made a left turn.

"I thought Roberto lived in the city," Nick said, noticing the change in direction.

"No, he lives near the eastern shore, close to the beach where we found you." Anthony said.

"Oh," Nick said. He had wondered about the beach and how it looked. *Maybe they could go by there first*, he thought.

"How far is the beach from Roberto's house?" Nick asked.

"If you are talking about mileage, it's probably five miles away. Time wise, it's close to thirty minutes because the beach is off of a dirt road with a slow speed limit. Why do you ask?" Anthony said.

"I was hoping we could go by the beach first. I want to see it," Nick said.

"Sure. That shouldn't be a problem. Roberto lives off of the main highway that runs across the island from west to east. The road that leads to the beach is at the most eastern end of that highway. Roberto's house is actually one of the closest to the beach. That's how we found him."

Nick looked out the window at the thick jungle that lined the road as they drove down the highway toward the eastern shore. Once outside of the hotel district, the island was sparsely populated. On the way to the beach, they passed a sign with an arrow that read, "San Gervasio Ruins." Nick read about the ruins when he did an internet search on sites to see in Cozumel. He made a mental note to ask his parents to go by there later. After fifteen minutes of driving on the highway, Anthony started to slow down as the road ended in an unpaved cul-de-sac. Anthony drove the car off the road and into the sand. Nick saw a dirt road to the left marked with a sign that signified the distances to various towns. Below the directional sign was another sign written in English with red paint. It read: NO RENTAL CARS BEYOND THIS POINT. Nick expected his dad to pull over; uncharacteristically, he ignored the sign and proceeded down the dirt road.

"Dad! Didn't you see the sign? It says no rental cars are allowed down this road!" Nick exclaimed.

"Yeah, that sign was there fifteen years ago. I ignored it then, and I'm going to ignore it now! There is no way I'm going to walk five miles to the beach in this sun," Anthony said, smirking at Vanessa.

"Wow, you guys were rebels back in the day, huh?" Nick joked.

"Yeah, don't get any ideas," Vanessa said, smiling.

As they continued down the dirt road, Nick realized why they did not want rental cars on the road. Every few feet, Anthony had to bring the car almost to a complete stop in order to drive over enormous potholes. The thick brush frequently protruded into the road, causing the branches to hit the sides of the car, leaving Nick to seriously question how his parents traveled this road in the middle of the night.

"You guys came out here at night?" Nick asked.

"Yeah, I was trying to impress your mom with a romantic evening on a secluded beach. Of course, it turned out to be one crazy night," Anthony said.

"You guys were pretty brave to come out to the middle of nowhere at night. You know, that's the stuff that inspires horror movies," Nick said, smiling.

"I told you we were rebels," Anthony reiterated.

"Right," Nick said.

They crept along the pot-hole-ridden road for twenty more minutes. Finally, they came upon a small clearing and an old sign that read: Playa Bonita. Anthony parked the car under a palm tree and they all exited the car.

"Wow, this place has changed since we were here last," Vanessa said, looking around.

"Yeah. It looks like there is a restaurant and some straw beach shelters now," Anthony said.

"Look! They built some restrooms, too. Thank goodness for that! Remember how badly I had to pee that night? I ended up having to go in the bushes!" Vanessa laughed.

"Ha! Oh, I remember!" Anthony exclaimed.

Anthony and Vanessa led the way. Nick tagged along, admiring the breathtaking beach. Playa Bonita was true to the name. The beach was breathtaking. The sun reflected off of the emerald sea, and the sand was powdery white. With palm trees randomly scattered about and the gentle breeze, it was truly a postcard-worthy scene. There were only five other people on the beach. For some reason, Nick felt that visiting the beach would help him understand why he was abandoned there. He was not sure what he expected to find or see, but at the very least, it would be a relaxing stroll on the beach. They walked along the water for a minute. Anthony and Vanessa came to a stop in front of a crumbling ruin that was partially hidden by sand dunes and sea oats.

"Do you remember that being here?" Anthony asked Vanessa.

"No. I guess because it was dark, we couldn't see it," Vanessa said

"Yeah, I guess so," Anthony said, staring at the ruin.

"Is this where you found me?" Nick asked.

"Yes. You were lying right around where we are standing," Anthony said.

Nick stood still and took in the surroundings. He tried to imagine what it was like that night. As he closed his eyes to take in the full effect, he was overcome with an illusion of a woman holding a vase. She turned the vase over and his stone necklace fell out. Four other necklaces followed. The necklaces fell onto a platform that had a strange symbol engraved in the middle. Shocked by what he was seeing, Nick snapped open his eyes and found himself starring up at the sun, lying in the sand.

"Nick! Nick! Are you all right?!" His parents were shouting, as they knelt over him.

"I don't know. What happened?" Nick asked.

"One minute you were standing here and the next minute, you were on the ground. I think you fainted. Have you been drinking enough water?" Vanessa asked, with a concerned look on her face.

"I had some juice at breakfast," Nick replied.

"Well, with the sun as hot as it is, I think you need to be drinking more water." Vanessa instructed.

"Are you sure you are all right? Do you want to go back to the car?" Vanessa asked him.

94

"No, I'm fine. I'm probably just dehydrated. Let's check out that ruin," Nick said, walking away from her toward the ruin. He could tell his parents were worried and wanted an explanation for his sudden collapse, but he did not want to tell them about the vision. If he informed them that he was seeing visions, in addition to still hearing the voice, it might prompt them to call upon the doctors again. *That was the last thing Nick needed right now!*

The ruin was a small, square, four-wall structure without a roof. There were no windows and just a single doorway. Most of the walls were crumbling. Nick, Anthony and Vanessa entered the small structure and saw the tourist graffiti on what was left of the walls. Nick scanned the graffiti. So many couples branded the building with their names and the word "forever" underneath. Nick smiled. He wondered how many people were actually still together.

"It's a real shame that people do that," a sweet voice from behind them said. They all spun around to find the silhouette of a beautiful Mexican girl standing in the doorway. Her long, black hair waved gently around her slender figure. As she stepped closer, Nick could not help but gawk at her in her black, bikini top and cut-off jean shorts. *She was probably close to his age*, he thought.

"Yes, it is," Anthony replied.

"I'm surprised you made it out here," the girl said in a Mexican accent. "Most tourists never leave the hotel district. If you guys came out here for surfing, today would not be the day for that. However, it is a lovely day for snorkeling. I'd be happy to give you the grand tour of our beautiful reef."

"No, thanks, we're just here taking in the scenery," Anthony said. "Maybe later in the week we will come back and take you up on your offer. Do you live around here?"

"Yes, my name is Roslyn. I'm here every day, as long as the weather is nice."

"Ok, good to know! My name is Anthony. This is my wife, Vanessa and, my son, Nick."

"Nice to meet you," Roslyn said, shaking their hands.

Roslyn moved away from the doorway to allow them to exit the ruin. She followed them out onto the beach.

"Do you know the history of this ruin?" Anthony asked Roslyn.

"Local legend describes this ruin as a boundary marking the end of the Mayan civilization. The Mayans believed that the world stopped where the sun rose, so the ruin was built on the most eastern point on land where they could see the sunrise," Roslyn said.

"That's very thought-provoking. You seem to know your history," Vanessa said.

"Yes. My ancestors are Mayan. I heard many of the myths and legends when I was a little girl. My grandfather Roberto loved to tell me Mayan bedtime stories.

Anthony, Vanessa, and Nick all looked at each other, as Roslyn spoke the name Roberto.

"Your grandfather's name is Roberto?" Anthony asked.

"Yes. Why do you ask?" Roslyn asked, quizzically.

"I'm sure it's not the same person, but we were just on our way to visit with a man named Roberto," Anthony said.

"Really? Does your Roberto have a last name?" Roslyn asked.

"I can't fully remember his last name. It's something "chez", I think. Velasquez maybe?"

"Sanchez?" Roslyn suggested with a worried look.

"Yes! That's it! Roberto Sanchez. How did you --?" Anthony did not finish the question, as he came to the same disturbing conclusion that Roslyn did.

Roslyn's friendly demeanor suddenly became defensive. "What do you want with my grandfather?" She asked.

"It's kind of a long story. Vanessa and I met him fifteen years ago, while we were on vacation. He did us a really huge favor. We just have some questions for him," Anthony said.

"That's going to be a problem. You might as well go back to your hotel. You're not going to be asking my grandfather any questions," Roslyn said.

"I promise, we don't mean any harm. It will only take a few minutes. You are welcome to join us if you want," Anthony pleaded.

"You don't understand. My grandfather cannot answer your questions. Last year he had a heart attack and never recovered. He passed away six months ago."

Nick's stomach dropped. Without Roberto, there was little chance of them getting to the truth. Anthony and Vanessa seemed discouraged, as well. While mulling over what Roslyn just relayed, Nick came to a realization. *The pictograph card was only delivered about two months ago. Roberto died six months ago. Roberto could not have been the person who sent it!*

"Wow. We're sorry to hear that," Vanessa said, sympathetically.

Roslyn must have sensed that they were all disappointed. She seemed to relax a little after the apology.

"What kind of questions did you have for my grandfather? Maybe, I can help. I lived with him my whole life. My mother and father separated when I was two, so my mom and I moved in with my grandfather," Roslyn explained.

"I'm not sure you can help us, but since your grandfather has passed, I guess it won't hurt to tell you. I think I'm getting sunburned. Is there someplace we can all sit down out of the sun?" Anthony asked.

"Sure," Roslyn said. "There are some tables over by the little restaurant. They won't mind if we sit there."

As they all approached a table, Nick could not help but notice Roslyn's beauty. Anthony and Vanessa rattled off the story of the romantic night on the beach that changed their lives forever while Nick thought about the vision of the woman and the necklaces. He reached in his pocket and grasped the stone in his hand. First, he had the dreams. Now, the vision with the necklace flashed again. *Maybe the necklace was more than a simple keepsake*, he thought. Sitting on the beach, where it all began, felt strange. He was determined to discover what happened there so many years ago and why all his efforts at finding the truth led to more mysteries.

CHAPTER EIGHTEEN

Roslyn's first impression of the Murphys was unremarkable. She assumed they were the average tourists looking to sightsee or take excursions. Originally, she approached them for a business opportunity, hoping to take them snorkeling or kayaking. When they mentioned her grandfather's name, chills ran up and down her spine. Everyone on the island knew of her grandfather's death. When they spoke of him as if he were still alive, it immediately struck a nerve. Of course, since they were foreigners, it made sense. Nevertheless, she was still skeptical of the Murphys and their reasons for visiting Cozumel. Growing up in Mexico, Roslyn had to be street smart. It was drilled into her at a young age that trust must be earned. Everyone is out to get you.

Roslyn had mixed feelings after hearing the Murphys' story. It seemed to her that the Murphys kidnapped Nick on the advice and assistance of her grandfather. Now, they probably feel guilty and want to make amends for their felonious crime. Roslyn lived with her grandfather for almost her entire life and never heard any mention of the Murphys and what they described. Granted, the events supposedly took place a year before Roslyn and her mother moved in, but Roslyn did not understand why her grandfather would not have mentioned it. The story was incredible. After all, it is not every day that some American tourists find a baby on the beach and decide to take him home with them.

"So, your grandfather never mentioned anything about us?" Anthony persisted.

"No. I already told you. He never mentioned anything," Roslyn asserted.

"How old were you in November 1996?" Anthony asked.

"I was born in June of 1996, so I was only five months.

"You were too young. Is it possible he told your mother?"

"I was much closer to my grandfather than my mom. She worked days and nights to support us. We didn't move in with him

99

until I was a year and a half old. Trust me, though. He would have told me at some point. Besides Mayan legends, he used to make up bedtime stories based on events in his life, so I'm sure I would have heard some version of your story."

"Well, did he ever mention having any friends at the US Consulate?" Nick probed her.

Roslyn thought for a moment. She did know someone who was affiliated with the consulate, but she was unsure how close that person was to her grandfather, and she did no want the Murphys to run off to badger the person for information. She decided to make something up for the time being.

"I'm not sure. My mother might have the answer to that question. How about you guys come back later in the week for some surfing or snorkeling, and I'll let you know," she suggested.

"I guess we don't have much of a choice," Anthony said, disappointed. "You're not available tomorrow?"

"I have some important errands to run in the morning. I wouldn't be able to make it back to the beach until around 3:00 P.M. You guys wouldn't have much daylight left. Thursday is much better for me. I can meet you as early as you like," Roslyn said.

"Ok. Thursday it is. How about 10:00 A.M?" Anthony said.

"Perfect," Roslyn said, smiling at Nick. "Where are you staying? If the weather doesn't cooperate, then I will have to call you to reschedule."

"The Seaside Reef Resort and Hotel. We are staying in the Starfish Villa Suite," Anthony said.

Roslyn and the Murphys all stood up to leave. They shook hands and started heading in opposite directions. Roslyn was half way down the beach on the way to her rental hut, when she heard someone calling her name from behind her. She turned around to see Nick running toward her.

"Hey! I wanted to ask you for a favor," Nick stammered, out of breath.

Roslyn giggled. "Sure. What do you need?"

"Since you seem to know your Mayan history, I was hoping I could convince you to give me a tour of the San Gervasio ruins," Nick said, smiling.

Roslyn was caught completely off guard. Normally, she was quick to discourage advances by tourists. Having a fling with a foreigner was not her idea of a good time. However, Nick was different. His demeanor was more mature, and he did not have the typical reckless, teenage attitude she experienced so often. Most guys her age that came to Mexico had two things on their mind, partying and drinking. He seemed genuinely interested in seeing the ruins and preferred to have her as a guide. His mesmerizing, piercing, blue eyes met hers, and uncharacteristically, she could not refuse.

"Ok. When do you want to go?" Roslyn asked.

"I was hoping we could go now. I don't see too many people ready to go snorkeling, so I thought you could get away for a few hours."

"What about your parents? Are they coming?" Roslyn asked.

"My mom wants to do some shopping. My dad is going to take her to lunch, and they'll spend the rest of the afternoon downtown. They can drop us off on the way."

"I guess I can take an early lunch and give you a tour for a few hours. You can tell your parents to go ahead without us. We can take my car. I'll drop you back at your hotel when we are finished," Roslyn said.

"You sure you are old enough to drive?" Nick questioned.

"I've been driving for a year now. Don't worry; the laws are rarely enforced here. As long as you can reach the pedals and see over the steering wheel, the cops assume you are legal," Roslyn laughed.

"All right, I'll let them know. I'll be right back," Nick said, turning around and sprinting back to the parking lot."

Nick intrigued Roslyn. In addition to being pleasing on the eyes, he seemed ambitious and confident. Of course, she only knew him for an hour, so he could end up being a complete jerk.

However, since her grandfather apparently trusted the Murphys, she felt she could, too.

Just to be safe, she decided to call her mom and tell her where she was going. Roslyn and her mother were not that close and rarely spent more than an hour together. Her mother was always working, sleeping, or going on dates with random men, while Roslyn was either in school, at a friend's house, or working at the beach hut. In addition to their conflicting schedules, Roslyn tended to avoid her mother purposely. She was lonely, probably depressed, and attempted to discount Roslyn's optimistic outlook. Every time Roslyn tried to express herself, her mother would barrel over her and ramble about all of her own problems. Roslyn did not think her mother meant to be rude but her mother's thoughtlessness upset her, intentional or not. Regardless, Roslyn was respectful enough to keep her mother apprised of her whereabouts.

* * * *

Nick jogged back to his parents with a smile stretching ear to ear. There was no question that Roslyn was stunning but that was not the reason that Nick sought her company. Roslyn seemed very savvy about the Mayans. With Roberto gone, Roslyn might be his last chance at finding some answers. He hoped that the excursion to San Gervasio would help him better understand the Mayan culture and hopefully give him some clues to the meaning of the pictographs.

Nick found his parents waiting for him in the car.

"Where's Roslyn? She didn't want to come?" His mom asked sounding disappointed.

"Roslyn wants to take her car. Are you guys okay with that? She says she can drop me back at the hotel when we are done," Nick reassured them, unable to contain the excitement in his voice.

"Well, considering this island only has about five major roads and the maximum speed suits a turtle, I think you'll be okay. Just be careful. Remember, we will be downtown if you need us.

We plan on returning to the hotel about 3 or 4 o'clock. Any idea how long you guys will be?" Anthony asked.

"It's 11:30 now, so I think we will go get lunch somewhere, and we will spend a few hours at the ruins. So, I guess I'll be back around the same time as you guys," Nick concluded.

"Unfortunately, our cellular provider is not supported down here, so our cell phones are useless. If you are going to be any later than 4 o'clock, please call the hotel room. If we are not back, leave a message for us," Vanessa requested.

"Okay. I'll see you guys later," Nick said, shutting the door.

He watched them drive away and turned to find Roslyn standing behind him. She wore a pink tank top over her bathing suit with matching sandals. She slung a black beach bag over her left shoulder and perched sunglasses on her head.

"Ready? My car is over by the restrooms. It's the little blue one." She pointed to an older, blue sedan.

Nick followed Roslyn to her car. He was, thankfully, more excited about the upcoming tour of the ruins than he was uneasy with the idea of Roslyn driving him there. Once they reached the ruins, he planned to show her the pictographs and the corresponding translations, in case she might recognize something about them. At the very least, she might be able to come up with a new theory or translation.

"So, what kind of food would you like?" Roslyn asked, starting down the long and bumpy road back to the main highway.

"I can eat anything!" Nick replied. "Do you have a favorite place that I can try?"

"Yeah. How about some local food?' Roslyn suggested. "I know a quiet place in the middle of nowhere that makes amazing food."

"Sounds perfect!" Nick said.

On the way to lunch, Nick and Roslyn talked about topics ranging from their day-to-day lives, to music, to sports. Nick was impressed by how much Roslyn knew about life in the United

States. When he brought up the subject of politics, she knew more than he did regarding current events and the upcoming election. When he asked her how she knew so much, she laughed and attributed it to much eavesdropping on the American tourists.

It took about an hour to get to the place Roslyn chose for lunch. Nestled in a pigmy, secluded village on the southern side of the island, the place was not a traditional restaurant. Comparable to an outdoor cafeteria, there was an open pavilion with picnic tables and a dilapidated structure with a thatched roof for food preparation. Off to one side of the hut was a huge fire pit with multiple spits suspended above it. Three of the five spits held whole piglets while the other two held small goats. Nick loved animals and hated to see them rotating over the fire but he could not deny the delicious aroma wafting through the village. Next to the fire pit was a rectangular, red brick structure. Nick assumed it was an oven. The scene kind of reminded him of summer camp, featuring roasting meat instead of marshmallows.

Nick trailed behind Roslyn to the hut. Behind the makeshift counter, two portly men were busy preparing food. One man chopped meat with a large meat cleaver, while the other shucked corn. Nick noticed the menu engraved in a large, wooden sign behind the counter.

"Do you eat pork?" Roslyn asked.

"Absolutely!" Nick responded.

"Okay! I'll place our order. You go find a place to sit," Roslyn said, gesturing toward the picnic tables.

Nick walked over to the tables and found the last, vacant one under a shady tree. He sat down and took in the scenery. The village was adorned with modest Christmas decorations. Instead of the new LED lights that were becoming common in the United States, Nick noticed the old fashion, screw-in bulbs dangling from random rooftops. Wreaths hung on almost every door and a faded, "Feliz Navidad" banner swayed in the breeze. A couple of children ran by, quarrelling over what Nick assumed to be their new Christmas presents.

"Peaceful, isn't it?" Roslyn said.

104

Nick turned around to see Roslyn placing two huge plates of food on the table in front of them. "Yeah, I was admiring the Christmas decorations. That is an enormous amount of food!" Nick exclaimed.

"I hope you enjoy it. That's cochinita pibil with rice, a traditional pork dish marinated in citrus. The other things are fried yucca, roasted corn, and homemade coconut bread," Roslyn added, pointing to each food. "I got the same thing, so if there is something you don't like, you can pass it over to me."

"It's mouthwatering!" Nick said, taking a bite of the tender pork meat. "Wow, this is definitely the best pork I have ever tasted! It's delicious!"

"I'm so glad you like it!" Roslyn commented, clearly pleased that she could offer something new and special for him to try.

Throughout their lunch, Nick told Roslyn about the break-in at the hotel and their subsequent upgrade. Roslyn found it peculiar that nothing valuable was stolen. Usually, local thieves only robbed for the money. The whole story was not sitting well with her.

"It sounds like they were after something specific," she proposed.

"My dad had the same line of thinking. I just think they were in a hurry and didn't get a chance to grab anything," Nick said, with a mouth full of pork.

"Mexican thieves aren't that stupid. I don't know why they left empty-handed. That's really strange." Roslyn said, pondering more in silence. "Did the hotel call the police?"

"My dad did. Unfortunately, when the police arrived, the hotel management told them they took care of the situation and sent them away. The free upgrade was the hotel's solution to the problem." Nick said.

"Unbelievable." Roslyn said, shaking her head.

They finished their lunch and Nick took his wallet out to pay. Roslyn pushed it away. She laughed and told him that it only cost eight dollars for both plates and it was her treat. He thanked her and they walked back to the car.

"Can I interest you in some ice cream?" Roslyn chirped.

"Ice cream! I gorged myself so much that you may have to roll me to your car!" Nick kidded.

Nick wondered how she kept her model figure. She matched him bite for bite, and she still had room for ice cream! He politely declined the ice cream, and they drove back toward the beach and the San Gervasio ruins. As fun as this pseudo-date was, he could hardly wait for Roslyn's tour.

CHAPTER NINETEEN

Elliot and Walter arrived in Cozumel on the afternoon of Tuesday, December 27th. It did not take much effort from Elliot to coerce Walter into making the trip. After Elliot offered to pay for the trip in full, Walter stopped complaining and started packing. Elliot did not need Walter to come on the trip but he wanted to bring someone trustworthy who could be easily manipulated. As a teacher, Walter was way better with kids. He had the time off from work, so it worked out nicely.

Elliot could not help but laugh at Walter's reaction to the luxury accommodations. He was like a kid in a candy store with his eye's bulging more and more at every turn. They flew first class to Mexico on Delta. Judging by his behavior, it was likely the first time Walter ever experienced such a thing. When the flight attendant came through the aisle with a hot towel before the meal, Walter hesitated, apparently unsure of what to do. When he started to wipe down the armrest, Elliot had to turn away and bite his lip to hold back from laughing hysterically. Sensing his mistake, he observed the other passengers wipe down their hands and faces before following suit.

Upon arrival at the Cozumel International Airport, a private limousine was waiting to take them to the Presidente Regio Resort and Spa, one of the finest resorts in Cozumel. Walter marveled at the hotel and the two-bedroom suite Elliot reserved. Walter was aghast at the large balcony with spectacular views of the ocean and a private butler service. For Elliot, luxury accommodations were commonplace, along with all the luxurious amenities that were included. Reared in a wealthy family, Elliot always enjoyed a lavish lifestyle. He could understand why Walter was impressed. On a teacher's salary, Walter would be lucky if he could afford an economy car payment and a modest mortgage. This trip to Cozumel was probably the first and the last time Walter would experience all the grandeur that Elliot's life had to offer.

Once Walter informed him that the Murphys were traveling to Cozumel for Christmas, it was easy to determine where they would stay. Cozumel was a small island with a limited number of accommodations. Elliot simply called the most popular hotels, impersonated Mr. Murphy, claiming he lost his reservation details. When the hotel employee informed him that there was no record of his stay, he abruptly hung up and dialed the next one. After calling about ten hotels, the employee at the Seaside Reef informed him that his itinerary included arrival on December 26th and departure on January 2nd. From that point on, all that remained to be arranged were flights, accommodations, and Walter.

After much contemplation, Elliot's theories about Nick's presence in Cozumel were taking shape. Elliot believed that Nick Murphy possessed an ancient treasure that could unlock the mystery of Atlantis. As farfetched as it seemed, all of his research brought him to the same conclusion. The stone that Nick mentioned was quite possibly a legendary Tuaoi Stone. These powerful quartz crystals are purported to have belonged to a legendary Atlantian emperor. There were many theories about the exact purpose of the stones if they existed at all. Elliot was not concerned about the importance of the stones, yet; he just wanted to confirm that they did, in fact, exist. Elliot was determined to find the truth. He hypothesized that he may need Nick for ferreting out details. This was why he solicited Walter's help. Walter dealt with Nick on a daily basis and could be useful if Nick decided to be uncooperative. The pictographs provided some clues but without Nick to decipher the true meanings, the possibilities were too numerous to contemplate.

Once they were settled into their room, Elliot excused himself onto the balcony to make a phone call. Elliot believed that one of the best things about Mexico was the rampant corruption; and he planned to avail himself to it. Elliot surmised that he could convince anyone to do just about anything for the right price. Prior to his arrival, he contracted for the services of a local thief. The thief was supposed to obtain the stone with minimal conflict. Having yet to receive word from the thief, Elliot decided to check-in with him. He dialed a local number the man gave him and waited for an answer. After about six rings, a voicemail recording answered that said, "It's me. Leave a message." Already irritated, Elliot left a message that said, "It's me. I'm in Cozumel. Call me back." He hung up the phone and sat down in one of the two cushioned, patio chairs. He slid a cigar out from his shirt pocket, cut off the tip, and lit the end with a match. As he puffed on his cigar on the balcony, he could not help but marvel at the glorious ocean view.

* * * *

Walter sat on the oversized couch in the common area of the two-bedroom suite, studying the room service menu. The choices were overwhelming! In fact, everything on the trip so far was overwhelming! From the flight, to the limo, to the hotel, Elliot must have already spent close to what Walter earned in a month. When Elliot asked him to come to Mexico, he was not enthusiastic about spending the majority of his Christmas break chasing down Nick Murphy in Cozumel. However, after Elliot discussed his theory about the meaning of the pictographs, Walter was sufficiently intrigued. Just as he suspected, Elliot believed the reference to The Isle of Flame was Atlantis. Regrettably, Walter got the feeling that Elliot was withholding pertinent information. When he asked Elliot about the reasons for following Nick to Mexico, Elliot gave him a vague answer about needing to find the origin of the pictographs and retrieving something that Nick possessed. Walter was not sure he believed the explanation, but when Elliot offered to pay for the whole trip including his meals, Walter happily agreed to accompany him.

After Elliot stepped onto the balcony to make a phone call, Walter decided to call in his room service order. He decided on the bagel and lox with cream cheese and capers. After deliberating for five minutes over desserts, he decided that he was in the mood for a slice of key lime pie. Walter picked up the phone on the table next to the sofa and was surprised to find that the line was dead. He inspected the back of the phone to see if the line came loose and discovered there was no phone line connected at all. In fact, there was no phone line anywhere. The closest phone was in Elliot's room. Walter opened the door and walked to the phone on the bedside table. He picked up the receiver and smiled when he heard the dial tone on the other end. He dialed room service and placed his order. When he finished with room service, he dialed the number for the butler service. Walter learned the hard way that a butler was not the same thing as a maintenance man. Annoyed, the butler bitterly explained the difference and promptly transferred him to the correct extension. He explained the phone problem to a maintenance man and was assured someone would be up to fix it shortly. Walter hung up the phone and proceeded to leave the room but something on the bed caught his eye. Elliot left a stack of papers and folders on the bed. In big, black letters, the top folder was marked: NICK MURPHY. Walter peeked out of the room to check that Elliot was still on the balcony. He went back to the bed, opened the folder, and spent about forty-five seconds skimming through the contents. Evidently, Elliot had Nick under surveillance. There were pictures of him at his home and at school along with pages of notes. Additional pictures depicted Nick's friends and his parents. As Walter shuffled through the photos and miscellaneous items, he came across a print of a painting that was particularly peculiar. It appeared to be a depiction of a tribal chief holding a large stone up toward the heavens. The print was labeled: TAZLAVOO'S TREASURE. Bumbling, Walter crammed the contents of the folder back and hustled out of the room. Just as he was sitting back down on the couch, Elliot pulled the sliding glass door open and came in from the balcony.

"Everything okay?" Elliot asked, clearly noticing Walter's flustered demeanor.

"Oh, everything is fine. I'm just upset with the phone situation. I went into my bedroom to call room service because the phone out here is missing the phone line. I called the butler service and they said they would have someone come to fix it in a few minutes," Walter said.

"You called the butler?" Elliot mused, looking at Walter with a confounded look before walking over to the phone and inspecting it himself. Elliot was about to say something, but a knock at the door stopped him. Walter walked over to the door and greeted the butler and the maintenance man who accompanied him. The butler informed them that the suite was recently painted. Whoever brought the furniture back in forgot to replace the phone line. The maintenance man went behind the couch, plugged in a new line, and ran it along the floorboard behind the table where the phone was placed. He plugged in the phone and was gone in under three minutes. The butler shot Walter an appalled look, excused himself, and closed the door behind him.

Elliot turned on the television to an international news channel and went to the mini bar to pour a drink. He asked Walter if he wanted anything, but Walter declined because his lunch was on the way. Elliot brought his drink over to the recliner next to the sofa and sat down.

"Are you pleased with the accommodations?" Elliot asked.

"Everything has been splendid!" Walter replied. "I'm curious about how you plan to find Nick."

Elliot sipped his drink, pensively. "Don't worry. I've taken care of that," Elliot answered with a smirk.

"What do you mean? Did you locate him already?"

"Something like that," Elliot smirked again.

"Well, exactly what is your plan? What are we trying to accomplish?"

"We are here to follow Nick where ever he goes," Elliot said.

"What are you hoping to find?"

"Walter, don't be naïve. Nick is eventually going to lead us to The Isle of Flame."

Walter sat on the couch staring at the television but not really watching it. *Did Elliot actually believe that Nick could lead them to the most elusive historical find of the century? Maybe he was just baiting him*, Walter thought. *Either way, once they found him, Walter would not let Nick out of his sight!*

111

CHAPTER TWENTY

The road that led to San Gervasio was just as long and bone shaking as the road that led to La Playa Bonita. The jungle was exceedingly dense. It seemed implausible that a popular tourist attraction was nearby. After a long drive, Roslyn pulled into a clearing designated for parking. They got out of the car, and Nick followed Roslyn down a tapering, dirt path. They followed the path to a small building behind a gate with a sign that read: Visitor Center. In front of the gate, a man sat on a stool collecting money. Nick reached for his wallet but Roslyn stopped him. She walked up to the man and was greeted with a warm smile. They exchanged some words in Spanish and the man waved them through. While they ventured through the visitor center, the line of souvenir merchants called and whistled for their business. Nick decided he would stop on the way out and see if he could find something worth buying. After they passed the merchant area, they came to another gate resembling the first one. An older man was collecting money. Roslyn was not received with the same welcoming smiles as the first gatekeeper. She addressed him in Spanish and he replied in a stern tone and began shaking his head. Roslyn persisted more, matching his Spanish pace and tone. The old man gave her a hard glare of uncertainty and reluctantly waved them through. Roslyn and Nick walked through the gate and followed the dirt path toward the ruins.

"What was that all about?" Nick asked.

"Just a little local charm." Roslyn chided. "The admission to see the ruins is 16 U.S. dollars per person. You have to pay 8 dollars at the first gate and 8 dollars at the second gate. The man at the first gate was my cousin; so he wasn't going to charge us. The second gatekeeper didn't know me, so he was insisting that we pay. I told him that we already paid the full amount at the first gate, so we weren't going to pay again. He didn't believe me, so I told him to go ask the guy at the front gate. I guess he was too lazy and decided it wasn't worth the walk."

"Yet another perk to having you for a tour guide! Free admission!" Nick laughed.

"Yes, but now I'm going to have to charge you double for my services!" Roslyn laughed with him.

"Oh really?" Nick challenged playfully. "Well, with all your charm, savvy negotiating, and Mayan knowledge, I'm sure I'm still getting a bargain." Nick said. Roslyn smiled, appreciating the compliment. He loved her personality. Nick wondered if Roslyn felt the same attraction to him that he was feeling toward her.

They continued down the path until they came upon a large sign suspended between two posts. As Nick glanced at the sign. "San Gervasio - Archeological Site," was written in big, brown letters at the top. In the middle was the familiar image of an old woman with an upside down vase. The words under the image took his breath away: Mayan Sanctuary of Goddess Ixchel.

"What's the matter?" Roslyn asked, with a concerned stare.

Nick felt like a train hit him. He was speechless. His eyes were plastered to the sign. Finally, he took a deep breath and spoke.

"The story my parents told you was not the whole story," Nick said, digging into his pocket.

"What do you mean?" Roslyn inquired.

"When my parents found me on the beach, I had this piece of paper rolled up in my hand," Nick revealed, holding up the small paper roll. His hand was shaking as he passed it to Roslyn. She unraveled the paper, and her mouth dropped open in amazement.

"Wow. . .This is incredible! You realize this is authentic Mayan writing, right?" Roslyn asked.

"Yeah, and that's not the only one. I have another one that was sent to me on my birthday last month," Nick added, handing her the other pictograph, still shaking. "This is why we came to Cozumel. We thought your grandfather could help us decipher their meanings. We anticipated that he could help us find the author. Ultimately, we hoped his insight could lead to my biological parents. One of these pictographs specifically mentions Ixchel."

"The entire San Gervasio site was used to worship Ixchel. You didn't know that?" Roslyn questioned, as she examined the second pictograph. However, her excitement turned into befuddlement and trepidation.

"What's wrong?" Nick asked, becoming anxious.

"Do you know what these say?" Roslyn asked in a serious tone.

"Yeah, I had them translated by an expert in Mayan picto –

"Wait!" She interjected. "Did your parents show the original pictograph to my grandfather?"

"Yeah, I think so. They told him everything. He said he had no idea what it meant. Why?" Nick asked.

"I don't know why my grandfather would have said that. He knew the ancient writings better than anyone I know. I'm positive that he could interpret these." Roslyn confirmed.

Nick was confused. *If what Roslyn said was true, then, that meant her grandfather read the pictograph and still encouraged my parents to take me. If the pictographs provided some sort of a clue about who left me on the beach, then, why would Roberto lie and tell my parents he did not know what the pictograph said?* Nick wondered. He turned his attention back to Roslyn. She looked as if she was going to be sick.

"What's wrong?" Nick asked her.

"The name at the top of this card says: NACXIT," Roslyn said.

"Yeah, so?" Nick said. "That's my given name."

Despite the fact that they spent the last few hours together, Roslyn stared at him as if she were seeing him for the first time. "Oh my --." She did not finish the sentence. Instead, she started pacing back and forth.

"Roslyn! Why are you acting like that?" Nick asked, getting upset.

"A few months before my grandfather died, he started teaching me how to read pictographs like these. We didn't get very far before he passed. The night my grandfather died, he called me into his room and told me a story. The story was about a child born from a god, destined to be a fearless leader. Minutes before my grandfather died, he whispered something in my ear that I will never forget, 'Help Nacxit, the great leader. He holds the key.' Those were the last words he ever spoke."

Roslyn's eyes met Nick's as she uttered those last words. They starred at each other then looked down at the pictographs, both coming to the same realization. Nick was so flabbergasted by the sign and what he just heard that he had to sit down. He found a large, flat rock under a tree and sat down to wrap his mind around what was just revealed. Since Nick received the translations from the professor, he assumed that the mention of Ixchel, was a representation for something else. Roslyn's insights made him believe the symbols should be taken literally. Her grandfather read the pictograph fifteen years ago and somehow knew that Nick would return to Cozumel. They both ruminated for a few minutes longer.

"Do you have the translations?" Roslyn broke the silence.

"Yeah, I have the report right here." He pulled out the papers the professor prepared and handed them to her. She looked over them and handed them back.

"Do you know what this means?" Roslyn asked him.

"I don't know how to answer that. I've read the translations probably one-hundred times, and you told me your grandfather's story. The conclusions I'm coming up with are just too farfetched." Nick shook his head, as if trying to wake himself from a dream.

"Well, let me spell it out for you," she said. "According to my grandfather and these translations, you are Nacxit, a savior child of Ixchel, and you are destined to lead us to salvation."

"And who is 'us'"? Nick asked.

"The world, the entire civilization, I suppose."

116

Nick wondered how she could have answered that question so casually. "I was afraid you were going to say that," Nick said, dropping his head dramatically into his hands.

CHAPTER TWENTY-ONE

Nick and Roslyn sat in the shade speechless. Roslyn's last statement sent his mind in a thousand different directions. He did not know what to think, or what to do next. Nick never felt so lost, yet so calm and sure about his identity. The voice increased in volume, frequency, and urgency to the point that it was giving Nick a pounding headache. It was clear to him that the voice wanted him to believe the idea that the pictographs presented. Until now, his explanations were reasonable or viable. The mere idea that he was the offspring of an ancient Mayan goddess was so unbelievable that he could hardly keep his lunch down. *How was it possible that just a few months earlier, I was stressing about homework and soccer practice, and now I'm expected to save the world?* Nick thought.

"So?" Roslyn said, interrupting the long silence.

"So, what?" Nick questioned.

"What do we do now? Do you want me to take you back to your hotel, or do you still want me to give you the tour of San Gervasio?"

"I don't know. I'm so confused. None of this is making any sense. I don't know what to do." Nick sighed.

"Well, you are here already. At least, have a look around. We can explore the ruins while you pull your thoughts together," Roslyn suggested.

"Okay," Nick said reluctantly. "Maybe the walking will calm me down."

Nick and Roslyn both stood up and started down the rocky path toward the ruins. The entire site was surrounded by the rain forest. Iguanas, smaller lizards, and birds were everywhere. Nick watched curiously as Roslyn retrieved a large stick from the bushes.

"What's that for?" He questioned.

"Lizards!" She scoffed. "When I was little, I woke up one morning and found a huge, slimy, one in my bed! Ever since, I cringe when I see one. They are disgusting and they freak me out!" Armed with her stick, the two of them continued down the path.

Roslyn began the tour by explaining to Nick that San Gervasio consists of eight major structures and multiple minor structures built out of stone blocks. None of the structures have roofs. Their wood construction rotted away long ago. Almost every one of the structures has a designated place for worship. Roslyn explained that the primary purpose of the ruins was to worship Ixchel, the fertility goddess. Mayan women from all over Mesoamerica made pilgrimages to the site and prayed to Ixchel for fertility. Every Mayan woman was expected to make the journey at least once in her lifetime to give offerings for her family and the crop fertility. It was believed that the site was first inhabited as early as 200 AD through the sixteenth century. When the Spanish arrived in 1519, the site was already abandoned.

Some of the structures are in close proximity. Others are off of secluded pathways. Maintained by a division of the Mexican government, all of the ruins are marked with a sign that presents a detailed description in English, Spanish, and French. The first ruin they encountered was called Manitas, or Little Hands. The building is named for its small, red handprints that are evident on one of the interior walls of the building. Thought to be the residence of Ah Huneb Itza, Overlord of Cozumel, Manitas is divided into an outer room and an inner room. The outer room was probably used as the main dwelling. The inner room is thought to be a personal shrine and used for worship.

They moved on to the next two structures, Chi Chan Nah, or Small House, and Murcielagos, or Bats. Chi Chan Nah is the smallest structure at San Gervasio and Murcielagos is the first structure constructed there. Because of the small size, Chi Chan Nah lent itself to be a place to leave offerings. Murcielagos, the original center of the site, is a collection of smaller structures that were used for shopping, storage, worship and opulent residences. As more and more pilgrims began to make the journey to San

Gervasio, a need arose for a larger venue. Thus, approximately six-hundred years later, the Plaza Central was developed.

The Plaza Central would have been equivalent to the modern-day town square. Nick's eyes widened with fascination. It is composed of nine small structures that form a closed courtyard. The majority of the structures appear to be places of worship, due to the large, vast areas with benches encircling the interior walls. Alters accompany most of the buildings. Two of the temples contain colorful, wall decorations including bands, spirals, and handprints in blues, reds, and yellows. There is a building that served as a tomb and a structure. It is known as the Palace. Most likely the residence of someone with astronomical wealth during the time period, the Palace contains three, small rooms that are thought to be bedrooms. Almost all Mayan dwellings are nothing more than single-room villas or huts, so this is quite an exception!

The Ka'na Nah, Pet Nah, and Nohoch Nah are the three remaining ruins on the site, and all three of them were ceremonial places of worship and devotion to Ixchel. Ka'na Nah, or Tall House, is the most remote of all the ruins and was probably the main point of worship to Ixchel. Pet Nah, or Round House, is considered unusual for Mayan architecture because circular-shaped buildings with two, rounded platforms and an altar in the center are uncommon. Nohoch Nah, or Great House, the largest of all the structures at San Gervasio, has a large altar in the center of the enclosure. The entire exterior is stuccoed and decorated with extravagant reds, yellows, and blues.

In addition to the architectural ruins, Roslyn educated Nick on what remained of the sacbeob, or walkways. These paved walkways and roads run to and from each of the temples, plazas, and ceremonial centers. She pointed out the dry cenotes, or wells, which were the main source of water for the settlement. Two hours later, they made their way back to the visitor center. They passed by a large, stone archway that marks the original entrance. It was baffling to contemplate the different purposes for each of the ceremonial buildings. Especially since they are all dedicated to a single goddess. Nick concluded that Ixchel was extremely important for an entire settlement to be erected in her honor. Nick was dying for a bottle of water when they finally returned to the visitors' center.

"Waterrrrrr," Nick cried, theatrically, dragging himself into the gift shop.

Roslyn smirked. "I'll go get some."

While Roslyn went to get water, Nick found a bench in the shade next to the entrance gate.

"So, did you like the tour?" Roslyn asked when she returned with the waters.

"It was incredible! You're an excellent tour guide," Nick said, smiling. "I had no idea that San Gervasio was centered on the worship of Ixchel. What are the chances that I requested to explore some ruins that were dedicated to the goddess in my pictographs?"

"Nick, maybe you shouldn't question every little detail and what everything means. Whoever or whatever is responsible for the pictographs and all the events up until this point is clearly guiding you in the direction you are supposed to go."

"This whole thing is just so crazy to me. I mean, why would I believe that I am the son of a Mayan deity? Furthermore, how am I supposed to believe that this goddess is orchestrating my life so that I can save a world that doesn't need saving?"

"An overwhelming majority of the world believes in some sort of Supreme Being, right?" Roslyn asked in a matter-of-fact tone.

"Yeah, but --"

"But what? Millions of people throughout the world flock to churches, synagogues, temples, etcetera, to talk to a higher power. They sing songs, celebrate holidays, and recite prayers. Is it so unbelievable that one of those higher powers decided to talk back?" Roslyn nonchalantly sipped her water.

Nick thought about Roslyn's statement. "When you put it that way, I guess it doesn't sound so crazy. But why me?"

"Why not you?" Roslyn asked. "You seem to be just as capable of saving the world as the next guy."

"Sure," Nick said sarcastically. "I'm a real James Bond."

"Maybe you don't need to be James Bond to save the world. You were chosen for a reason. Just go with it. Besides, if Ixchel is indeed influencing you and saving the world is your destiny, then your fate is pretty much put in the stone."

Nick looked at her sideways, trying to contain his laugher. "I think you mean 'set in stone.'"

"Put in stone, set in stone, whatever! You get my point." Roslyn shouted with a grin.

They both burst into laugher. "Oh! That reminds me!" Nick said, anxiously reaching into his pocket. "I forgot to show you this." Nick pulled out the hemp necklace with the large stone and handed it to her. "What do you think about that?"

Roslyn took the necklace from him and examined it with a confused look on her face. "Well, it's obviously a necklace. Why are you showing this to me? Did you buy it at a local gift shop somewhere?"

"No. When Anthony and Vanessa found me, that necklace was around my neck. I thought the stone might be significant in Mayan folklore."

"It's possible. Nothing comes to mind, though. I would have to ask around. It's very pretty!" Rosyln observed, handing the necklace back to him.

"It's almost four o'clock. We should probably start heading back toward my hotel," Nick said

"All right. Let's go," Roslyn said, finishing off her water and walking toward the gate.

CHAPTER TWENTY-TWO

Nick and Roslyn returned to the car and started back down the bumpy road toward the main highway. There was a recent accident on the highway, so traffic was at a standstill. Roslyn let out a sigh of frustration and mumbled to herself in Spanish about the obscene number of idiots on the road. If traffic continued to inch along, it could take two hours to get to the hotel. Nick was oblivious to it all. He was focused on the previous events of the day.

"So, how do you feel?" She asked, breaking his train of thought.

"Besides sunburned and tired, I feel fine. Why do you ask?" Nick chuckled.

"No silly! I don't mean like that. I mean, do you feel different? Do you feel empowered or anything?"

He couldn't help but laugh. "Oh, I see. You want to know if I can shoot lightning out of my finger tips or light things on fire with my mind?"

"Noooo! I was just hoping you could teleport us out of this traffic," Roslyn joked with a grin.

"No, I don't feel any different, but I will let you know when I become endowed with my superpowers!" Nick kidded, but then he became serious. "The only weird things that are happening to me are the visions."

"Visions? What kind of visions?" Roslyn probed.

"Until today, I thought they were of a random woman. But now, I recognize her as Ixchel. At first it was just dreams, predominately of the necklace I showed you. Today, I blacked out on the beach and had a vision of Ixchel with five necklaces identical to mine. I told my parents I was dehydrated, so I did not have to tell them about the vision. I didn't want them to freak out and accuse me of going insane again."

"Again? What do you mean?" Roslyn questioned.

Nick was mad at himself for letting it slip out. No one besides his parents and the doctors knew about the voice and his "condition." How was he going to explain this to a beautiful girl he just met? He remained silent. Roslyn was beginning to look uncomfortable.

"You're not some psycho killer, are you?" Roslyn stammered, only half joking.

"Ha!" Nick laughed. "No, I'm not that insane. Just your standard 'hearing voices in my head' crazy. The doctors say it's a mild form or Schizophrenia. Besides my parents, you are the first person I have ever told."

"Voices in your head? What do the voices say?" Roslyn asked, looking skeptical.

Immediately, Nick regretted telling her. He was sure she was going to look at him differently now. He went from the cool foreign kid to the crazy guy from America that hears voices. There was no turning back now. He might as well tell her everything.

"Well, it's just one voice. Occasionally, she gives me advice. And she never seems to be wrong. Usually she doesn't say much. Lately, though, she's been annoying. She keeps repeating the word 'BELIEVE'. I'm pretty sure she's referring to the pictographs," Nick explained.

"She? So the voice is female?"

"Yeah. Since I can remember, she's been with me. She's overly-motherly."

"Motherly?" Roslyn repeated with a look of concern. At first, Nick feared that she was about to start mocking him, but suddenly, he realized what warranted her concern. Once again, the sick feeling returned to his stomach. How could he have missed the connection? It was so obvious that Roslyn, someone he only knew for a few hours, realized immediately.

"I can't believe it," Nick whispered, looking out the window. "She's been with me the whole time. Since I found out about my birth story, I have been wondering why I was abandoned on the beach. In reality, Ixchel never left. She's been guiding and looking out for me."

Roslyn was unusually silent. "Well, what are your thoughts?" Nick asked her.

"Sorry, I don't know what to say. There have been some serious revelations in the past few hours. I thought you might want to reflect in silence for a change," she offered.

Nick appreciated the gesture. They continued down the highway in stop-in-go traffic for another five minutes in silence. They came upon the accident. It appeared that a group of tourists rented scooters to explore the island and one of them crashed into a taxi. An ambulance and police were on the scene. There was a significant amount of blood on the road, and the crowd of onlookers stood by with worried expressions. As Roslyn slowly drove by the crash, she rolled down the window and spoke to a woman in Spanish. The woman shook her head, sadly, and replied. Roslyn nodded, rolled up the window and continued down the highway toward downtown.

"What did she say?" Nick asked, breaking the silence.

"I asked her if the person is alive. She said he is alive, but barely. They are not sure if he is going to survive."

"That's terrible," Nick acknowledged.

"Yeah, but it is a reminder to be thankful. You never know when it all will end."

Roslyn's last statement did not sit well with him. Nick mulled over the pictograph message. Fear washed over him. *What if the pictographs lead me into danger? If Ixchel intends for me to be some kind of hero, what kind of perils will I encounter?* Nick forced himself to dismiss the idea and tried to focus on something else. Ixchel would protect him, or so he hoped.

CHAPTER TWENTY-THREE

Elliot walked back out onto the balcony of the suite and finished the last half of his cigar, contemplating his next course of action. The braggadocious, local thugs he hired to keep tabs on the Murphys touted themselves as world-class criminals. In reality, they were bumbling fools who did not appear competent enough to handle a petty theft. They botched the attempt to retrieve the necklace from the Murphy's hotel room. Because of the failed attempt, the Murphys would be more prudent and vigilant. Elliot cursed. It would be even more difficult to obtain the mysterious piece of jewelry! Also, Elliot was concerned about Walter's commitment to his purpose. Initially, Walter was biddable if it meant uncovering information about Atlantis. Lately, he did not seem so invested. He was acting unsure and hesitant. Elliot was beginning to wonder if bringing him along was such a bright idea. He took the last puff of his cigar, stamped it out on the tile floor, brushed it off the balcony with his foot, and went back inside.

"Get ready. We're leaving." Elliot barked, as he walked by Walter and into his bedroom.

"Where are we going?" Walter asked, choking down the last bite of his key lime pie."

"To observe." Elliot replied.

Elliot gathered the files from his bed, put them in his briefcase, and walked back into the living room to find Walter standing by the front door.

"I assume we are not going to take the limo," Walter smirked.

"Of course not," Elliot said. "I have a car waiting in the parking lot. Yesterday, I had someone leave it for us."

There was nothing remarkable about the car that was waiting for them in the parking lot. It was a white, foreign model, four-door sedan. Fairly new, the paint was already scratched in numerous places and dents were scattered all over the body.

"This is it?" Walter asked, in a surprised tone.

129

"Yes. Is there a problem?" Elliot shot back.

"No, no. I just didn't expect something so --. He didn't finish the sentence.

"So frugal?" Is that the word you were looking for, Walter?"

"I guess you could put it that way."

"When you are attempting to be discreet, it is not smart want to parade around in a Bentley.

Elliot got into the driver's seat as Walter got settled into the passenger side. They left their hotel and headed northeast, back toward downtown and the airport.

"Where are we headed?" Walter asked.

"My local contacts informed me that Nick visited San Gervasio today. Supposedly, he made friends with a local girl and they just left the ruins. The site is dedicated to Ixchel, so I suspect he went there for a reason. I want to go by the Murphy's hotel first. Then, we will go by San Gervasio."

Walter shrugged apathetically, which annoyed Elliot. *What got into him? Wasn't he excited about the potential of finding a city that was lauded as the richest in history? If the money did not excite him, surely the prominence should.* Things could get difficult with Nick. Elliot had no intentions of hurting anyone, but if the need arose, he would not hesitate to subdue whoever was impeding his progress. Though, he preferred blackmail to violence. Violence was for uneducated thugs. Encouraging someone to cooperate by eliminating all their other options required more finesse and skill.

After passing through downtown San Miguel, Elliot spotted the Seaside Reef Hotel and Resort and veered into the parking lot. There was a small, blue sedan under the drop off area at the entrance to the hotel, and to Elliot's surprise, Nick Murphy was sitting in the passenger seat. Elliot quickly drove by and parked the car where he could see Nick, but Nick could not see him. The driver was a striking, Hispanic girl. She must be the local girl, Elliot guessed. Their expressions hinted of the importance of the conversation. Finally, Nick climbed out, waved goodbye, and

130

went inside. The girl waved goodbye and exited the parking lot. Elliot had to decide whether to follow the girl or stay with Nick. He decided to follow the girl. He could come back to the hotel any time. *Who was she? How did Nick know her?* He was not sure if the girl knew anything, but another easy opportunity to follow her might not present itself. As the blue sedan pulled out of the parking lot, Elliot backed out of the parking space he just pulled into and warily followed after it.

"What's happening?" Walter asked, clearly confused by Elliot's sudden departure.

"You see that blue sedan? The girl behind the wheel just dropped Nick off. We're going to follow her and see if we can learn anything worthwhile."

"Like what?" Walter questioned.

"Like who she is and what happened at San Gervasio today. It will be easier to get it out of her than Nick. Once Nick knows we are here, he will surely be suspicious."

They shadowed the blue sedan down the main road toward downtown. The car pulled into a two-story plaza called Plaza Punta Langosta, which meant Lobster Point Plaza. While Elliot majored in Mesoamerican studies, he minored in Spanish and was fluent in both the language and the culture. They parked a few spaces down from the sedan and watched the Hispanic girl disappear into one of the buildings. Elliot and Walter got out of the car and casually trailed behind. They approached the door that the girl entered. The emblem on the glass piqued their interest. Gleaming in the sunset was the seal of the United States of America. Elliot and Walter exchanged quizzical looks.

"It appears that this is the local U.S. Consulate," Walter said.

"Yes, I can see that. I wonder what business she has here," Elliot said.

"Maybe she came here on Nick's behalf?" Walter suggested.

"I don't think so. Nick was just with her. Why wouldn't they just come together?"

Elliot accessed the office with Walter right behind him. The office was small for a main consulate and definitely lacked security. Elliot assumed it was a satellite location served by another larger consulate on the mainland. There were chairs lining three walls, with a door and a reception window on the fourth wall. Before they could reach the window, the door opened and a woman peered out to look at them. Like a deer in headlights, Elliot froze. He was not sure if he should turn around and leave, pretending their entrance was a mistake, or stay and lie to explain their presence. Deceiving government employees was quite perilous.

"May I help you?" The woman asked.

"I hope so," Elliot said, trying to sound desperate. "My friend and I were on the public beach earlier today and our passports were stolen. We need to get emergency replacements."

"Oh dear," the woman said, sounding sympathetic. "I'm sorry to hear about that. Regrettably, we don't handle things like that here. You will have to go to the regional consulate in Merida."

"I understand. Is there someone here who can at least advise us about the paperwork involved? I would hate to make the trip all the way to Merida and found out I'm missing documents."

"Well, we are about to close, and there is only one agent here. Her niece just walked in, but she can probably give you all the information you will need. Come on back. Let me see if she can attend you before she leaves," the woman said, motioning them to follow her.

Elliot shot a smile in Walter's direction as they followed the hallway. They entered a large room with cubicles and the woman gestured for them to take a seat. She approached the cubicle where the Hispanic girl was sitting. Elliot tried to interpret some of the conversation between the Hispanic girl and the agent in the cubicle, as he walked by, but could not decipher anything. Elliot and Walter took a seat in the chairs that lined the back wall while the woman summoned the agent.

"She's almost ready for you. She just needs to wrap things up with her niece," the attendant shared, after a few minutes.

"Thank you," Elliot said. When she was gone, he whispered to Walter in urgent exasperation, "I have to know what they are saying! It could be the cornerstone to our entire operation!"

"Don't worry. Once they are done, I'll tell you everything. Let me concentrate," Walter promised, intently staring at the agent.

Elliot did not know exactly what Walter was doing, but he did not have another alternative. He kept quiet and waited for the agent and the Hispanic girl to finish their conversation. Ten minutes later, they exchanged kisses on the cheek, and the girl left the room. The agent motioned for Elliot and Walter to come over to her desk. They exchanged greetings while Elliot stealthily scanned the papers on her desk, trying to ascertain the purpose of the Hispanic girl's visit.

"I understand your passports were stolen?" The agent asked.

"Yes," Elliot said. "We were told we would have to go to Merida to apply for replacements, but we are unsure of the required documentation."

"Okay. I would be happy to print out a checklist for you. Is that all that you need?"

"That should do it," Elliot said.

The agent typed something into the computer and clicked the mouse a few times. Then, she excused herself to collect the documents from the printer. The agent returned about two minutes later and handed Elliot an envelope.

"Everything you need to know is in the envelope," the agent said. "I'm sorry you both had to endure this. The world is full of thieves, I guess."

"Unfortunately, you are right." Elliot said, inwardly smirking at the irony of the situation.

Elliot and Walter shook the agent's hand and made their way out of the building and back to the car. Inside of the vehicle, Elliot took out a notebook and a pen. Spastically, he wrote down

133

everything he saw and heard that he thought was paramount. Next, he turned to Walter.

"So, what did they say? Tell me now!" Elliot queried, in a demanding voice.

"Yeah. The Hispanic girl's name is Roslyn. They were discussing something about Roslyn's grandfather, which I assume is the agent's father. Roslyn asked her about something involving a baby on the beach and her grandfather. Her aunt seemed surprised, but said she would check it out. That's all I got." Walter said, breathing a sigh of relief.

"How did you know what they were saying? I couldn't hear a thing!" Elliot admitted.

Walter smiled as he replied, "It's a skill I acquired accidently. When I was sixteen, my friends and I were playing with some fireworks. To make a long story short, things went terribly wrong and I ended up rupturing both of my eardrums. I was completely deaf for a few months. In those months, I became a proficient lip reader. I have maintained the skill over the years by teaching classrooms full of teenage history students. They are always whispering back and forth and trying to communicate test answers without being heard. Needless to say, it's almost impossible to cheat in my class."

Elliot was impressed. Walter was proving to be more useful than he expected. He thought about everything he observed on the agent's desk along with Walter's interpretation of the conversation. The mention of a beach was intriguing because Nick told him one of the pictographs was found on a beach. While scanning the agent's desk, Elliot observed a note that read: Murphy, 1996. 1996 was the year that Nick told him the pictograph was found on the beach. The Hispanic girl, Roslyn, spoke of a baby. Elliot wondered why they spoke about a baby. He did some quick calculations in his head and came to a shocking realization. Nick claimed to be adopted. If the pictograph was found in 1996 on a local beach and there was a baby involved somehow, the baby must have been Nick Murphy. Nick admitted his given name was Nacxit and that he did not know his biological parents. Elliot assumed that Roslyn was inquiring about the adoption, but he was not sure why. *Why did she choose not to bring Nick with her?*

"Where to now?" Walter said, interrupting Elliot's thought process.

"We need to go back to the Seaside Reef. There is something that we are missing."

"Like what?" Walter asked.

"I think Nick Murphy has a secret."

Elliot started the car and drove back to the Seaside Reef Hotel and Resort with multiple theories and questions racing through his mind. Initially, he thought that the necklace was the lynchpin of the story, but the developing mystery surrounding Nick's adoption was causing him to reconsider this conclusion. Either way, Elliot was going to get the truth and the necklace out of Nick, no matter what the cost.

CHAPTER TWENTY-FOUR

When Nick got back to the hotel, he was disappointed to find that his parents still were not back from their trip downtown. He was eager to discuss the day's events with them. He was not sure how to explain it all. As unbelievable as it was, he knew they would listen and try to understand. He decided to go down to the pool and have a swim while he waited for them to return.

The pool was Olympic-size with a narrow walkway going through the center, which divided it into two smaller pools. At the end of one pool, there was a swim-up bar, and at the end of the other there was a shallow area for children. The pool area was not as busy as Nick thought it would be. Two couples were sunbathing and a family of four was playing in the pool farthest away from the swim-up bar. Nick jumped in the pool closest to the bar and swam over to order a drink. He ordered a soda and sat at the bar where he could enjoy the view and see through the large glass windows into the lobby. This way, he could see when his parents returned through the front entrance. Sipping his drink, he envied the family that was playing at the other end of the pool. They were complete strangers, but their sense of perfection angered him. He always wanted a sibling, and now it appeared he did not even have "real" parents. Tears welled up in his eyes. He dropped his head, and with the back of his hand, he quickly wiped them away and tried to regain his composure. *Why am I crying?!* It was not as if he had a bad life. Anthony and Vanessa were everything he could have desired. They were probably better than most parents. He had no right to resent his life, but for some reason, the model family at the other end of the pool was agitating him. He diverted his attention and decided to ignore them.

Nick reflected on his day with Roslyn. He was still in a state of disbelief. He wondered if the conclusion that they came to was a mistake. In Nick's opinion, it was really the only logical explanation, if one could call being the lost child of a deity logical. He thought about the pictographs and wondered about the key and the great altar. Could one of the altars they saw at San Gervasio be the great one? He realized that he would need Roslyn's help. She was way more versed in Mayan history, and he felt in over his head.

Nick finished his soda, as he saw his parents enter the lobby. He hopped out of the pool, grabbed a towel, and walked over to the lobby doors. He opened the door and yelled out to his parents who were waiting at the elevators. They turned toward him and he waved for them to join him at the pool.

"Hey! How was your trip to the ruins?" Anthony asked, following Nick to a table area by the pool.

"Very enlightening," Nick replied. "I think I know how I ended up on the beach."

"What?!" They both inquired. "I thought you were going to the ruins for some sightseeing?" Anthony asked. The color faded from their faces, and Nick found himself staring at two very worry-stricken parents. He spoke up quickly.

"Yeah, we did. That's how Roslyn and I figured it out," Nick said.

"How?" Anthony asked.

"Well, there's a lot to discuss so let's go up to the room and go over the details in private. To make a long story short, I think I'm a gift from a god."

His parents both took a sigh of relief. "Of course, you are. We are all God's children, and the minute I laid eyes on you, I knew you were a gift from God," his mom said, smiling.

"No, Mom, you don't understand. I mean literally. I was put on that beach by a Mayan goddess, Ixchel," Nick said, already regretting his decision to tell them.

Anthony and Vanessa looked at each other and then back at Nick.

"How in the world did you come up with that?" Vanessa asked, fear-stricken.

"I know it seems unfathomable, but it's really the only explanation that fits. Let's go to the suite, and I will tell you the whole story."

Nick adjusted his towel and followed his parents to catch the lobby elevator. Since the break-in, Anthony insisted on entering the room first to ensure everything was safe. Nick found this to be a little silly, but he cooperated, anyway. Once inside the suite, Nick changed into some dry clothes while his parents put away their shopping bags. They all settled in the living room.

"I guess I'll start from the beginning," Nick stated. The tension in the room could be cut with a knife.

"Yes, please do," Anthony said.

Nick adjusted his recliner and began the story with his lunch excursion and the savory, delectable food. He described the location meticulously, so he could paint the full mental picture. Although his parents were listening, he could tell they were more interested in hearing about his god theory. When he began explaining the ruins and the subsequent conclusions that he and Roslyn came to, the intense silence that seemed to radiate from his parents' side of the room gave way to a barrage of questions.

His parents were usually very supportive, but they were not receptive to the idea that he was the offspring of a Mayan goddess. In fact, if he told them he came on a spaceship from Pluto, they might have accepted that idea better. Their problem with the Mayan goddess theory was the implications it imposed on their faith. Both of his parents were Christians. Vanessa was raised Catholic, while Anthony was brought up Methodist. Currently, they were not attending a church, but Vanessa mentioned a few weeks ago that they should start attending a new church together as a family.

Though they needed spiritual refreshing, as Christians, they were wholeheartedly monotheistic and could not accept the ancient Mayan's polytheistic practices. Nick's whole theory was sacrilegious. Nick never gave much thought to religion. He definitely believed in a higher power, but he could not defend why. Consequently, he was undecided about whether he believed in one Supreme Being or many. Nick did not understand why it mattered. He planned to live his life knowing that there would be consequences for poor choices and he would strive to make reasonable and rational decisions. Whoever, or whatever dispensed the final judgment was irrelevant.

A few days earlier, he might have gone along with his parents' point of view. He even found himself willing to try out a new church with them. Though, after he visited San Gervasio, he felt pulled away from that idea. After verbalizing his theory and defending it, Nick realized that something beyond his understanding was happening. He could feel it. For the first time, since the mysterious postcard arrived in the mail, Nick was at peace. He had a feeling of warmth and comfort, like an invisible blanket wrapped around him. Of course, he was still anxious to decipher the pictographs, but the thought of Ixchel and his divine origin made him feel complete, like he finally found his place in life.

After about an hour of discussions and arguments, they all agreed to disagree. Nick was disappointed. He really wanted his parents' support and approval. Nick wondered if Ixchel chose them to find him on the beach or if it was purely a coincidence. *If it was divine, why did she choose to put me into the hands of non-believers?* Nick's thoughts were interrupted by the sound of the telephone ringing. Anthony went over to answer it. It was Roslyn. Before handing Nick the phone, Anthony informed him that he and Vanessa were going to the pool for a swim before dinner. Nick told him he would come down after the phone call and took the receiver.

"Hello?" Nick said.

"Hey, it's me," Roslyn said. "I just wanted to make sure we are still on for snorkeling tomorrow."

"Yes, of course. We are all looking forward to it." Nick realized the lack of enthusiasm in his voice almost made his statement seem like sarcasm.

"Ok, terrific. So, did you tell your parents about everything?" Roslyn asked, sensing the frustration in his voice.

"Yeah. It's not going well," Nick reluctantly admitted. "They refuse to believe in Ixchel or anything related to her. They still think I have actual birth parents somewhere."

"Well, that is still possible. In fact, after I dropped you off, I went by the U.S. Consulate to see if my aunt knew anything about your adoption," Roslyn said, hoping to lighten the mood.

"Really? Why didn't you take me with you?" Nick asked.

"I just thought it would be easier if I went by myself. If she turns up anything, I will let you know. Hopefully, whatever she finds will help us convince your parents one way or the other," Roslyn said, sounding as optimistic as possible.

"I hope so. Right now, they think I'm crazy."

"Don't worry. Everything will work out. It always does. Oh, I wanted to ask you about the necklace you showed me. Is it quartz?" Roslyn questioned.

Her question peaked his curiosity. "Yes, I think so. Why do you ask?"

"Later tonight, I'm meeting a friend who might know something about it. If the stone has any significance in the Mayan culture, she should be able to tell me."

"Okay, please let me know what she says," Nick requested, trying to remain hopeful.

Nick and Roslyn spoke a little while longer before Roslyn told Nick she had to go and they said their goodbyes. He sat on the couch and gazed out of the window. He hoped Roslyn could unearth some explanations. His conversation with Roslyn had cheered him up a little but his resentment toward his parents still burned inside him. He needed them to understand. *My explanations are ludacris, but so what? As my parents they should respect my thoughts and ideas, instead of dismissing them and citing religious exemptions. Nothing was concrete in religious practices. Christianity certainly did not have all the answers. The multiple outlandish stories that littered the Bible were attributed to miracles. Why can't my parents just accept my birth as a miracle and Ixchel as my guardian angel? Ixchel, I wish you could give me more guidance. I need answers! What emotional, physical, and mental hardships will I endure to fulfill your prophecy? What are your limits, if any? What if I selfishly refused to continue?* Nick yelled with frustration. He was done with speculation. He knew with absolute certainty that the moment he learned of the Ixchel, there was a connection; it was like magnets slowing closing a gap and suddenly crashing together. This truth would be his driving force. Suddenly, he felt silly for expecting his parents' approval. His quest and his purpose where beyond trivial things like parental permissions. He knew what he had to do. Tired of brooding, he decided to go back to the pool and watch the sunset with his parents.

CHAPTER TWENTY-FIVE

Nick took the elevator down to the lobby and proceeded to the pool area. As he walked by the large glass windows, he saw something that confused him and scared him at the same time. His parents were in the pool sitting on one of the numerous ledges that ran along the perimeter. Directly across from them, sitting in one of the lounge chairs on the pool deck, was his high school history teacher, Mr. Ambrose. Nick froze for a brief moment. Then, he quickly ducked behind an enormous, potted plant. He peaked out from behind the plant to take a second look and make sure he was not hallucinating. Just as before, Mr. Ambrose sat in chair fully clothed, and eavesdropped on his parents. *What was he doing here?*

Nick was unsure whether he should approach him, or stay behind the plant and continue observing. He decided to stay hidden and observe them a bit more. Crouching behind the plant, Nick realized that Mr. Ambrose never met his parents. He contemplated the idea of it all being one big coincidence. *It's not unreasonable for Mr. Ambrose to come to Mexico for his Christmas holiday, but what are the chances that he would come to the same city, same hotel, and sit across from my parents? No way! This is intentional*, he asserted.

Just as he was about to go and demand answers, a debonair man came and sat down next to Mr. Ambrose and handed him a drink. Nick eyed him. He recognized him, but could not remember a previous introduction. He wracked his brain trying to identify him. After mentally scrolling through all his acquaintances, he finally remembered the man. Nick had trouble recalling the man's face because they had never met in person. He had seen him on the internet. Under a section titled "About Us" on the website for The Center for Mesoamerican Studies was a picture of the founder and CEO, Professor Elliot Shelton.

Nick moved from behind the plant to an inconspicuous sitting area that gave him a direct line of sight to the pool area. He watched Professor Shelton, Mr. Ambrose, and his parents for fifteen minutes before his parents climbed out of the pool. As they toweled off, it appeared that Professor Shelton and Mr. Ambrose were talking to his parents. *What were they telling them?* In fear of being noticed, Nick swiftly ran to the stairwell. He took the stairs two at a time to the second floor and caught the elevator the rest of the way. Nick had just enough time to slide his shoes off and sit down on the couch, before his parents came through the door.

"Hey, what happened to you?" His mom asked as she stepped through the doorway. "I thought you were coming down to sit by the pool with us?"

"I was, until I saw my history teacher eavesdropping on you," Nick said in a concerned tone.

"What do you mean? You saw your history teacher at the pool?" His mom asked incredulously.

"Yes. And remember the professor that took forever to translate the pictographs and stopped returning my emails and phone calls? He was with him. They were sitting in lounge chairs on the side of the pool where you guys were swimming. They were listening to your every word! What did they say to you?"

Nick's parents were both in a state of confusion. "They said they were archeologists from the states studying the ruins at San Gervasio. They overheard us talking about that Mayan goddess and struck up a conversation with us." His mom defended. "We told them that our son visited the site earlier today and was so captivated that he returned to share that he felt spiritually connected to Ixchel."

Nick's blood began to boil. *It was one thing for them to differ in opinion, but it was another thing for them to go and joke with strangers about it!*

"Spiritually connected! That is not what I said! Why would you be discussing this with complete strangers? It's obvious that you are not taking my feelings, or anything I've told you, seriously!" Nick fumed.

"I know what you said, but I certainly wasn't going to tell them your 'offspring of some goddess' story. For your information, we did not intend to talk to anyone. As you said, they were eavesdropping and started the conversation with us," his mom retorted.

"Look, everyone needs to calm down," his dad demanded, brusquely. "Nick, we respect your opinion and your feelings, but your theory is just too far-fetched for us. We agree that there are still some things that need further explanation, but our hearts cannot accept that you were born from a Mayan goddess. We hope you can equally respect that. Now, more importantly, why are your history teacher and that professor here at our same hotel in Mexico? Did you tell them you were coming here?"

Nick was still angry, but he agreed with his dad. He tried to focus on why Mr. Ambrose and Professor Shelton were in Cozumel because they might lead to further enlightenment.

"I'm just as confused as you. I only told a few friends I was coming to Cozumel. Maybe Mr. Ambrose was eavesdropping on one of those conversations, too. I do not believe it is a coincidence. They are here because of me. I'm sure it has something to do with the pictographs; I'm just not sure what," Nick said.

"The pictographs? What do they want with those? Both of them have already seen them, right?" His dad questioned.

"Yes, they have both seen them," Nick answered, as he tried to imagine a reason for Mr. Ambrose and Professor Shelton to follow him to Mexico. Still in their wet swimsuits, his parents went to their room to quickly change their clothes and afford him a moment alone to think.

Mr. Ambrose had limited exposure to the pictographs and Nick tried to keep his distance from him. Because he now knew that Mr. Ambrose was in close contact with Professor Shelton, it was safe to assume that they both had the same information. Nick thought about his conversations with the professor. When they talked about the translations, Professor Shelton asked Nick numerous questions. He remembered that Professor Shelton

145

seemed shocked by some of his answers. It was obvious to Nick that the message in the pictographs was important to the professor, but he did not know why. As far as Nick could determine, the pictographs were a personal message to him about saving the world. *What value did the professor see in that? Could he suspect, as I do, that divine forces are at work?* Nick contemplated Mr. Ambrose's and the professor's motives for a few more minutes before his parents returned and started with more questions.

"If they don't want the pictographs, then what are they doing here?" Anthony asked, pointedly.

"I don't know. Maybe they know something about the pictographs that I don't," Nick suggested.

"I think the best way to approach this is to be direct," Anthony said. "I'm just going to call the front desk and ask to be connected to their room. Then we can all sit down and ask them what they want."

Before Nick could object, Anthony was at the phone dialing the front desk. He gave the desk clerk both Ambrose and Shelton as names to look under. After a few minutes, Anthony hung the phone up with a look of confusion on his face.

"They said there is no one registered under either of those names," Anthony said, baffled.

"I didn't think it would be that easy," Nick said. "Those two are up to something. Obviously, they don't want anyone to catch on to their devices. Otherwise, they would have just told you who they were and what they wanted at the pool."

His mom chimed in, "They seemed harmless to me. I think we should just chalk it up to a coincidence and continue on with our vacation. Speaking of which, are we still going snorkeling with Roslyn tomorrow?"

"Yes, she called and confirmed our excursion for tomorrow," Nick replied.

"Fantastic. Now let's talk about where we are going for dinner. I'm starving," Vanessa said.

Even though he knew that Mr. Ambrose and Professor Shelton's presence was no coincidence, Nick decided to drop the issue. He really did not have any answers and it was useless arguing about his suspicions. They talked about what they wanted to eat for dinner and decided on a seafood restaurant his parents saw downtown.

When they arrived at the restaurant, it was close to eight o'clock. Normally, their dinner conversations were long and detailed, but tonight, everyone was reticent. They briefly talked about his parents shopping trip downtown and the snorkeling trip in the morning. Nick was worried. He wondered about the two men's intentions. His mind rewound to the conversation he had with Professor Shelton. They went over the translations together. Professor Shelton asked him some questions, requested more information about the necklace and then Nick never heard from him again.

The answer came to him like a slap in the face! *Professor Shelton wanted the necklace!* Nick took the necklace out of his pocket and examined it.

"You brought that with you?" His mom asked, noticing the necklace in his hands.

"Yeah. Since you gave it to me, I always keep it with me," Nick said.

"It's very resplendent and a bit mysterious, don't you think? His mom asked.

"Yes, it is. Maybe that's why they are after it," Nick commented.

"Maybe that's why who wants it, dear?" His mom questioned.

"Mr. Ambrose and Professor Shelton." Nick said, curling his lips into a smile.

CHAPTER TWENTY-SIX

After dropping Nick off at the hotel, Roslyn went to see her aunt who worked at the local U.S. Consulate. She wanted to inquire about the Murphys' story and Nick's adoption. Her aunt said she would not be able to check into the adoption until tomorrow due to the late hour. In order to get some more immediate information, she planned to meet with an old friend of her grandfather, Lucia. Since she was elderly and living alone, Roslyn made a point to visit her at least twice a month and take her shopping or out to eat. Her grandfather never asked her to do this, but she felt he would be happy knowing someone was looking after her. Ironically, Roslyn remembered being terrified of Lucia when she was little. There was nothing overwhelmingly creepy about Lucia, except maybe her crooked, rotten teeth. Not to mention, she resided in a dark, dank-smelling house that was cluttered with a myriad of Mayan artifacts and artwork. It was a bit much for a five-year-old.

An atypical, pleasant aroma greeted Roslyn as she rang the doorbell to Lucia's house. Lucia answered the door promptly. Roslyn was delighted to see that Lucia was cooking. Usually Roslyn and Lucia would go out to dinner, so it was a nice surprise to have a home-cooked meal. They enjoyed chicken enchiladas with rice and black beans. They had their usual chit-chat over dinner until Roslyn decided to bring up Ixchel and the necklace. Just like her grandfather, Lucia was knowledgeable about the ancient Mayan culture and rituals. Initially, Lucia seemed somewhat defensive about the subject of Ixchel, almost as if she were defending someone she knew personally. Roslyn began reciting Nick's story in an effort to ease Lucia's tension, but her demeanor changed from guarded to concerned and anxious. Lucia stopped Roslyn right as she was explaining how the Murphys met her grandfather, Roberto. Confused, Roslyn sat in silence, while Lucia composed herself. When she finally spoke again, the story she told Roslyn only added to the mystery of Nick, Ixchel, the pictographs, and now, the necklace.

Lucia already heard Nick's story before. Roberto contacted Lucia the same day he met the Murphys and told her their story. Lucia said Roberto was in a state of panic and unsure about what to do. Lucia assured him that the baby was probably abandoned by a local who wanted someone to think the baby was special, so they would take him home and raise him properly. She advised Roberto to help the Americans take the baby back to the United States with them and tell them he knew nothing about the pictograph or the necklace. Lucia admitted that she did not truly believe a local abandoned the baby, but at the time, it seemed like the right thing to do. She and Roberto were in no position to raise a child and it would be irresponsible for them to put the baby in an orphanage. The Murphys seemed to be well off, young, and full of life. Lucia thought about the baby everyday and told herself that if he were in fact a child of Ixchel, he would return one day. Lucia explained to Roslyn that Roberto felt the same way and he swore he would help Nacxit fulfill the prophecy. When Lucia brought up the word prophecy, Roslyn was intrigued.

"Prophecy? What prophecy?" Roslyn asked.

"Roberto and I believe the pictograph is referring to a lost, forgotten prophecy spoken by Ixchel before she died," Lucia said.

"So you know what the pictographs mean?" Roslyn said, becoming excited and moving to the edge of her seat.

"Not exactly. I've only heard about the pictograph that Nacxit, who I guess is going by Nick, had with him on the beach that night. Are there others?" Lucia questioned.

"Yes, there is one more. Nick said it showed up in his mailbox back in November on his fifteenth birthday. He had it translated, along with the original pictograph, and it says something about five keys at an altar will bring salvation."

"I see," Lucia said, thinking intently.

"So, what exactly is the prophecy?" Roslyn asked again, getting impatient.

"Roberto and I were not exactly sure. I believe my mother told me a watered-down version when I was little, but I really don't know.

"Tell me the story. I want to hear it," Roslyn said.

"When I was a little girl, I came home from school one day in tears. Some boys at school were teasing me and telling me that girls were useless and dumb. Basically, they meant we had no place attending school. I told my mother that I was not going back to school unless she could change me into a boy. That afternoon, my mother told me a story about a powerful goddess named Ixchel. She said that Ixchel was one of the most powerful women in the Mayan culture and was responsible for making children. In addition to creating children, Ixchel was a renowned healer. Some go as far as to say that she had psychic powers. Her mysterious abilities were said to come from a rare stone that was given to her by her husband as a wedding present. She used her powers to make female babies smarter than male babies, so that no man could ever outsmart her.

My mother gave me a hug and told me that because of Ixchel, women were smarter than men. They could not be bullied because Ixchel's strength and wisdom was inside of all women. I took tremendous comfort in the story. I never forgot about Ixchel and years later, when I was a teenager, I asked my mother about the goddess's powerful stone. She told me no one knew for sure what happened to it. Some claimed it never existed at all, while others said it was hidden deep inside a lost Mayan temple somewhere. As an adult, I was still fascinated with Ixchel, so I tried to research all I could about her. Unfortunately, the only additional things I discovered were the details about her death. Supposedly, Ixchel's husband discovered her favoritism toward women and had her exiled and eventually executed. The prophecy says her final words put a curse on humanity somehow and only she can remove it."

"So, that's it? You don't know what the curse is?" Roslyn asked, upset that there was not more to the story.

"I'm afraid not. Based on that, and what is common knowledge about the Mayan civilization, Roberto and I believed that Nick, the pictograph, and the necklace are Ixchel's way of finally removing the curse before the Mayan calendar ends."

"If the curse is not removed before the calendar ends, what do you think will happen?"

"Honestly, I don't know. The pictograph suggests that removing the curse will bring salvation. I can only assume something disastrous. Besides being associated with the moon, Ixchel is sometimes referred to as a rain goddess. Perhaps Ixchel is warning of a deluge."

"What about the necklace? Do you think the stone could be Ixchel's power stone?" Roslyn asked.

"Anything is possible, but I doubt it. All the descriptions of the stone I ever heard described it as a large pyramid shape." Lucia answered.

"Both pictographs reference an altar. Do you think the altar could be at San Gervasio?" Roslyn questioned.

"San Gervasio was built in Ixchel's honor. It did not exist in her lifetime, so I don't think it's a site that she would consider sacred. I think the altar would be much older, presumably built close to the time the Mayan civilization first appeared."

"You mean someplace like Chichen Itza?" Roslyn offered.

"No. Chichen Itza is also too young. The oldest Mayan settlement that I know of is a place called Cuello in the northern part of Belize. I'm not sure what is left of the site, but I read about it in a book a few years ago. The site sits on private land owned by the Cuello family. It was discovered in 1973 by British researchers. I think the site has been excavated extensively. It dates back to 1200 B.C," Lucia said.

Roslyn was astonished by everything Lucia said. She could not understand why her grandfather never mentioned anything about Nick until his last hours. Maybe he thought she would not believe him. The guilt from letting the Murphys take Nick must have weighed on him heavily over the years, especially if he believed the prophecy as Lucia did. However, he knew that Nick would return and that explained his last words to Roslyn.

Lucia spoke some more about Roberto and all the fond memories they shared. Roslyn secretly wondered why Lucia and her grandfather never married. Roslyn's grandmother died in her early forties from tuberculosis, and as far as she knew, there was not a man in Lucia's life. She heard Lucia speak of a daughter one time, but Roslyn assumed they were not in touch that often. As close as her grandfather and Lucia were, the thought must have crossed their minds. Perhaps they thought the marriage would ruin their friendship or maybe they were both still in love with their previous partners.

They concluded the evening with some delectable homemade flan and a re-run of a telenovela. Roslyn preferred to be outdoors as much as possible, so she never really watched a lot of television. Despite her dislike of television in general, she sat happily on the couch with Lucia and enjoyed the wonderful food and delightful company. *Besides*, Roslyn thought, *why watch a soap opera when I can just watch Nick's life unfold?*

CHAPTER TWENTY-SEVEN

La Playa Bonita was busy for a Wednesday morning. The weather was superb, and the sea was so calm that it looked like glass. A random tour bus pulled up at 8:00 A.M. and tourists fanned out in all directions to enjoy a day at the beach. Roslyn was not complaining. She had more business this morning than she would normally have in a week. She rented three of her five kayaks, the majority of her snorkel gear, and all of her beach chairs and cabanas were sold out. Her sunglasses, sunscreen, and batteries were also running low. The majority of the tourists appeared to be Asian, which explained why she did not expect their arrival. The Asian tour groups were few and far between, so it was impossible to know when they were coming. Most of the other tour groups came on set days at set times, so Roslyn could be prepared for a crowd. Roslyn checked her watch. It was 9:45 A.M. The Murphys would be arriving shortly. Roslyn was looking forward to seeing Nick all morning. Not only did she enjoy his company but she was also dying to tell him about what Lucia said last night.

The Murphys pulled into the parking lot just a little after 10:00 A.M. She wondered if Nick made any more progress convincing his parents about his presumed divine conception. Lucia's story further confirmed her belief that Nick was connected to the legendary goddess. *At some point, his parents will have to accept the overwhelming evidence*, Roslyn thought.

"Hey stranger!" Nick called out, as he and his parents approached her beachside hut.

Roslyn returned his greeting with a smile and a wave. Nick was shirtless, which was a pleasant surprise. In more traditional beachwear, his dad sported swimming trunks, and his mom wore a modest tankini. Over her shoulder, she carried a cumbersome, beach bag with decorative stitching and the word COZUMEL written across the front.

155

"Good Morning," Mr. Murphy said, as they approached the front of her hut.

"Good Morning! Are you guys ready to have some fun?" Roslyn asked.

"Absolutely!" Nick said, grinning.

They all walked to the backside of the hut where the kayaks were stored. Nick helped Roslyn with one kayak, while Mr. and Mrs. Murphy grabbed the other one. Roslyn left the Murphys by the shore and jogged back to close up the hut. She grabbed a couple bags of snorkeling gear, closed all the doors, and took the keys over to her friend, Arturo. Arturo managed the café. Occasionally, he watched over her hut when she had to run an errand or shop for more supplies. She instructed him to only allow people to return rented items and to call her on her cell phone, if he had any problems.

Cozumel was home to some of the best snorkeling and diving in the world. However, the majority of the reefs were on the western side of the island, which was too far to kayak from Playa Bonita. Roslyn decided that the best place to take the Murphys was Punta Morena. If they wanted to swim up to the beach, the reef there was relatively shallow and close to shore there. Roslyn was happy that the weather was nice and the waters were calm. Trying to kayak in choppy seas was physically demanding and would take away from the intended enjoyment of the excursion.

Roslyn returned to the shoreline and helped Nick push his parents' kayak. Nick instructed Roslyn to get in their kayak so he could push it out. Once both kayaks were in the water, Nick and Roslyn took the lead, while Mr. and Mrs. Murphy followed. On the way to Punta Morena, Roslyn commented on some points of interest and shared some history about Cozumel and its people. It took them about thirty minutes to reach Punta Morena and Roslyn was happy to see that not many people were on the beach. That was one of the best things about the beaches on the Eastern side of the island; not many people ventured that far from the cruise port so the beaches were usually deserted.

"Is this the place?" Mr. Murphy asked.

"Yes, sir," Roslyn replied. "The reef is directly under us. It stretches for about a mile in both directions. You guys are free to start exploring. I don't want the kayaks to drift away, so I'm going to swim them up to the beach."

"I'll help you with the kayaks," Nick said.

They all got out of the kayaks and put on their snorkeling gear. Nick took the lead rope of one kayak and Roslyn took the other, and they swam toward the beach. Mr. and Mrs. Murphy explored the reef. Roslyn was glad that Nick offered to help with the kayaks. Not only was it less work for her but, it gave her a chance to privately discuss her conversation with Lucia. Nick made it to the beach first and pulled his kayak up onto the sand. Next, he came and did the same with Roslyn's.

"Thanks," Roslyn said.

"It is my pleasure," Nick said, dramatically bowing to her.

"Wow! I'm getting the royal treatment today, huh?" Roslyn laughed. "I should be bowing to you. Word has it that you are the divine one."

"You're correct! Go fetch my chariot!" Nick teased.

"Right away, sir," Roslyn said, smiling.

"Thanks again for arranging this little venture. I can't wait to see the reef," Nick said as he headed back into the water.

"Hey, wait a minute!" Roslyn called. "Let's take a walk on the beach. I have some things I want to tell you."

"Oh, yeah? Did you find something out about the necklace?"

"Actually, yes. Now, come on, and we'll walk and talk."

Roslyn and Nick headed north on the Punta Morena beach as Roslyn recounted her conversation with Lucia. She told Nick about the lost prophecy and about the mysterious stone that was the supposed source of Ixchel's powers. Nick stopped her at this point and asked if his necklace could be the power stone. Roslyn gave him the description that Lucia mentioned and told him it was possible but unlikely. She told him about the night his parents

157

found him on the beach and why her grandfather encouraged the Murphys to raise Nick in the states.

"So, what does this all mean?" Nick asked. "Does Lucia know the meaning of the pictographs?"

"No. Though, she did speculate that Ixchel placed a curse on humanity and you are supposed to remove it somehow. She believes the reference to time running out is referring to December 21, 2012, the date the Mayan calendar ends."

"Well, I agree with her about the date. That is the only obvious interpretation for the end of time. The curse thing is interesting. Did she reveal the nature of the curse or what it means?"

"No. She said the prophecy has been long forgotten and she has not been able to track down anyone who can tell her anything more about it. She said most people thought the prophecy was a hoax made up by teenagers to scare little children. Personally, I find it a little farfetched but it's all the information we have at this point."

"Great. So, I guess the only thing left to do is go back to San Gervasio and see if there are any clues as to what the rest of the pictograph means. I was thinking that maybe one of the altars there is the 'great altar.'"

"Oh! That was the other thing we discussed!" Roslyn exclaimed. "Lucia believes that San Gervasio was built as a shrine to Ixchel after her death. It is much too young to hold any meaning to her. She suggested a much older site called Cuello. It would have been present during Ixchel's estimated lifetime. It is possible that it could have been her village. The problem is that it's in northern Belize, so it's very far from here."

Roslyn expected Nick to respond immediately, but he remained silent as they walked along the shore. She wondered how he was coping with everything. *His life was becoming more complex by the day. The fact that his parents were not entirely supportive probably was not helping. He was clearly a strong person, but one could only take so much,* she thought.

"There is something I should tell you," Nick suddenly said.

"Ok, go ahead," Roslyn said.

"Yesterday, I saw the only two other people who know about the pictographs, my history teacher and a professor, at the hotel. They seemed to be eavesdropping on my parents.

"Okay. So, what's wrong with that?" Roslyn questioned.

"Don't you find it incredibly odd that they are suddenly in the same resort location, in the same hotel, at the same time?"

"Oh, wow," Roslyn hushed, realizing Nick's point. "What do they want?"

"I'm not sure, but both of them know exactly what the pictographs say and one of them definitely knows about the necklace."

"Did they say anything to you?"

"I was so surprised by the whole thing that I ran back to our hotel room before they could see me. I'm not sure if they intended to talk to me or not. They lied to my parents about who they were and what they wanted. They told my parents they were archeologists studying San Gervasio. That prompted my mom to tell them about our excursion there and she insinuated that I was obsessed with Ixchel. I think they were fishing for information."

"Do you think they are dangerous?" Roslyn asked.

"Maybe. I believe they are the ones that broke into our hotel room."

"Really? Why?"

"My dad's laptop and my mom's Kindle were in plain sight, but they were untouched. That's why I think it was the professor and my teacher. I think they were looking for the necklace. The professor is an expert on ancient Mayan culture. I think he knows something that we don't. I don't know their intentions, but I sense that the situation might get ugly and become dangerous."

"Don't worry about me," Roslyn said, flattered that he was trying to protect her. "I'm worried about you. You are the one drawing all the attention."

They turned around and started walking back toward the kayaks. Roslyn was not sure whether she should continue on the

159

same topic or change the subject all together. Nick seemed worried and she did not want to upset him. Luckily, he spoke before she could.

"I'm dying to check out the reef!" Nick exclaimed.

"Yeah. It should be full of life today. The waters are calm and there isn't a cloud in the sky! If you're lucky, a sea turtle might float right past you," Roslyn said, disappointed that he changed the subject.

"That would be awesome! What about sharks? Any chance of getting attacked?" Nick asked.

"There are plenty around, but don't let them scare you. Unless you're bleeding heavily or carrying bait, sharks tend to mind their own business. It's the barracuda and jellyfish that are the real menaces. The barracuda are extremely aggressive and will attack unprovoked. The jellyfish are sometimes hard to see and usually travel in schools so by the time you see one, you are surrounded by hundreds."

"Suddenly, I'm not looking forward to the reef," Nick joked.

"Don't worry. I'll point out the barracuda, so you know what to stay away from. Just keep an eye out for jellyfish. Fortunately, they are slow moving," Roslyn said.

They walked back to the kayaks and swam to the reef to join Nick's parents. The captivating marine life stimulated great conversation. Roslyn practically grew up in the water and was happy to answer all their questions. So far, their favorite sightings were the colorful parrotfish and blue head wrasse. Roslyn explained the parrotfish's ability to make sand. Remarkably, one parrotfish could produce close to two hundred pounds of sand annually. Equally interesting was the fact that all blue head wrasse were born as females and changed into males later in life. Roslyn gave them the grand tour, pointing out some lobster, a couple of eels, and some large grouper. The highlight of the day, much to Roslyn's surprise, was the dolphin sighting. Just as they were all swimming toward the beach to retrieve the kayaks, Roslyn spotted a pod feeding about a hundred feet to the north. They all snorkeled toward the pod, but the dolphins whirled past them and back out to sea. It was still an awesome experience for the Murphys, if only for a few seconds.

By the time they got back to La Playa Bonita, it was almost one o'clock. Roslyn and Nick dragged the kayaks up to her hut while his parents went to use the public shower. As Nick was helping Roslyn open the windows on her hut, her cell phone rang. It was her aunt from the U.S. Consulate.

"Hola," Roslyn said.

"Hola. I looked into the name you gave me. There isn't much to tell. I see that the Consular Report of Birth, but there is an issue. Normally, there is some kind of supporting documents from the government, but I can't find anything. The whole thing is weird. How do you know this person?" Her aunt questioned.

"Uh, he's a friend of a friend," Roslyn quickly lied, glancing at Nick.

"Well, whoever this person is, their file is missing a myriad of crucial information. I'm surprised the U.S. issued the report in the first place," her aunt said.

"Yeah, that is weird. Well, I have to go. My shop just got really busy. I'll call you later. Thanks a lot for looking into that for me," Roslyn said, hurrying her off the phone.

"Who was that?" Nick asked.

"That was my aunt at the U.S. Consulate. Remember, yesterday, I went by there to see if she could find anything on your adoption?"

"Yeah. What did she find?" Nick asked, anxiously.

"That's the strange part. She said she couldn't find anything except the Consular Report of Birth. She said there are supposed to be government documents that go with it, but she couldn't find any. She started getting suspicious, so I hung up."

Nick was silent again. His latest trend of not talking about things was starting to exasperate her! She knew everything that happened was a lot to take in, but ignoring the problem would only make it worse. She decided to push him a little.

"So, what are your thoughts?" Roslyn asked.

"About what?" Nick said.

Roslyn almost wanted to slap him! "About everything. You know, about these crazy guys following you and what Lucia said. How do you feel about everything?"

"I think –" They were interrupted by the sound of Mrs. Murphy's voice calling to Nick from the restrooms. She was calling and beckoning him.

"Be right back," Nick said as he turned and jogged toward the restrooms.

Annoyed, Roslyn walked to the backside of the hut. She filled up a bucket with water and dish soap. She gathered all the snorkel gear that they used on their kayak trip and dunked it, piece by piece, in the soapy water. In the middle of cleaning the snorkel gear, a customer walked up. He was having trouble with his beach umbrella. Roslyn left the hut to help him. By the time she finished, Nick and his parents were waiting for her.

"We are leaving to go to lunch." Mr. Murphy said. "What a sensational tour! Let us thank you by treating you to dinner tonight."

"Oh, you don't need to thank me. It was my pleasure," Roslyn said. "And regarding dinner, that's not necessary. We are all friends now. You don't need to repay me."

"Nonsense. I insist. It's the least we can do. Just consider it an evening among friends, if that makes you feel any better," Anthony insisted.

"Well, if it's just an evening with friends, I will gladly accept," Roslyn said.

Still thanking her profusely, they began walking toward the parking lot. Nick hung back and quickly walked over to Roslyn. "Sorry I ran off earlier. You're not mad are you?"

"Not at all." Roslyn said, trying to force a smile.

"Okay. So, I guess I'll see you tonight?" Nick asked, while he turned and headed toward the parking lot.

"Yep. What time?" Roslyn shouted after him.

"Six o'clock should be fine," Nick shouted back, jogging after his parents.

Roslyn turned back toward her beach hut and saw that the man with the umbrella problem was waiting on her again. She rolled her eyes and went to attend him. *It is going to be a very, long day*, she thought.

CHAPTER TWENTY-EIGHT

Roslyn arrived at the Seaside Reef Hotel a few minutes before 6:00 P.M. Dressed in a khaki mini-skirt, wine-colored blouse, medium heels, and sparkly, dangly earrings, she hoped that she was not overdressed. She was not sure if she should wait in the lobby or go up to the Murphys' room. Just as she was about to walk over to the front desk, the Murphys stepped out of a nearby elevator. As they walked toward her, she realized she had never before seen them in a semi-formal setting. She was relieved to see that her choice of attire was appropriate. In his khaki pants and short-sleeved dress shirt, Nick looked very handsome. Although he was only fifteen, he could pass for eighteen. As Nick stepped closer to her, the inviting scent of his cologne lingered. She noticed that Nick was acting unusual. He seemed upset.

"Wow! I barely recognize you. You look beautiful," Mr. Murphy said.

"Thank you. All of you look wonderful," Roslyn said, returning the compliment. "So where are we going to dinner?"

"There's a restaurant downtown that has stellar reviews. It's called Kondesa. Have you ever been there?" Mrs. Murphy asked.

"Oh, yeah. I've been there a few times. The food is sensational! You guys will love it!"

"Excellent. Do you want to ride with us or meet us there?" Mr. Murphy asked.

"I'll ride with you guys, if you don't mind," Roslyn replied.

They all walked to the parking lot, got into the rental car, and began the short drive to the restaurant. Mrs. Murphy asked Roslyn about the local schools and if many students went to college in the United States after high school. Roslyn explained that many students never completed high school and the ones that did usually could not afford a higher education. In addition, entering the workforce was usually more appealing than going to school, so the drop-out rate was fairly high.

Nick was reticent, so Roslyn was surprised when he interjected. "What are your plans? Will you finish high school and continue to get a degree?" Nick asked her.

"I'm not really sure. I absolutely love working outdoors. I don't think I could ever go to an office all day. If I do go to college, I would love to pursue a degree in ecology, marine biology, or even archeology. I love ancient history and the idea of a fossil dig! What about you?" Roslyn asked.

"I definitely want to go to college, but I haven't figured out my passion. Though, I like math and excel at it. Architecture is something I could see myself doing. I'm just not sure if that is my calling. Since art is not my forte, architecture probably wouldn't be the best career choice." Nick said, cracking a smile.

Roslyn laughed. She loved his smile. Mr. Murphy parked the car in a lot and they began the two blocks' walk to the restaurant. Mr. and Mrs. Murphy walked side-by-side in front of Nick and Roslyn. Halfway to the restaurant, Nick abruptly put his arm around Roslyn and pulled her close to him. Normally, her instinct would have been to pull away, but his embrace felt so natural and comforting that she found herself leaning into him.

"I need you to pretend that you left something in the car." Nick quickly whispered in her ear.

"What?" Roslyn whispered back, surprised.

"Tell my dad you forgot something in the car!" Nick whispered again, more demanding. He let her go and began walking normally again.

"Oh, no!" Roslyn said in a louder than normal tone. She stopped walking and began scrounging through her purse.

"What's the matter?" Mr. and Mrs. Murphy both questioned, as they turned around to look at her.

"I think my cell phone fell out of my purse in the car. Do you mind if I go back and check?" Roslyn asked desperately.

"Not at all. We can all walk back with you," Mr. Murphy offered.

166

"No. No. I'll walk with her," Nick insisted. "There's no need for us all to go. You guys go ahead and get a table. We'll find her phone and be right behind you."

"Okay. Be careful," Mr. Murphy cautioned, handing Nick the keys.

Roslyn and Nick turned and started walking back toward the car. When his parents were out of earshot, Nick started talking.

"Sorry to spring that on you, but I needed to talk to you alone," Nick said. He seemed nervous and frustrated.

"It's fine. What's going on? You seem upset," Roslyn commented.

"To make a long story short, I fought with my parents and I've made some radical decisions. I told them about the prophecy. I made it clear that I intend to pursue whatever clues I can find to help decode the pictographs. I told them they were not being open-minded and I needed them to be supportive. They said I was being unreasonable and that this whole trip was getting out of control. They don't want to hear anything more about Ixchel and they regret coming back to Mexico."

"Whoa! So, what are you going to do?" Roslyn asked, staring at him. She had never seen this side of Nick.

"The only thing I can do," Nick said. "I'm going to leave without them."

"What?! What do you mean leave? Where are you going?" Roslyn asked, not fully prepared for the answer.

"My plan is to go to Cuello. I was hoping I could convince you to come with me."

Roslyn was stunned. It was as if she were speaking to a completely different person. Nick went from being confused and overwhelmed to centered, determined, and dominating in a matter of hours. She was not sure where this new side of Nick came from, but she liked it. Of course, his idea to go to Cuello by themselves was crazy, but the fact that he was determined to go was impressive.

"It's admirable that you want to go to Cuello and pursue this Ixchel mystery, but Mexico and Belize are not exactly the

167

safest places for two teenagers to prance around alone. Maybe you could try talking to your parents again and—" Nick cut her off before she could finish the rest of her sentence.

"Not going to happen! I told you they don't want to hear any more about it, and now I have Ixchel telling me to go, too! Of all people, I thought you would understand! If it truly is my destiny to be a leader, then, now, is the time to lead. I'm going to Cuello with or without you," Nick snapped, turning away and walking back toward the restaurant.

"No! Wait!" Roslyn called, chasing after him. "I do understand and I want to help. I promised my grandfather I would, and I don't think you will get very far without speaking any Spanish." She paused for a second and said, "What do you mean that Ixchel told you?"

"The voice, you know. Ixchel. She is now saying, 'He waits at my resting place. Go to him.'"

"Who's 'he?'" Roslyn asked.

"I don't know but the best plan I have is to go to Cuello," Nick said, despairingly.

"Okay. I'll go with you," Roslyn said reluctantly. "But I need at least a day to arrange—" Nick cut her off again.

"Sorry, but you've only got a few hours. We are leaving tonight," Nick said.

"What?!" Roslyn exclaimed. "How do you expect me to pick up and leave in the middle of the night? I'm not ready to make last minute arrangements for my shop, much less cover my tracks with my mother!"

"Look, I'm leaving tonight! Either you're coming with me or you're not." Nick said, matter-of-factly.

They continued walking toward the restaurant. Roslyn brainstormed what she could do with her shop. *I can keep the shop closed for a few days, but concocting an explanation to tell my mother is going to present a challenge. New Year's Eve would be on Saturday, and mom will be suspicious if I closed the shop on a holiday. Furthermore, I will need cash because my savings are depleted from Christmas.*

"Okay. I'll go, but give me an hour or two to talk to my mom and pack a bag." Roslyn conceded.

"I knew I could count on you!" Nick smiled and gave her a hug.

Normally she would have enjoyed his embrace, but she was so worried about how she was going to sneak off in the middle of the night that she barely noticed it.

"I want to catch the last ferry to Playa del Carmen at 10:00 P.M. Once we get there, we can hop on the bus," Nick said with a hint of excitement in his voice.

"The bus? That's going to take foreverrrrrrr," Roslyn whined.

"Not forever, but close to it. It only takes around six hours," Nick said, smirking.

"Only," Roslyn said sarcastically. "This ought to be interesting. You have never ridden a bus until you've ridden a Mexican bus."

They entered the restaurant and found the table just as the waitress was bringing Nick's parents their drinks. They asked Nick and Roslyn what took them so long to get back to the restaurant. Nick lied and told them Roslyn's cell phone fell between the seat and it took them a while to find it. They accepted his answer and changed the subject to the menu. Everyone's meal was extraordinary. The Murphys could not have been happier with their restaurant choice. Roslyn tried her best to participate in all the small talk during and after dinner, but her mind was focused on the adventure ahead. *Nick and I are only fifteen. Crossing from Mexico into Belize is not going to be easy. Someone is sure to question our age and the absence of an adult.*

When they returned to the Seaside Reef Hotel, Nick offered to walk Roslyn to her car on the other side of the parking lot.

"It's eight o'clock now, so I'll meet you at the ferry terminal at 9:45," Nick said.

"How are you going to get there? Should I come back for you?" Roslyn asked.

"No. I'll find my way. Don't worry about me," Nick said, opening the car door for her.

"Okay. Guess I'll see you at the dock," Roslyn said, climbing into her car.

Nick closed the car door behind her and turned to walk back to the hotel entrance. She watched him walk across the parking lot and disappear behind the door. *What am I doing? I have only known Nick for just over forty-eight hours and now I'm planning to travel to Belize alone with him!* She just could not say no to those incredibly fierce, blue eyes! They were like vivid blue sapphires, hypnotizing her with their beauty. She hoped that what appeared to be the dumbest decision of her life would have a positive outcome. After all, the fate of the world may hang in the balance.

CHAPTER TWENTY-NINE

Elliot was beaming. Eavesdropping on Mr. and Mrs. Murphy paid off, and he was one step closer to unlocking the mystery. The idea to go to the Murphys' hotel was a last minute decision, and Elliot did not have time to strategize. When Elliot and Walter walked into the hotel lobby, it was sheer luck that Nick's parents passed by on their way to the pool. Elliot was elated he hired someone to take surveillance photos weeks earlier. Otherwise, he would not have recognized them. Fortunately, Nick did not appear to be with them. He could not have asked for better circumstances.

Getting information from the Murphys was incredibly easy. With Walter's lip reading abilities and a little eavesdropping, Elliot was able to interject and steer the conversation to his advantage. The story the Murphys told was unbelievable. Nick was claiming to be some sort of a prophet and his parents, understandably, thought he was crazy. If Elliot did not have a background in Mesoamerican studies, he would have a hard time accepting Nick's story, as well. However, the pictographs, the necklace, and the circumstances surrounding Nick's birth all added up to some compelling evidence in Nick's favor.

Although Elliot was familiar with Ixchel before Nick consulted with him about the pictographs, the mention of her name and The Isle of Flame prompted him to research her further. Whether it was considered fact or fiction, Elliot went from books to newspapers to journals to the internet to obtain any information he could on the legendary goddess. During his search, he came across an obscure text, mentioning a prophecy. Out of all the articles and documents he read, it was only mentioned once and not in its entirety. This forgotten text compelled Elliot to focus all of his attention and resources on Nick. It was not much to go on, but it gave credit to the authenticity of the pictographs. The Isle of Flame could indeed exist.

Contrary to the prophecy, many documents mentioned Ixchel's power crystal. This intrigued Elliot because Nick mentioned a quartz necklace. His initial attempt to retrieve the necklace failed but that would not deter him. Elliot had not seen the necklace for himself, yet. For all he knew, it could be worthless, but the mystery and subject matter surrounding it was just too enticing to forget.

Elliot discovered an ancient parable, which spoke of a prominent Atlantean emperor known as Tazaloo. The parable claimed that Tazaloo possessed a powerful crystal. In addition, he found an old painting depicting Tazaloo holding his magnificent stone, which was created by a peasant artist back in the early eighteen hundreds. In some of the writings Elliot encountered, Ixchel and her husband, Itzamna, were described as fair-skinned and said to have arrived in the Yucatan from an Eastern homeland that was destroyed by a flood. When they landed in the Yucatan, they brought the knowledge of all the arts, such as city-planning, astronomy, agriculture, writing, mathematics, and government. They were credited with starting the Mayan civilization. If the assumption was made that Ixchel and Itzamna were Atlanteans fleeing from the great city of Atlantis, then it was possible that Ixchel's power stone and Tazaloo's power crystal were one and the same. In the same vein, the Quiche-Mayans described Nacxit as the leader of a sunken kingdom across the Atlantic, who possessed a powerful crystal. Before the kingdom's demise, Nacxit gave the stone to a fearless warrior, named Ballam-Qitze, whose description could double as Itzamna. Many texts mentioned that Ixchel received her powerful stone from Itzamna as a wedding present.

Elliot did not feel that Nick's given name of Nacxit was a coincidence. It was a message from whomever or whatever was orchestrating the events that transpired, in order to connect Ixchel to Atlantis. He wondered if Nick made the connection. Without the extensive research and familiarity with the culture, he doubted many would connect the Mayans with the mythical Atlantis. While Elliot did ponder the idea of disclosing his findings to Nick, he wondered whether Nick's involvement would hinder his designs on taking credit for any subsequent discoveries. Elliot came to a sudden realization.

Nick needed an ally! Besides his Mexican girlfriend, everyone else thought he was crazy. I could be the one person of real substance to stand at his side. All the better position for stabbing him in the back! Elliot chuckled at himself for being so brilliant. He would not have to rely on all of the incompetent morons he employed, either. Of course, Nick would be suspicious, so he would have to find a way to earn his trust. His thoughts were interrupted by his cell phone.

"Yes?" Elliot answered.

"Yeah, boss. The kid left the hotel and I followed him to the ferry terminal."

Elliot checked his watch. It was ten minutes until ten o'clock. "It's kind of late for him to be out. Are you sure it's the kid I told you to follow?" Elliot asked.

"Yes. It's him."

"Is he by himself? Are his parents with him?"

"No, boss. He met the girl here. They just boarded the last ferry to Playa del Carmen. I overheard the girl say something about Belize."

"Don't let them out of your sight!"

Elliot hung up the phone and paced back and forth in the living area of the suite. Walter looked up from the television with an inquisitively.

"Why are you pacing?" Walter asked.

"Nick and the girl just hopped on the ferry to Playa del Carmen. My employee said that he overheard them say something about Belize."

"What? At this time of night? What business do they have in Belize?" Walter asked, sounding just as shocked.

"I can only assume they are absconding in the middle of the night because Nick's parents either do not approve or do not know. Regarding Belize, I surmise they intend to visit another Mayan site. Unfortunately, I have no idea which one. There are oodles of

173

them. I'm hoping my associate can tell me more when they reach their destination."

"What do we do in the meantime?" Walter asked.

"We pack. Looks like we are going to Belize," Elliot said.

CHAPTER THIRTY

Nick's breaths drew quicker when he heard his parents close their bedroom door. It was time. He grabbed all the cash he could find in this mother's purse and left a note explaining himself. *At least that gives me until morning before they come looking for me*, he thought. He included Roslyn's cell phone number, ready to inform them that he was in Cuello by the time they called. *The last thing I need is the police chasing after me. It is easier to ask forgiveness than permission, right?* He snuck out of his room, closed the door behind him, and tip-toed out of the suite. His convictions to pursue his quest were stronger than ever. He truly felt his parents failed him. He could only rely on Roslyn. He knew she understood and supported his decision.

By the time Nick got to the hotel parking lot, it was already 9:40 P.M. He planned to walk to the ferry terminal, but he was short on time. By a stroke of luck, a cab pulled into the hotel parking lot, just as he began walking toward the street. He jumped in and paid the driver the standard flat rate of $5 to take him to the ferry terminal. He exited the cab and bolted to the ticket booth. Roslyn was waiting for him. Reaching the ticket booth, he purchased the tickets in a fluster. Just as their feet hit the ferry, the captain gave the order to push off from the dock.

The ferry ride to Playa Del Carmen lasted about forty-five minutes. During the ride, Nick and Roslyn talked about the pictographs and what they planned to do once they got to Cuello. The local bus line would take them to Chetumal, Mexico where they would have to change buses and take another one to Orange Walk, Belize. Once they reached Orange Walk, Cuello would be just four miles outside of town. Nick realized that he had not fully developed his plan for their arrival at Cuello. He asked Roslyn what her thoughts were and it seemed that they both reached the same conclusion; Ixchel would let them know if they were in the right place. Ixchel got him this far and it appeared she was determined to see him through to the end. Of course, what and where the final destination was still remained a mystery. *Maybe Cuello will have all the answers*, Nick thought. Roslyn asked him about his parents and how they were going to react when they found out he was missing. He told her about the note he left them and that he included her cell number. She told him that she struggled to convince her mom to let her travel to Belize. She had to make up an elaborate story in order to convince her. As Nick listened to Roslyn tell the story, he could not help but admire her beauty. The moon-lit water accentuated her pulchritude. They spent the remainder of the ride people-watching and pretending to translate the random passengers' thoughts. Roslyn was much better at it than Nick. Her stories were so detailed that even Nick would have believed them.

When they arrived at the ferry dock, they caught a cab to the Playa Del Carmen bus station. The bus to Chetumal was scheduled to leave at 11:30 P.M., which gave them thirty minutes to spare. Nick purchased their tickets and they looked for their designated bus. Nick still could not get used to how cheap everything was in Mexico. For the two one-way tickets, it was only forty dollars. They boarded their bus and selected seats near the middle. In an effort at chivalry, he let Roslyn have the window seat. Nick expected the buses to be similar to a Greyhound bus, but they were far from it. They were comparable to school buses! Void of air conditioning and a commode, the tattered seats reeked of smoke. Suddenly, the ticket prices made sense. Roslyn was not fazed by the lack of amenities.

"What's wrong? You weren't expecting the Taj Mahal, were you?" she joked.

"Well, I was hoping for at least a bathroom and air conditioning," Nick said.

"Ha!" Roslyn laughed. "This is Mexico. You're lucky this thing has four wheels."

Nick could not help but laugh with her. Roslyn had a contagious sense of humor. They watched, as the rest of the seats filled with passengers. There was a man carrying a live chicken. Nick found it to be strange until Roslyn explained that

176

cockfighting was a popular sport in most Latin American countries. An elderly woman clutching a rosary hobbled into a seat after the man Nick dubbed "the chicken guy." After ten others boarded, the engine finally roared to life. There were about thirty passengers in total. Nick and Roslyn took out their MP3 players and squirmed to get comfortable for the four-and-a-half-hour drive.

Nick planned to sleep the entire trip to Chetumal, but that was easier said than done. In addition to the bumpy roads and constant stops to let people on and off the bus, every so often, he was roused by the intermittent wafts of live chicken stench from the seats in front of him. He was thankful that, at the very least, the seats reclined. Roslyn seemed equally annoyed. Occasionally, she opened one eye to peer around and then went back to sleep. Eventually, Nick managed to fall asleep and his dreams were filled with images of Ixchel, the pictographs, and Roslyn. There was no real sequence to them. Only random scenes with random actions and speech played through his mind. It was in the middle of one of those dreams that he was awakened by Roslyn's voice.

"Nick, wake up. It's time to get off," Roslyn said, slightly nudging him."

"What's going on?" Nick said, rubbing his eyes.

"We're here. It's time to go," Roslyn said, poking at him.

"Wow, I must have been really out of it. It seems like I just went to sleep," Nick said, groggily. Nick grabbed his backpack from underneath the seat in front of him, shoved his MP3 player inside, and moved to disembark from the bus.

The Chetumal bus station was much larger than the one in Playa Del Carmen. There were many shops and concession areas with significantly more seating. Even though it was four in the morning, the place was very lively. Nick looked for a ticket window to arrange the remaining leg of the trip while Roslyn went to buy some snacks. He found the window, purchased the tickets, and scouted the station for Roslyn. He walked back the way he came and found her trying to jam a dollar bill into a soda machine.

"These things! They never work!" Roslyn grumbled, frustrated that the machine was not accepting her money.

"Here. Let me try," Nick offered, laughing and trying to ease the moment. "You have to talk nice and be gentle with it," Nick joked. He took the dollar bill from her, smoothed it out some and, gingerly fed it into the machine.

"Unbelievable! You just got lucky," Roslyn jeered as the dollar bill went in and did not return.

"Sorry, it must not have liked your attitude," Nick said, unable to contain his laughter.

Roslyn made her selection, retrieved her soda, and stomped off to a nearby bench. Nick purchased his soda and joined her. Fifteen minutes remained before their bus boarded at 4:30 A.M. Conversation was dwindling due to their sleep deprivation. They sat on the bench sipping their sodas until it was time to board. They selected the same seats as the first bus. Immediately, Roslyn put her head against the window and fell asleep.

Their destination, Orange Walk, Belize was only ninety minutes away, so Nick decided to use that time to formulate his plans. Upon his earlier research, he was disappointed to find no hostels. However, he found a guesthouse that charged only ten dollars a night. He did not expect it to be glamorous, but the reviews said the place was clean. He hoped Roslyn would not mind the sub-standard accommodations. He must have dozed while deep in thought because he was suddenly awakened by the sound of multiple people yelling in Spanish. The bus was stopped and two men in uniforms were arguing with the bus driver. Nick lightly shook Roslyn to wake her up.

"What's going on?" Roslyn asked, sleepily.

"I'm not sure. Looks like the police are harassing the bus driver," Nick said.

Roslyn rubbed her eyes and stood up slightly to get a better view. "We are waiting at the border to cross into Belize. We must present our passports. Those are Mexican border patrol officers," Roslyn said.

"Oh, I didn't realize crossing the border was such a big deal. I thought it was like Europe where you can just go from country to country," Nick said.

"I think they just check your passport and let you go. Don't worry," Roslyn said.

Nick watched as the two uniformed officers began walking down the aisle. They scrutinized every passport, before they handed it back. When they reached his row, he gave the officer a casual smile and handed over both his and Roslyn's passport. The officer looked at both passports and instead of handing them back over, he called for the other officer to join him. They said a few words to each other in Spanish and then nodded in agreement.

"Tu y tu, ven conmigo." The officer demanded, motioning for them to follow.

"What does he want?" Nick whispered to Roslyn.

"He wants us to follow him off the bus." Roslyn answered. Nick and Roslyn both stood up and Roslyn initiated more Spanish dialogue. They went back and forth a few times, while Nick stood silent. Finally, Roslyn turned to Nick.

"They are detaining us. We have to get off the bus and go with them," Roslyn said with a slight hint of panic in her voice.

"Detaining us? For what?" Nick responded.

"The officer claims that we either have to be accompanied by a parent or have written permission from one in order to cross the border since we are minors," Roslyn explained.

Nick and Roslyn gathered their belongings and followed the officers off of the bus. Nick was in a state of shock. *How could this happen?! Of all the things I thought should worry about, the border crossing was not one of them! I planned for a tight budget, places to sleep, and I worked up an explanation to give my parents. Now what am I going to tell them?* Reality set in and he felt sick to his stomach. Roslyn seemed equally distraught. They followed the officer into a small building next to the border crossing. He led them into an interrogation room, barked at them to take a seat, and left the room, slamming the door behind him.

"I can't believe this is happening!" Roslyn wailed as she sat down at the table and put her head in her hands.

"I'm so sorry. This is completely my fault," Nick said. "I should have done better research. I had no idea they would stop us at the border."

"Yeah, well, normally they wouldn't. Apparently someone called in a kidnapping early this morning; hence, they increased border security. You couldn't have known," Roslyn said.

"The officer told you that?" Nick asked.

"Yes. I lied and told him my cousin crosses this border alone all the time, and she's only sixteen. I thought the whole thing might be a shake down for money," Roslyn said.

"Great. So, now, what are they planning to do with us?" Nick asked.

"I guess they are going to make us call our parents and have them come and get us," Roslyn speculated.

"I have no idea what I should tell my parents. I know they will be angry that I left, but being detained in a police station is going to infuriate them!" Nick said.

"I'm sure we will have plenty of time to figure it out. It's only 5:00 A.M., so I don't see anyone in a rush to get us out of here. I think I only saw two other officers working. I'm going to try and get some sleep," Roslyn said.

"Me too," Nick said. He flipped the light switch off and joined her at the table. Roslyn rested her head on her arms and was asleep in a matter of minutes. She could sleep anywhere!

Meanwhile, Nick felt terrible. He dragged her out in the middle of the night and put her on a smelly bus for five hours only to wind up in a police station. *Some super hero I am*, he thought. *The trip to Cuello was supposed to go off without a hitch! Now, it appears we're not going to make it out of Mexico!* He wondered if Ixchel was impeding his progress because Cuello was not where she wanted him to go. Like countless times before, he took out the necklace from his pocket and examined it. The early morning light from a small window near the ceiling reflected off the stone and caused tiny specks of light to dance all over the room. If the stone did have some king of supernatural powers, he wondered how they would be activated. He looked at the distinct edges and grooves of the stone and noticed how they resembled the shaft of a ---

"A key!" He shouted, holding the stone up in front of his face.

Roslyn stirred from his outburst, but did not fully wake up. He decided to let her sleep and fill her in later. *The stone was the key! How could I have been so stupid? The pictograph mentioned a "key of salvation." The stone must be the key.* Nick was so excited that the reality of being detained in a police station suddenly did not seem like a big deal. He took out the pictograph translations and re-read them. The exact wording was: Leader at the end of time brings first key of salvation. *I am the leader and the stone is my key! Wait, why does it say, "first" key. Are there other keys? Do I have other keys and not realize it?* Nick looked at the translation for the card he received in the mail. It said, "Union of five at great altar will give rise to salvation." Nick wondered if the "union of five" was a reference to five keys. *If I only have one of the keys, where are the others?* Pacing feverishly, Nick tried to make more connections with the pictographs. He read them over and over again, but he was unable to come up with any new ideas. He was desperate to discover the "isle of flame." Cozumel was an island, but as far as Nick knew, there was no flame or fire. That was something else he would have to ask Roslyn when she awoke.

They were locked in the small room for almost three hours. Finally, an officer checked in on them. He flipped the light switch a few times to wake them up. Abruptly, Roslyn sat up and tried to focus on the officer's rapid-paced Spanish through sleepy eyes. Nick sat quiescently. During the succinct conversation, the officer gestured toward Nick a few times. His glare made him nervous. The conversation ended with Roslyn standing up and motioning for Nick to follow her. They left the room and followed the officer to a desk where Roslyn and Nick were each handed a pen and a document that was completely in Spanish. Nick hesitated.

"Just sign at the bottom and we are out of here," Roslyn urgently whispered in his ear.

Nick knew better than to start asking questions. He signed the document and placed the pen down on the desk. Roslyn did the same. The officer collected the documents and returned their passports. Roslyn and the officer exchanged a few more words. Roslyn took Nick's hand and led him out of the police station and onto the street to greet the warm Mexican sunrise. Briskly, they walked away from the border crossing

"Oh, man! What just happened?" Nick exclaimed, halting a block from the station.

"I was just about to ask you!" Roslyn shrieked. "Whatever you told your dad must have done the trick."

"Told my dad? What are you talking about?" Nick questioned.

"The officer said that he spoke to your father and was able to rectify everything. That was why they let us go," Roslyn said, confused.

"He spoke to my dad? How is that possible?" Nick asked, his heart palpitating.

"I guess maybe your dad called back to the station, or something, after you called him," Roslyn suggested.

"Roslyn! I never called anyone! I was locked in the room with you the entire time! Even if they were somehow able to look up my information from the passport, there is no way they could know that my parents are in Cozumel or the name of our hotel," Nick said, his voice rising with every exclamation.

Roslyn's facial expression turned from confusion to worry. "Look, I don't know how or why, but the officer specifically said your father called and took care of everything and asked them to release us," Roslyn said.

Nick was quite disconcerted. *How could my dad have called the police station? He did not know we were detained. In fact, no one knew we were detained. Could Ixchel have done this?* Paralyzed, Nick and Roslyn stood on the narrow sidewalk in deafening silence for a few moments.

"If your dad didn't call, who did?" Roslyn dared to ask.

182

"I have no clue. I know this is going to sound crazy, but maybe Ixchel was involved?"

Roslyn looked skeptical. "Look, I hate to change the subject, but I really gotta go," Roslyn said, dancing oddly on the sidewalk.

Nick erupted into laughter. He could count on Roslyn to lighten the mood at just the right time. "I see a small bodega ahead. Maybe, they have a restroom, he offered.

They walked to the bodega and were relieved to see it was open. Roslyn hurried inside. Nick paced outside, trying to calm his nerves. He followed the dilapidated sidewalk down to the next block and then turned around. He repeated this path a few times. Ten minutes passed, so he decided to check on Roslyn. *What is taking her so long?* He entered the bodega and briefly surveyed the store. He approached the employee behind the counter.

"Bathroom?" Nick asked, hoping the man would understand him. The man stared at him, clearly confused.

"BAÑO!" Nick was surprised by the voluminous tone that he displayed.

The man pointed to a nearby door. Nick walked over and opened the door. There was a small hallway with another door that displayed the word "BAÑO" on a handwritten sign. Nick went over to the door and gave it a gentle knock.

"Roslyn, are you okay in there?" He asked. There was no response. He knocked a little harder and raised his volume again.

"Roslyn, is everything all right?" Again, there was silence. Nick grabbed the doorknob. It turned freely, so he opened the door to find a cramped room with a toilet and a sink but no Roslyn. He went back out to the man at the counter to check if he saw Roslyn. No luck. The man did not speak a word of English and Nick could not come up with the proper words in Spanish. As he frantically searched aisle after aisle, the knot in Nick's stomach tightened. He searched the entire bodega, but Roslyn had vanished!

Nick was in a state of panic. He had no idea what to do. *Did Roslyn go into another store without me noticing?* Nick only took his eyes off the bodega for a few minutes. She could not have gone too far. Besides the bodega, Nick could not find any other stores that were open. He returned to the bodega and searched to no avail. Nick wondered if Roslyn went back to the police station. He dismissed the idea after he thought about how quickly she dragged him out of there. Standing outside the bodega on the street corner, Nick did the first thing that came to mind. He turned in every possible direction and yelled Roslyn's name at the top of his lungs. He waited, in hopes of something, anything that would indicate Roslyn's presence. Again, there was nothing. Just as he was about to re-enter the bodega and scour it a third time, he felt pressure between his shoulder blades and heard an unfamiliar voice with hot, rank breath whisper in his ear.

"If you want to see your girlfriend again, do exactly as I say. That pressure you feel is my gun. Don't make me use it," the voice threatened in broken English.

Nick was frozen in place. At first, he thought he was being mugged. When a black van pulled up and forced him inside, he knew the situation was much more dire. He had seen enough movies to know that this was no mugging. He sat in darkness, blindfolded and gagged, feeling the dilapidated roads beneath him. He knew he was being kidnapped.

CHAPTER THIRTY-ONE

Although Nick was terrified and unsure of his own fate, he could only focus on Roslyn. *Could she be near him in the same vehicle? They better not hurt her!* From what he could tell, he was alone in the back part of the van and his abductors rode in the front seat. He could hear their voices, but they were muffled. Due to fear or lack of sleep, it took Nick a few minutes to realize that he had free use of his hands. He wondered why his captors did not tie his hands. Ever so carefully, he reached up and adjusted the blindfold. He peeked out from the bottom and saw a window partition between the front and back part of the van. There were two Hispanic men in the front seat. Nick did not recognize either of them. He looked around the back part of the van. There were no seats, nor windows. The entire area was grossly carpeted. Roslyn was not there.

Just as he began thinking about ways to escape, the van slowed down, made a right hand turn, and came to a stop. The two men got out, flung the side door open, and pulled Nick out of the van. He felt a firm grip on his upper arm and the gun at his back.

"Keep moving!" The man vociferated, pressing the gun further into his back.

He saw gravel under his feet as he was led into a building and forced into a chair. One of the men bound his hands to the chair with plastic zip ties and removed his blindfold. He was relieved to see Roslyn a few feet to this left, though she was also tied to a chair and gagged. She appeared to be unharmed, but certainly frightened.

With its large, open space, high ceilings, and dirty windows, it seemed to Nick that they were in an old industrial building. Nick could smell gasoline and the floor was covered with oil stains. Due to the restraints, he could not see directly behind him, but he got a peripheral view of a large, roll up door. *We must be in a mechanic's garage*, Nick concluded.

The two men conversed briefly in Spanish. After, one of the men departed through a side door. The other man walked over to a makeshift table with a small television on top and sat down to watch. Nick re-directed his attention back to Roslyn. Her eyes were filled with terror. *How could I have allowed this to happen? What do these men want? Is this just about a ransom, or is it related to the pictographs?* He struggled to loosen his hands from the restraints, but was unsuccessful. He fought with the gag in his mouth to no avail. He recalled all of the action movies he had seen and how the hero always escaped. Something surged inside of him. He wanted to be the hero right now! His legs were free, so maybe he could use that to his advantage.

Just as Nick began struggling with his restraints, he heard gunshots coming from outside. *Maybe the police are outside trying to rescue us!* Instantaneously, the man watching television got to his feet and drew his gun. He slowly walked toward the side door and waited, aiming at the door. There was more commotion outside. Nick, Roslyn, and the man with the gun all stared at the door, unsure of who or what was on the other side.

After about two minutes of intense staring and nothing happening at the door, the man relaxed his arm and jammed his gun in the front part of his belt. He approached the door and put his ear against it. Apparently satisfied with whatever he did or did not hear, the man slowly turned the doorknob and peaked through the cracked door. A few seconds later, he closed the door with a confused look on his face. He took out his cell phone and returned to his chair in front of the television. Just as the man sat down, there was a large crash from behind their chairs. Dust filled the air, as the rumbling of a large engine echoed around them. Gunfire erupted. Still tied to the chairs and blinded by the dust, Nick and Roslyn sat in horror and hoped that guns were not aimed at them.

* * * *

Elliot was impressed with himself for executing such an ingenious plan on short notice. Everything was going like clockwork. When he learned that Nick was ditching his parents

186

and vamoosing to Belize in the middle of the night, he knew it was a prime opportunity to gain Nick's trust. No matter what the cost, he would figure out what Nick and his little girlfriend were up to and turn it to his advantage. A straight drive from Cozumel to Chetumal would normally take five hours. Of course, Elliot was not about to sit in a car and navigate deplorable, Mexican roads in the middle of the night. He contacted a scenic helicopter tour operator and paid for the whole day. It was the only way to ensure that he and Walter would arrive in Chetumal before Nick and Roslyn.

In order to get to Belize, the bus Nick boarded had to cross the border in Chetumal. Normally, the Mexican police boarded the buses crossing into Belize to collect a small departure tax. They rarely asked questions or detained anyone, unless something like a kidnapping was reported. Elliot made sure that several kidnappings were reported to ensure that the border patrol would be on high alert. He knew two teenagers traveling by themselves would surely catch the attention of any border agent. Once Nick and Roslyn were detained, it was fairly easy for Elliot to call the station and pretend to be Nick's father. Because Walter was Nick's teacher, he had access to all his vital information. Answering the border agent's questions was quite simple. Convincing the officer to release them was slightly precarious, but Elliot smooth talked his way through that too. He was a born manipulator.

Once Nick and Roslyn were released from the authorities, the second part of his conciliatory plan was set into motion. Elliot theorized that in order to gain Nick's trust, he would need to demonstrate genuine qualities to Nick. He needed to be a hero. To achieve this, Elliot staged a kidnapping. Nick and Roslyn were the helpless victims, and in few minutes, Elliot would come to the rescue as their proverbial knight in shining armor.

Elliot sat in a black limousine across the street from where Nick and Roslyn were being held captive. He zoomed in his phone's camera feed, just as the car crashed through the garage door. Sheer terror was written across Nick's face. *I'll have to compliment the boys on the gunfight. Nice touch!* He decided to let the shooting go on a bit longer. He wanted to instill as much fear as possible. Nick and Roslyn needed to feel that there was no escape, and they would not make it out alive.

* * * *

The gunshots rang out for what seemed like an eternity. Nick assumed the police were attempting a rescue and things went terribly wrong. Finally, the dust from the crash settled. The shooting halted and silence hushed over the building. Nick could barely see the outline of a crumpled body where he last saw the man who was guarding them. Still restrained, he could only see a portion of the vehicle that crashed through the garage door. He glanced over at Roslyn, longing to hold her and reassure her. Although, for all he knew, they both could be dead in the next minute. His ears were ringing and his heart was racing. He forced himself to calm down. Again, he wrestled with the plastic ties that bound his wrists. He could feel the plastic edges gouging into his skin with each pull and twist. He winced in pain and struggled, until the blood ran down his hands. Roslyn seemed to be doing the same. Suddenly, he heard footsteps and muffled voices quickly approaching from behind. Nick stopped struggling and tried to decipher what the voices were saying. He wished he paid more attention in Spanish class. Within seconds, two well-dressed Hispanic men were standing over them with their guns drawn.

"Senor Murphy?" One of the men asked, touching Nick's forehead with the cold barrel of his gun.

Nick was unsure how he should answer. Obviously, if the men were here to rescue him, he should say yes. However, if these men were survivors of the supposed botched police rescue, maybe he would be better off denying his identity. He decided not to give the men a response to see how they would react but, to his surprise, Roslyn rapidly nodded in affirmation. The men lowered their weapons and removed Nick and Roslyn's restraints. The minute their restraints were gone, Nick and Roslyn instinctively ran to embrace each other. Tears streamed down both their faces while the two men stood silently observing them. Nick began wiping the blood from her bleeding wrists.

"Are you police?" Nick stammered at the men, trying to regain his composure. Neither of the men responded. Assuming they did not hear him or understand, he repeated the question. Again, both men were silent. Suddenly, a third voice boomed from behind them, "No, they certainly are not the police. They are MY employees." The voice was strikingly familiar. As Nick tried to recall it, the last person he expected to see emerged from the shadows.

"Professor Shelton?" Nick uttered in disbelief.

"Hello, Nick. I'm so glad we found you! Are you injured?" The professor asked, seeming genuinely concerned about the blood on his hands.

Nick stayed silent, took Roslyn's hand, and took a few steps backwards.

"There's no need to be frightened. We are here to help," Professor Shelton said.

Surprisingly, Nick was not frightened. After surviving the kidnapping and gun battle moments earlier, Nick felt numb. His steps backwards were purely instinctive. Maybe he was disoriented from all that transpired, but the professor's presence was disturbing.

"We're fine. What are you doing here?" Nick snapped.

"Saving your life, of course," Professor Shelton calmly replied with a smile.

"How did you know I was in Mexico and how did you know I needed saving?" Nick shot back at him.

"Calm down, Nick. I'll explain everything in the car. Follow me. My car is parked right across the street," Professor Shelton replied, motioning for them to follow him.

"We're not going anywhere with you," Nick stated belligerently, holding his ground.

The professor turned back around and glared at Nick. The friendly smile vanished from his face. "If I wanted to harm you, I wouldn't have wasted so many resources on your rescue. Now, I

189

suggest you show a little bit of gratitude and get in the car," Professor Shelton warned.

Nick was ready to continue the protest until he heard the two thugs cocking their guns behind him. It was obvious that Professor Shelton's intentions were to keep them alive, but beyond that, Nick was uncertain. Nick and Roslyn followed Professor Shelton to a black limousine parked in an unpaved lot. One of the armed thugs got into the driver's seat while the other took the front passenger seat. Nick followed Roslyn into the rear passenger area. Nick gasped as he was met by another familiar face, Mr. Ambrose. Mr. Ambrose sat comfortably in the corner, sipping a drink. Professor Shelton took his seat next to Mr. Ambrose and the car roared to life and pulled out of the lot.

"Hello, Nick." Mr. Ambrose said through a nervous smile.

"I should have known you would be involved," Nick scoffed.

"You are going to have to work on that attitude, Nick." Professor Shelton interjected. "I already told you we are simply here to help."

"Ok, then," Nick snapped, sarcastically. "You can start helping by telling me how and why you are here."

"Very well. As you know, your pictographs are not just some ordinary tourist trinkets. All along, we've been suspicious. Your last-minute vacation to Mexico interested us."

"How did you know about that?" Nick interrogated them.

"You go to a high school. Teachers hear things." Mr. Ambrose explained.

"Sure," Nick scoffed.

"Our plan was to meet up with you in Cozumel to discuss the meanings of the pictographs. We had some difficulties with our travel arrangements, so when we sought you out at your hotel, we only saw your parents. We were not sure what you told them about the pictographs, so we decided not to bring it up."

"How did you know that we were in Chetumal?" Nick challenged.

"Since you were not at your hotel when we came by, I asked someone to watch your hotel for your return. When our surveillance guy told us you were heading to the ferry dock in the middle of the night, we became concerned for your safety. For no other reason than your well-being, we insisted that he follow you. He told us about the bus to Chetumal and about your unfortunate experience with the police. Walter and I were on our way to meet you at the police station when we witnessed the kidnapping. At that point, I called everyone I knew to find you and rescue you. So you see, Nick, we are not the bad guys. You should trust us. Though, even if you don't trust, you should believe that we have your best interests in mind. I think we've earned that much, at the very least."

Nick was not buying into the fairy tale that Mr. Ambrose and Professor Shelton were simply good Samaritans out to save the world. Their story seemed contrived. Only three of his friends knew about the Mexico trip and Mr. Ambrose did not accidentally overhear anything. Also, he suspected they were responsible for the hotel break-in, but he decided not to mention it. Instead, he decided to play along with their game and use them to get to Cuello. Once they arrived, he would try to lose them.

"I guess that makes sense." Nick said, trying to sound hopeful.

"I knew you would come around!" Professor Shelton exclaimed, slapping Mr. Ambrose on the back.

"So, what now? Where do we go from here?" Nick asked, innocently.

"I'm glad you asked," Professor Shelton said with a grin. "That's entirely up to you. Where would you like to go?"

"We were headed to Belize City," Nick lied. "We planned to spend the night in Orange Walk and continue to Belize City the next day."

"Why Belize City? What do you hope to find there?" Professor Shelton asked.

Right away, Nick knew that Professor Shelton was pretending to be uninterested but his body language told a different story. Nick was still unsure of exactly what the two men knew, or thought they knew, but whatever it was, it prompted them to follow him through Mexico. He certainly was not going to tell them anything about Ixchel speaking to him or what he believed the pictographs actually meant. From the moment that their restraints were cut, Roslyn remained silent. He was eager to hear her thoughts and reveal that the necklace was a key. He would wait until they had a minute alone.

"There are a couple of Mayan ruins near the city. We explored San Gervasio and didn't come up with much. I thought we could explore the ruins in Belize City and gain insight into the true meanings of the pictographs," Nick offered.

"Yes. About that. . ." replied Professor Shelton. "The last thing we heard from you was that a family member found the pictographs on the beach. Is that all there is to the story? What else have you learned? Can you tell us about possible connections to how the pictographs were found and their meaning?"

Nick was uneasy with Professor Shelton's questions. He seemed to be asking things he already knew. He could feel Roslyn tensing up next to him. The less Professor Shelton knew the better, but Nick was fearful of the consequences. If Professor Shelton knew he was being lied to, there was no telling what he would do. He decided to tell half-truths.

"It's true that my parents found one of the pictographs on the beach. The other pictograph arrived in my mailbox last month. My parents found me on the beach with the pictograph. They adopted me. That's why we came to Cozumel. I want to find my birth parents. I think the pictographs are clues to find them. I researched Ixchel, since she is mentioned in the pictograph. That research led me to San Gervasio and another site in Belize City." Nick waited nervously to see if Professor Shelton accepted his answer.

"So, did your parents actually find you on a beach in Cozumel?" Professor Shelton asked.

"Yes. It was in the middle of the night. The beach was deserted and they heard crying. They said they tried to find my parents for weeks but were unsuccessful. They adopted me and brought me back to the States."

"And how do you think Ixchel relates to all this?" Professor Shelton asked.

"I think Ixchel is a representation for something else. If I know more about Ixchel, then, maybe I can understand who or what she represents in the context of the pictographs."

Nick could not tell if Professor Shelton was buying into his story or not. Shelton had a faint smirk on his face as if Nick said something funny.

"I don't think you are giving me the whole story, Nick," Professor Shelton warned. "I can understand why you may not trust me just yet. That's ok. I'll extract the truth out of you one way or another," Professor Shelton added, with a slight chuckle.

Nick did not like his tone. He sensed that the professor was threatening him, but he did not care. *Of course, I will never trust him! Does Professor Shelton think I am that naïve? If so, maybe I can use that to my advantage.* He decided that it was better to have Professor Shelton underestimate him instead of anticipating his every move.

"All right. Belize it is." Mr. Ambrose said, breaking the silence.

"I guess so." Nick said, glaring at him.

"We will stick to Nick's original plan," Professor Shelton obliged. "We will drive down to Orange Walk, spend the night, and head for Belize City first thing in the morning."

"I can't wait," Nick whispered under his breath, sarcastically.

CHAPTER THIRTY-TWO

The border crossing into Belize was ridiculously slow because the agents were still on high alert from the earlier kidnapping report. While crossing the border usually took half an hour, it took them almost two hours to cross. No one said a word, as they inched along, waiting for the border patrol to inspect the vehicle and their documents. As the border patrol approached, Professor Shelton spoke up with explicit instructions to Nick and Roslyn.

"Alerting the authorities would be the grandest miscalculation of your existence. Answer only what they ask you and nothing more," Professor Shelton warned.

Nick contemplated alerting the police at the border but quickly dismissed the idea. Not only would he have to go back to the police station but, he would have to involve his parents, and his quest of getting to Cuello would surely come to end. Roslyn was still silent. Nick was not sure if she was still traumatized from the morning events, or if she was angry, or both. When the finally were able to approach the checkpoint, the agents did not even care to look inside the rear part of the limousine. Professor Shelton must have seen the astonishment on Nick's face because he gave him an evil smirk along with a remark about it being their lucky day. From the border, it would take approximately two hours to reach Orange Walk. With nothing more to see and no desire to talk to his captors, Nick leaned his head on the car window and fell asleep.

Nick awoke to one of the men in the front seat informing Shelton that they arrived in Orange Walk.

"What time is it?" Mr. Ambrose asked Professor Shelton, groggily.

"Almost four." Professor Shelton answered, putting down the book he was reading.

Nick opened his eyes and surveyed his surroundings. Professor Shelton was still sitting on the back seat by the doors

195

while Mr. Ambrose moved to the passenger side bench and stretched out for a nap. Roslyn was still to his left on the driver side bench, her head resting on his left shoulder. Under different circumstances he might have put his arm around her, but this was not the time for romance. He turned his attention to the scenes outside the window.

The town of Orange Walk was not how Nick pictured it. For some reason, he thought that small towns in Belize would be nicer than the small towns in Mexico. This was not the case. The majority of the roads were a combination of dirt, gravel, and revolving dust clouds. Based on the numerous large trucks hauling loads of sugar cane, Nick deduced that the town only existed to cater to the nearby sugar cane processing plant. There were no quaint streets lined with houses or modern office parks. The buildings were wooden, old, and dilapidated, and livestock wandered the streets. The only semi-modern attribute was the clock tower at the center of town. The driver circled the town and turned down a couple of different streets, searching for a place to spend the night. After about ten minutes of driving around aimlessly, the car stopped in front of a street vendor. The man in the front passenger seat rolled down his window and spoke some Spanish to the vendor. The man gestured and indicated that they should go in the opposite direction. The driver followed the man's directions and finally stopped the car in front of La Casita Hotel.

Professor Shelton exited the vehicle while everyone else remained in the car. Roslyn was now awake but she still remained taciturn. Professor Shelton returned in a few minutes and requested everyone exit the car except the men in the front seat. He pulled three sets of keys from his pocket and distributed one set to the driver and one set to Mr. Ambrose. He kept the last set for himself. After addressing the driver in Spanish, he turned to Nick, Roslyn, and Mr. Ambrose.

"This way to our rooms," Professor Shelton said, turning back toward the hotel building. "I am sure you are all hungry. Once you are settled in your room, please feel free to order whatever you like from room service." Nick and Roslyn followed Professor Shelton with Mr. Ambrose close behind them.

"Hold on a minute. Let me check those backpacks," Professor Shelton said, yanking the bags from Nick and Roslyn's hands.

"What for?" Nick demanded.

"Just making sure you don't have anything you don't need," Professor Shelton smirked, while unzipping the bags. He searched both bags thoroughly and handed them back.

"Find anything?" Nick asked, snatching the bag back from him.

Professor Shelton ignored him and walked ahead of them toward the hotel.

Professor Shelton purchased three adjoining rooms. One room was for himself, one for Nick, Roslyn, and Mr. Ambrose, and one for the two thugs. All three rooms appeared to be identical and were far from glamorous. They were the run-of-the-mill hotel rooms. There were two double beds, a beat-up couch, and a repulsive bathroom.

Nick was already planning his escape. There was a window in the bathroom. He and Roslyn could easily fit through it. It was a viable escape route, depending on where Mr. Ambrose chose to sleep.

"This will be home-sweet-home until the morning," Professor Shelton said, lingering in the doorway of their room. "Walter, be sure to keep a close eye on these two. We would not want them escaping in the middle of the night. My two associates will be taking turns guarding the door from the outside."

"Of course," Mr. Ambrose replied.

Professor Shelton then reached behind him, withdrew his gun, and handed it to Mr. Ambrose. "This is to make sure that everyone behaves." Professor Shelton smirked.

Mr. Ambrose accepted the gun and jammed it in the front part of his pants. "I don't think we will have any problems," he said.

"Excellent. Please do not leave the hotel room. If you need anything, I will be in the room to your right and my associates will be in the room to your left. We are leaving here at 8 A.M. sharp for Belize City," Professor Shelton ordered, disappearing through the door on the right.

The next few hours were spent ordering and eating food, flipping through the five channels on the TV, and taking turns in the bathroom. While Nick was using the bathroom, he thoroughly inspected the window and peeked outside. They were on the fourth floor but there was a small ledge under the window that he hoped to utilize. Satisfied with his escape plan, he washed his hands and left the restroom. Mr. Ambrose took his turn in the bathroom next so Nick took the unsupervised moment to talk to Roslyn. It was the first opportunity he had to speak with her alone since she was kidnapped from the bodega.

"Roslyn, be ready to go tonight when Mr. Ambrose goes to sleep. I think we can escape out the bathroom window," Nick whispered.

"I will be ready, but what is this all about, Nick? How do you know these men? What do they want from us?" Roslyn demanded.

"Remember back on the beach when I told you about the two men I saw at my hotel pool? These are the two men. Mr. Ambrose is my history teacher. Professor Shelton is the Mayan expert. Mr. Ambrose gave me Professor Shelton's information, so I think they have been planning something from the beginning. This all revolves around the pictographs."

"I don't know what they are planning, but while we were tied up in the warehouse, I heard the two men talking about how their boss said to 'scare them good so they would trust him.' I don't think Professor Shelton is as innocent as he wants you to think. I think he orchestrated the entire fiasco," Roslyn said pointedly.

Nick was slightly dumbfounded. He knew Professor Shelton was far from innocent, but he was shocked that he would go to such tremendous lengths over some pictographs. Nick heard the toilet flush.

"They didn't hurt you, did they?" Nick asked.

"No. I was coming out of the bodega, and they grabbed me. They told me to be quiet if I wanted to live. After, they brought me to the warehouse. They brought you in about fifteen minutes later. Another thing I've been waiting to tell you is that your parents called my cell phone."

"What? When did they call?" Nick questioned.

"They called when I was in the bathroom at the bodega. I answered and spoke to your mom. I told her we were fine and you would call her back soon. She bombarded me with questions. Nick, she was very upset! I told her I didn't know anything, and that she should speak to you. Since then, she's called at least ten times, but I didn't answer."

"You still have your phone?"

"Yeah, I hid it in my shorts when they kidnapped me. It's on silent," Roslyn said.

"Nice! So, be ready tonight. I will signal you and we will sneak out through the bathroom window," Nick said, just before Mr. Ambrose emerged from the bathroom.

"What are you two discussing?" Mr. Ambrose snapped.

"The weather," Nick snapped back.

"Oh really? I hope you are a better meteorologist than you are a liar," Mr. Ambrose grunted, matching Nick's sarcasm.

Nick and Roslyn silenced their conversation and they all resumed watching television. It was almost 9:00 P.M when Mr. Ambrose moved the couch in front of the entry door and plopped himself down for the night. Nick and Roslyn each selected a bed and pretended to go to sleep. Mr. Ambrose attempted to turn the television off, but Roslyn requested he leave it on to help her fall asleep. Truthfully, she hoped it would muffle any sounds of their escape.

Mr. Ambrose started snoring about twenty minutes after they turned off the lights, but Nick wanted to wait until he was sure that Mr. Ambrose was in deep sleep. Lying in bed for an hour and trying to stay awake was very difficult. He had no sleep the night before and it seemed that tonight was not going to be restful, either. At 10:00 P.M., Nick decided it was time to make their escape. He crept out of his bed, grabbed his backpack, and stuffed pillows under his comforter to give the appearance that he was still asleep. He crouched down on the floor and crawled over to Roslyn's bed. He tugged on her comforter. She rolled over and slid stealthily out of the bed onto the floor next to him.

"Use the pillows to make it look like you are still in bed, then crawl over to the bathroom," Nick whispered to her.

Once in the bathroom, Nick could still hear Mr. Ambrose snoring loudly, like a flat-faced animal. He instructed Roslyn to keep an eye on Mr. Ambrose while he wrestled with the window. He was thankful that Roslyn requested to keep the television on because the squeaky window was louder than Mr. Ambrose's snores. Roslyn gave him the all-clear, and he pushed the window open. Nick climbed onto the toilet and leaned his head out of the window to get a better grasp of what lay below. There was another building attached to theirs with a lower roof at the end of the ledge. Hopefully, they could traverse the ledge to the roof and jump down to the alley. He stepped back to the floor and allowed Roslyn to go first. He instructed her to carefully walk along the ledge to the roof of the neighboring building and wait for him there. Roslyn acknowledged his instructions with a nod and quickly maneuvered through the window. Nick watched her slide along the ledge and successfully land on the lower roof. Nick followed in her footsteps and was so relieved to meet her on the roof that he hugged her for a few seconds before looking for a way to get down to the alley.

"What now?" Roslyn whispered, pulling away from him.

"Let's find a way down to the alley. Looks like we are still two stories up. We could jump, as a last resort, but we'd likely break a bone." Nick said. "Let's look around." After a few minutes of searching, Nick was overjoyed to find some rusty and dilapidated pegs jutting out of one side of the building. "Over here!" Nick called to Roslyn in a hushed voice. "I think this is supposed to be a ladder."

"Wow. That doesn't look safe at all." Roslyn frowned, peering over the edge of the roof.

"Well, it will have to work. It's better than jumping." Nick concluded.

Nick decided to go first. If the pegs gave way, he could catch Roslyn. He handed his backpack to Roslyn, dropped to his knees, and slid his foot down the wall until it caught the first peg. Thankfully, it seemed sturdy enough to hold him. Step by nerve-wracking step, he descended the side of the building, holding his breath each time he put shifted his weight. When his foot finally reached the cracked up pavement of the alley, he let out a huge sigh of relief. Roslyn tossed the backpacks down to him. He motioned for Roslyn to initiate her descent. Because she was shorter than Nick, she had difficulty reaching the first peg. He watched in horror as her foot slipped off the first and then the second pegs. Nick braced himself, even though he would not be able to properly break her fall. Fortunately, by sheer luck, she was able to catch the missed peg with her hand and dangled on the side of the building.

"Nick!" She pleaded, desperately. "My hands are slipping!"

"It's ok! Everything is going to be ok!" Nick stammered, trying to hide the fear in his voice. "There is a peg just a few inches to your right! All you have to do is reach your foot out!" After a short hesitation, she swung her foot out and made contact with the peg. Slowly, she made her way down the remaining pegs and joined him in the alley.

"I can't believe I'm alive!" Roslyn shrieked and collapsed into his arms. He could feel her shaking. "Those things look like they have been there since the Mayans," she whimpered, glancing up at the rusted pegs.

"For real," Nick said, trying to lighten the mood. "Are you hurt?"

As she pulled away from him, they both looked down to see numerous scrapes on her arms and legs.

"I got banged up, but I'll live," she said, still shaking.

"Can you walk?" Nick questioned, concerned.

"I'm fine!" She insisted. "Now let's get out of here before those creeps notice we are gone."

"Yes ma'am!" He exclaimed and comically saluted her. He took her hand and they ran into the night.

* * * *

It was exactly 10:23 P.M. when Professor Shelton heard the knock on the door that he was expecting. One of his associates informed him that Nick and Roslyn were on the run. He instructed him to follow them but to keep their distance. He knew Nick would escape. In fact, he would have been surprised, if Nick had not escaped. After settling everyone in the rooms, Professor Shelton informed his thugs of the plan to allow Nick to escape. He put Walter in Nick's room so he would believe he escaped undetected rather than having been set loose. He was disappointed that Nick did not believe his rescue attempt but was impressed at the same time. He thought Nick was a typical petulant teenager, but Nick's brains and determination surprised him more every moment. Unfortunately, Professor Shelton was unable to secure Nick's necklace from his possession. *He could not have left it back in Cozumel. It must be on his person somewhere,* he thought. All the same, Professor Shelton congratulated himself for a plan well-executed. Nick would now continue with his original plan without knowing that he was being followed. He smiled as he curled up in bed. *Tomorrow is going to be a day of truths,* he thought, and drifted off to sleep.

* * * *

Wandering through the streets of Belize at night was not something Nick anticipated. It would be one thing if he were by himself, but with Roslyn, things could get very dangerous very quickly. He wanted to get to the guesthouse he researched, but he was unsure of its location. Originally, he planned to ask for directions at the bus station in Orange Walk and take a taxi. Nick unfolded the map he printed, but only a few of the roads were marked with street signs. Whether it was just luck or Ixchel at work, they stumbled upon the bus station almost immediately. Nick felt the tension subside in him for a moment. If they had not found the bus station, Nick would have been forced to go into a local bar to ask for directions. Entering a bar in Belize at that hour would only insight trouble.

There were two taxis parked in front of the station. Nick and Roslyn quickly climbed into one of them and Nick requested the driver to drive to the guesthouse. After a ten-minute drive down a very dark, secluded road, they pulled up to Maria's Guesthouse. The room was even less inviting than the last. Two single beds and a nightstand were the only pieces of furniture in the tiny, tile-floored room. The price was economical, though, and they had a safe place to sleep. With everything that transpired within the last forty-eight hours, there was so much to discuss. However, the minute they climbed into their respective beds, they both fell fast asleep.

CHAPTER THIRTY-THREE

Walter awoke to the sounds of the housekeeping staff accessing a room across the hall. Two women discussed how the previous occupant could have made such a mess in one night while banging cabinets and slamming doors. He sat up on the couch and sleepily looked at his watch. It was 8:19 A.M. Heading to the bathroom, he switched off the television and glanced at the covered lumps in the beds. Something was amiss. He grabbed at what he thought was Nick Murphy's leg but found pillows. He grabbed at the other bed, guessing he would find the same. He uttered an obscenity as he abandoned his trip to the bathroom and ran toward Elliot's adjoining room door. "They've escaped!" Walter yelled, barging through the door. Elliot was sitting up in his bed sipping coffee and reading a local newspaper.

"Good morning to you, too," Elliot said, putting his paper down and placing the coffee mug on the nightstand.

Sure that Elliot did not hear him clearly, Walter repeated, "Nick and Roslyn have escaped!"

"I heard you the first time. How did this happen?" Elliot replied, nonchalantly.

Walter was dumbfounded by Elliot's laissez faire demeanor. "I'm not sure. The moment I noticed they were gone, I ran to inform you."

"I assure you that they have been gone for some time," Elliot said.

"I put the couch in front of the door just like you instructed! How did they get by me? Walter asked.

"They didn't get past you. They went out the window in the bathroom at ten o'clock last night. I assume you were asleep." Elliot responded.

Walter was confused. If Elliot already knew they escaped, why was he sipping his coffee and relaxing in bed like nothing happened?

205

"Yes, I guess I was asleep. Shouldn't we start searching for them?" Walter asked.

"You may search for them if you like, but I already know their exact location." Elliot replied.

"Where?" Walter asked, still confused.

"I knew Nick would escape. I was hoping he would escape. I requested an associate follow them to a guesthouse about ten minutes from here."

"So, are we going after them?" Walter pressed.

"Absolutely not. That would ruin everything."

"We're supposed to drive to Belize City today and explore the ruins," Walter reminded him.

"We still may be going to Belize City but that depends on Nick. He's smarter than I thought. He was never going to trust us. If he feels that he has gotten away then he will continue with his original plan. Wherever he goes, we will follow. Then, once I learn more about the true meaning of the pictographs and obtain the necklace, I won't need Nick anymore."

"Necklace? What necklace?" Walter asked.

"Don't worry about that now. Just be ready to go. We will be leaving shortly."

Walter stood in the doorway for a few minutes trying to comprehend exactly what Elliot was up to before returning to his room. He was livid that Elliot did not warn him about the escape or this mysterious necklace. *I don't appreciate being treated like a child! Elliot must not trust me or thinks I am inept. Either way, Elliot's supercilious attitude and his treatment are aggravating. If it were not for me, Elliot would be sitting in his office reading historical documents and living his boring life. Because of me, we are in South America searching for the greatest mythical city known to mankind, and I will see to it that Elliot acknowledges that fact,* Walter concluded.

* * * *

The copious amounts of sunshine beaming through the ramshackle curtains in their room made it impossible to sleep.

Nick rolled over to look at the clock on the nightstand that separated his bed from Roslyn's. It was 9:34 A.M. He looked over at Roslyn. "You awake?" he whispered, receiving no response. Nick decided to make his way to the communal bathroom. Nick got out of bed, tip toed to the door, and walked down the hall to the bathroom. He was thankful to find it was vacant. When he was finished, he returned to the room to find Roslyn sitting up in bed.

"Good morning," Nick said, shutting the door behind him.

"Good morning," Roslyn said, yawning.

"How did you sleep?" He asked.

"I slept like a rock, until I was nearly blinded by the sunlight," Roslyn said.

"Yeah! No kidding! It woke me up, too."

"So, what's the plan?" Roslyn said, rummaging through her backpack.

"As soon as possible, I want to get to Cuello. I'm sure Professor Shelton and Mr. Ambrose know we escaped by now. They are probably out combing the streets."

"That was a very scary situation. Do you think they would have hurt us?" Roslyn asked.

"I have no idea. I never would have imagined that my history teacher would go to such great lengths over some pictographs. I feel awful about dragging you into such a perilous ordeal. Please forgive me."

"Nick, I don't blame you! You couldn't have known those guys would go to such extremes," Roslyn assured him. "Do you think they know about Ixchel?"

"They obviously believe something extraordinary is going on. I doubt they will believe Ixchel is speaking to me. My own parents didn't believe me." Nick reflected.

"Speaking of your parents, you need to call them. I think they are really worried about you," Roslyn reminded him.

"Yeah, you're right. I'm just not sure what to tell them."

"Just call them," Roslyn persisted, handing him her phone. "If I'm not back in twenty minutes, come check on me." She handed her phone to him. Her long hair swayed as she shuffled off to the bathroom. Nick went to his backpack and retrieved a piece of paper with the hotel phone number. He dialed the number and entered the room number when prompted. After two rings, his mom answered.

"Hi, Mom." Nick said.

"Oh, my God, Nick! Are you okay?! Where are you?!" His mom shouted, frantically.

"I'm fine, Mom. We are in Belize." Nick replied.

"I know you are mad at us, but you shouldn't have left in the middle of the night! We love you very much and are looking out for your safety. When you didn't call us back, we became so worried! Dad left here this morning for Belize," his mom said, in tears.

"What? How is he going to get here?" Nick said, stunned.

"He hired a local guy to drive him down there in our rental car. We bought prepaid cell phones, so we can stay in touch. In hopes that you would call, I stayed here. Where are you? Dad is coming to get you."

"What?! I don't want him to do that! I'm fine. I'm in Belize to visit a place I believe was sacred to Ixchel. Nothing has changed!"

"You can't just go marching off into a foreign country without rhyme or reason! You are only fifteen years old! Besides, you have to be back for our flight on Sunday. Now, tell me where you are so I can tell your Dad where to get you!"

Nick dreaded the inevitable conversation. Today was Friday, and Nick was not sure what they would find at Cuello. He also doubted that whatever Ixchel had in store for them would be finished by Sunday. He understood his parents' concern but the night he left, he committed to Ixchel's cause and nothing would change his mind. Unfortunately, he knew that arguing with his mom was futile.

"I have your new cell numbers. Tomorrow, I'll call you. I love you. Bye," Nick said, abruptly ending the call. He set the phone to silent and placed it on the nightstand between the two beds, knowing full well it would ring and ring and ring. He ignored all six of his mom's subsequent calls while he waited for Roslyn to return from her shower. After a few minutes of waiting, Nick decided to visit the front desk to inquire about a taxi to Cuello. The clerk informed him that Cuello was about ten minutes away and offered to call a taxi for him. Nick accepted the offer but advised that he would not be ready to leave for another hour. The clerk said he would have the taxi waiting outside at 11:00 A.M.

Nick returned to the room, briefly spoke with Roslyn about the plans, and went to take a shower. While it had only been a little over forty-eight hours, Nick felt like he had not showered in weeks. The water was lukewarm and the pressure was horrible. It was wonderful and invigorating, though. The last few days were anything but dull and a relaxing shower was really what he needed. He reflected on the events that ensued and was happy that Roslyn agreed to this adventure. Obviously, he felt terrible about the kidnapping. However, now that it was behind them, he was getting excited about what they would find at Cuello. Ixchel was still echoing, "Go to him." Previously, she mentioned her "resting place." He hoped Cuello was the place she was referring to and that the "him" would be waiting for them.

While showering, he noticed that the faint birthmark on his left forearm looked different. Normally, it was barely noticeable, just a few shades darker than his skin. Now, it appeared slightly pink and irritated. Nick decided he must have scrapped it at some point during the escape the night before. He lathered it with extra soap and finished his shower.

Nick went back by the room to join Roslyn in the search for their next meal. The guesthouse breakfast left a lot to be desired. Nick had two, stale donuts, and Roslyn had some dry toast while sitting on a rusty, old bench outside the guesthouse. It was past 11:00 A.M. and there was no sign of the promised taxi.

"I guess taxis in Belize run on Mexican time," Roslyn commented with a smirk.

"Yeah, seems that way," Nick agreed.

"What do you think we will find at Cuello?" Roslyn asked.

"I'm hoping that the things Ixchel told me or something related to the pictographs will be there. Which reminds me, I completely forgot to tell you about what I realized back at the police station." He took the necklace out from his pocket and dangled it in the air. "What does this look like?"

"Ummm, a necklace?" Roslyn said, confused.

"Besides a necklace!" Nick urged.

"A rock on a string?" Roslyn said.

"No! A key! Don't you see? The pictograph says 'first key of salvation.' I think this necklace is a key!"

Excitedly, Roslyn grabbed the necklace from him. She spun it around a couple of times and examined it from multiple angles. "Wow! I think you're right! There are some distinct grooves. That's amazing!"

"Now, we just need to decipher 'isle of flame.'" Nick said. "I have to assume that it is referring to an island with flames or fire, but I don't think the island is Cozumel. You have any ideas?"

"No. Nothing comes to mind. There are lots of islands off of the coast of Mexico and Belize, though. Let's look at a map."

"Good thinking," Nick said as the taxi pulled up in front of them. They climbed in and simultaneously chimed, "Cuello!" Nick silently hoped that this leg of the journey would unveil the surmounting mysteries of the past few months.

* * * *

After finishing his routine morning coffee and newspaper browsing, Elliot prepared for his requested noon check-out. Nick and Roslyn were being followed so they could take their time. The last update from his associates indicated that Nick and Roslyn were heading west, instead of south toward Belize City. Elliot familiarized himself with all the Mayan sites in the area and when Nick mentioned exploring sites near Belize City, Elliot was skeptical. To his knowledge, there were no Mayan sites near Belize City. In fact, there were only four sites near Orange Walk and Belize City and all of them were in close proximity to Orange Walk. This was the primary reason that Elliot allowed the escape.

210

He believed that Nick planned to stay in Orange Walk and did not intend to go to Belize City. The only site west of Orange Walk was Cuello. Though a recent discovery, Cuello was considered to be the oldest site in Mayan history. The site was discovered in 1973 and not fully excavated until 2002. Elliot read about the findings in a scholarly journal a few years ago but lacked the time to evaluate the depths of what the researchers uncovered. One problem that Elliot saw with Cuello was that it was located on private property. Unlike a public site, permission from the landowner would be required for entry. Second, the site was probably not maintained. Elliot pondered what Nick expected to find at Cuello. Of all the Mayan sites in Central America, it was among the least popular. He read the pictographs numerous times and nothing indicated the significance of Cuello. There was mention of an altar but he was doubtful that Cuello was where they would find it.

Elliot changed out of his sleepwear and donned a pair of business slacks with a golf shirt and his holstered gun. He collected the few items he removed from his small suitcase and his thoughts turned to Walter. He seemed very unhappy about Elliot's exclusion of him. Elliot found this reaction to be utterly childish. Though, since Elliot viewed Walter as childish in general, the pouting came as no surprise. One could not expect much from a man who was never married and was still living at home with his mother. Having been married three times, Elliot was clearly not an expert on marriage, but he had not lived with his parents since he was eighteen. Elliot wondered if Walter ever had relations with a woman and shuddered at the thought. Even though his own relationships were unsuccessful, he still saw them as necessary life experiences.

"Walter, are you ready to go?" Elliot asked, knocking on the adjoining door.

"Sure," Walter replied from the other side.

Elliot reluctantly opened the door and entered Walter's room. He found him sitting on the sofa, with his packed duffle bag in his lap.

"I hope you are not still upset from this morning," Elliot said, knowing full well the answer. Walter remained silent. "If I can't rely on you to keep your emotions in check, then, I will continue without you. We came here to complete a mission. Need I remind you of the potential rewards that are at stake?" Elliot asked, annoyed. Sometimes Elliot felt like he was dealing with a petulant girlfriend instead of a grown male colleague. He had to restrain himself from slapping Walter square in the face and telling him to get it together.

"I just feel like you are treating me like a child and you don't trust me," Walter confessed.

"Put your feelings aside and let's focus on the task at hand. Trust is a non-issue. It's 11:30 A.M., and we need to be out of here by noon. Either you get it together and depart with us now, or we are leaving you behind," Elliot said pointedly. With that, he turned on his heels and left the room. He did not have time to sit around all day and play house with Walter. *What a pathetic excuse of a man*, he thought. Though he gave Walter an ultimatum, it was too late to cut him out. Walter was garrulous and he knew too much. Were he to continue excluding Walter, surely he would go home and get the media involved in an effort to fund some ridiculous expedition. *The last thing I need is media attention*, Elliot thought. *What if their entire pursuit was in vain? Instead of being a renowned and revered history professor, I will be a laughing-stock among my respected peers and colleagues. I will just have to put up with Walter's tantrums a little bit longer and try to appease him*, Elliot conceded.

CHAPTER THIRTY-FOUR

Nick and Roslyn were equally surprised, when the cab driver came to an abrupt stop in front of a large, modern building painted yellow and green featuring large white letters that read: CUELLO DISTILLERY, LIMITED. Slightly behind and to the right of that building was a tall, square building that reminded Nick of an oriental pagoda. *Is this the right place?* Nick thought. The driver's first language seemed to be Spanish, which was surprising because Belize is the only English speaking country in Central America. The native language of Kriol is also commonly spoken. Roslyn turned to Nick and informed him that they were, indeed, at the right place. The Cuello family owned the land where the ruins were discovered. That same land was home to the family's primary business, a rum distillery.

Nick paid and thanked the driver before exiting the vehicle. He and Roslyn walked up the driveway and through the chain-link gate to the building. More like a small warehouse than a retail store, the building had four loading docks facing the road. They knocked on a small window to the far right side of the building that resembled a drive-through window. Through the glass they could see a man sitting behind a desk having a conversation with another man standing in front of him. They ended their conversation and the man that was standing approached the window, sliding it open.

"Can I help you?" The man asked with a confused look.

"We are looking for the Mayan ruins that are supposed to be near here," Nick said. "Are we in the right place?"

"Oh! Yes! Of course! I'm sorry. I thought you were here for the distillery. Please come to the side of the building and follow the path between the rum still and the barn. Once you pass the barn, you will be at the animal pasture. Walk straight across the animal pasture and you will come to a wire fence with a small gate. The gate is the beginning of the area where the ruins are located."

"Ok. Thanks. Is there someone who can show us around?" Nick asked, just as the man was closing the window.

"There are guides you can hire back in town. I'm sorry but our business is the rum," the man said.

"Where do . . ." With that, he cut off Nick's question by firmly closing the window. "I guess we're on our own," Nick said to Roslyn.

"Guess so," Roslyn replied.

Following the man's instructions, Nick and Roslyn walked to the side of the building. They embarked down the dirt path running past the still and beyond to a typical barn. While walking past the barn and into the pasture, Nick felt that they were being watched. He could almost feel someone's eyes burning into the back of his head. He could not explain it, but he was sure. There were plenty of people around that most certainly noticed them walking through the pasture. Nick stopped dead in his tracks and did a swift about-face. He saw some workers by the still area they just passed, but they all appeared disinterested.

"What's wrong?" Roslyn asked.

"I feel like we are being watched," Nick said

"You don't think we were followed, do you?"

"No. For now, I think we are safe," Nick said, reassuringly. He took her hand and led them through the field. They walked for several more minutes, until they approached a wire fence with a gate. There was a sign on the gate that said: CUELLO RUINS, PRIVATE PROPERTY, NO TRESSPASING. Nick opened the gate, and they proceeded.

Unlike San Gervasio where the structures were clearly visible, Cuello presented more of a challenge. There were two, side-by-side, statuesque mounds. The immense amount of vegetation engulfing the structures made it difficult to tell exactly what they were observing. Beyond the mounds, myriad smaller structures littered the landscape, lacking the guide placards of San Gervasio. Overwhelmed, Nick wondered if they were in the right place. Walking around the mounds and through the brush, they saw remnants of a stairway exposed.

"I think these were pyramid structures," Nick speculated.

"Yeah, but this place is nothing like San Gervasio. If there is an altar here, I have no idea how we will find it. This place is not very organized," Roslyn said, sounding disappointed.

"I'm not sure what I expected from a place that is well over three-thousand-years old. The guy at the window mentioned that there are guides back in town. I think we may need to hire one. This place is overwhelming!" Nick admitted in exasperation.

"Has Ixchel told you anything else?" Roslyn inquired.

"No. Just the same 'Go to him' chant. I hope this is the right place. I'm worried we may not be where Ixchel intended."

"Oh, my! What happened to your arm?" Roslyn interrupted and turned his left arm over to expose his birthmark. In the shower, he noticed that it looked irritated. Now, it was bright red to the point that it was almost bloody and it itched.

"Wow! I'm not sure. It's my birthmark. I noticed something was wrong in the shower, but it didn't look that bad this morning. I think I scraped it during our escape yesterday." Nick said.

"It looks infected. I think you need an antiseptic. Maybe the distillery has a first aid kit we can use," Roslyn suggested.

"Let's walk around a bit more, and then, we can go back into town for some lunch and find a guide. I'll ask for a bandage when we leave." Nick said.

Nick was impressed by the amount of area the ruins covered. At some point, Cuello must have been a large, prominent settlement. In addition to the two at the entrance, there were remnants of at least two other pyramid structures. Finally, they came upon an area that looked like it was recently excavated. Nick wondered there were plans to excavate the area further. After spending another half-hour exploring the ruins, they exited the gate and walked back through the pasture. When they reached the barn, they saw a worker crouched over in one of the stables.

"Excuse me," Roslyn said. "We are sorry to bother you, but is there a first aid kit somewhere that we could use?"

The person working in the stables stood and turned to look at them. The young man removed his gloves and approached them with a warm smile. He probably was not much older than they were. He had red hair just like Nick, but longer, and blue eyes. As their eyes met, Nick was overcome with a very strange feeling. The young man standing before them looked familiar; so familiar, that Nick felt like he was looking in a mirror.

CHAPTER THIRTY-FIVE

Nick continued to stare in disbelief at the stable worker. Their height, build, skin tone, hair and eye color all were identical. There were clear differences in their facial features and hairstyle, but their resemblance was irrefutable. Nick overheard a muffled gasp from Roslyn as she clearly noticed their uncanny likeness. This had to be the person Ixchel wanted him to meet.

"Hi. I'm Nick, and this is my friend, Roslyn. We were just exploring the ruins," Nick explained, extending his hand for a handshake.

"Yes, I saw you in the field. I'm Amyas," he said, gripping Nick's hand. "You enjoyed the ruins?"

"We were a little disappointed that the site is so overgrown. We were having trouble identifying all the structures and their purposes. We are going back into town to try and find a guide."

"Not many people have interest in the ruins. You are students?" Amyas questioned. Nick noticed that English was probably not Amyas' first language.

"No. We are more interested in the Mayan history than the archeology," Roslyn answered.

"Yes, lots of history! I do not know if anyone in town knows of it," Amyas said.

"Really? Do you know anyone who does? We've had quite a journey getting here, and we'd like to make the best of the trip," Nick said.

Amyas looked at his watch and was silent for a moment. "I know of the Mayan history. Please join me for lunch, and after, I give you the tour."

"That would be fantastic!" Nick and Roslyn chimed, simultaneously.

"Ekselen! I will wash hands, and we go. There is a lady with her lunch cart in the parking lot. She is wife of one of the employees. Her food is very tasty. She makes most delicious tamales," Amyas said.

217

"Sounds wonderful." Nick said.

Amyas washed his hands at a nearby sink, then they all walked back to the parking lot together. The area was much more active than it was when they arrived. There were two semi-trucks at the loading docks and the man from the window was directing a forklift. At the far right end of the parking lot, Nick spotted the food cart parked under a large shade tree. They hurried to get in line.

"You both are from South America?" Amyas asked, walking toward the food cart.

"I live in the U.S. and Roslyn lives in Cozumel. I was born in Cozumel, though," Nick clarified. "Are you from Belize?"

"No. I have been in Belize for few years. I was born in Egypt," Amyas replied.

"Egypt? Wow! That's pretty far away. What brought you to Belize?" Nick asked.

Amyas was quiet for a moment, almost like he was thinking about how to answer the question. "Family," he answered, just as it was their turn to order. "Gloria! Meet Nick and Roslyn. They are here for the ruins, but first, I make them try your famous tamales. What are you serving?"

"Hello, Amyas. Very nice to meet you," Gloria said, smiling at Roslyn and Nick. "Today, we have chicken tamales, plantains, and rice."

"Bongou! Three orders please," Amyas said.

"Bongou?" Nick repeated. "Is that Kriol?" Nick asked, reaching for his wallet.

"Yes. Most people speak English in Belize, but many of my friends and co-workers speak Kriol," Amyas said. "Please put wallet away. Lunch is from me today."

Nick complied, and they took their food to a picnic table in a grassy area near the still. The food's aroma was exquisite. Normally, Nick would not consider eating from a street vendor in the United States. He only agreed because he did not want to be rude. Once he bit into the tamale, he was glad that he obliged.

The food was delicious. He was surprised that a little old lady and her meager food cart could produce such a culinary delight.

"You were saying that you have family here in Belize?" Roslyn said, resuming the conversation.

"Yes," Amyas hesitated. "You both come to Belize for vacation?"

"Actually, we just came to Belize to visit Cuello. I was on vacation in Cozumel when I met Roslyn," Nick said.

"Why Cuello? There are many Mayan sites than Cuello."

"Yes, but Cuello is the oldest," Nick said, reaching for a napkin.

"Oh! That has infection," Amyas exclaimed, staring at Nick's arm.

"Yeah, we were supposed to get a bandage from you. I guess I need to find some antiseptic to put on it," Nick said, turning his arm upward so he could examine the wound again.

While glancing at Nick's arm, Amyas' demeanor changed from nonchalant to stern. "How this happened?" He asked. A look of fear flashed in his eyes.

"I had a birthmark there, and I think I scraped it on something. I noticed it was red in the shower this morning. I'm sure it just needs some antibiotic cream and a bandage. Nothing to worry about," Nick replied. *Why was Amyas so concerned?*

"How many years do you have?" Amyas asked Nick, almost demanding.

"Is something wrong?" Roslyn asked.

"How many years?" Nick repeated, confused.

"Your age?" Amyas asked again, ignoring Roslyn.

"I'm fifteen. Why?" Nick said, annoyed.

"And your birth date?" Amyas questioned.

"November first," Nick said, getting concerned.

When Nick uttered his birthday, Amyas froze. He put down the fork he was eating with and folded his hands together like he was about to say a prayer. With his folded hands in front of his mouth, he starred at Nick. His eyes began to tear. "I cannot believe it. It is true," he whispered.

219

"Believe what?" Roslyn and Nick asked simultaneously.

Amyas unfolded his hands and extended his left arm onto the table with his forearm facing up. Nick and Roslyn both let out a quiet gasp when they saw the perfectly centered, large, brown mark.

"The mark on your arm will appear like mine in a week," he said. "When I arrived to Cuello, this infection happened to me. The mark was difficult to see, and then it became this. It is all her plan."

The mention of "her" was like a punch in the stomach and the feeling of winning the lottery at the same time. Nick was so caught off guard, he did not know what to say next. He felt that Amyas was the person he was supposed to meet at Cuello, but he was shocked that he had knowledge of Ixchel.

"What do you mean by 'her'?" Roslyn asked, skeptical digging deeper.

Amyas took a deep breath and reached in his pocket as he spoke. "You have come to Cuello for same reasons I did two years ago." He placed two very familiar items on the table, a piece of paper displaying pictographs and a hemp necklace with a large piece of quartz dangling from the center. "There are five of us. We share a birth date and a mother."

Nick was not sure why he was having such a hard time comprehending what Amyas was saying. It was the same story he attempted to convey to his parents a few days ago. Maybe it was just pure shock that everything he believed in his heart that seemed too incredible to conceive was now a reality. In this obscure little distillery in a small town in Belize, all of his struggles and confusion appeared to be validated.

"If we share a mother, than that would make us --" Nick said.

"Brothers," Amyas said. "I was a baby found at the Nile River in Cairo, Eygpt on 1st November, 1996. This pictograph and necklace were with me. By the river, my name, Ampheres, written with stones."

Nick and Roslyn were flabbergasted. The situation was so unbelievable that Nick almost expected someone to jump from hiding and declare the whole thing a practical joke. Nick reached into his pocket and retrieved the pictographs and his own necklace.

"Pleased to meet you, Ampheres. I was found on a beach in Cozumel, Mexico on November 1, 1996." Nick placed the pictographs and necklace onto the table. "A pictograph and necklace were the only things with me, also. Written in stones, on the beach, was my name, Nacxit."

CHAPTER THIRTY-SIX

It was almost 3:00 P.M. when the limousine pulled into the Cuello parking lot. Elliot was relieved that, despite his discontent, Walter continued on the journey rather than going home. After leaving the hotel, they stopped to eat at a local café. To Elliot, the food was insipid and the service was ridiculously slow, but Walter seemed to enjoy every last morsel. Elliot hoped that the meal would help take Walter's mind off their earlier disagreement. While at the café, Elliot's associate that was following Nick and Roslyn confirmed their arrival at Cuello. He reported that they had lunch with someone that works at the distillery. Elliot could not stop analyzing why Nick selected that site. *It has to be something about the age of the site*, Elliot thought. *Cuello was where the first evidence of Mayan civilization was discovered. Were they searching for another pictograph? Who did they have lunch with?* He was desperate to find out.

The driver parked the limo on a far side of the lot and Walter and Elliot stepped onto the gravel. They walked through the parking lot to a warehouse and stopped a man driving a forklift. He instructed them to follow a path that led behind the distillery and through a field. Obtaining access to the private property was much easier than he thought it would be.

"Nick and the girl are probably back at the ruins now. If they see us, they will run. I don't want to interrupt what they are doing. I just want to observe for a while before apprehending them," Elliot said to Walter. "Let's walk back there and see if there is someplace we can watch them from afar."

Walter nodded in agreement and they followed the path to the pasture. Instead of taking the direct route, they veered to the right, just in case Nick was headed in their direction. The sun was piercing in the open field.

"Did you bring water?" Walter wined. "I can't take much more of this heat."

222

"No," Elliot panted. "Let's just get to the ruins and we can sit in the shade for a moment."

By the time they reached the gate on the opposite side of the field, they were dripping in sweat. Elliot cursed for wearing long pants.

The site was overgrown and did not appear to be maintained. Normally, this would upset Elliot but the current state of disarray gave them adequate places to hide. Satisfied that Nick and the others were not nearby, they entered through the gate and took cover at the first structure in sight. The Belizean sun was unrelenting! From where they were crouching, there was no sign of Nick. After a brief rest in the shade, they vigilantly crept from structure to structure. They found Nick, Roslyn, and a third person standing in a large rectangular trench. *Probably an excavation trench*, Elliot thought. The unknown male was speaking while pointing down at the ground. However, nothing about Cuello was as enthralling as the striking resemblance between Nick and the young man standing next to him and Roslyn. Elliot and Walter watched and listened while Nick's doppelganger explained the mysteries of Cuello.

* * * *

Despite knowing their given names, Nick and Amyas agreed to continue to use their nicknames for simplicity. Nick never went by the name Nacxit, and Amyas adopted his nickname when he arrived in Belize. Using their adopted names just felt natural. After finishing their lunches, Amyas suggested they tour the ruins before he returned to work. Nick was in shock from the recent revelations. Not only did someone believe his story, but that believer was a brother he never knew existed. *The strangest part is that our birth stories are so similar*, thought Nick.

With Amyas guiding, Nick and Roslyn were able to see the Cuello ruins from a completely new prospective. Amyas knew everything there was to know about the structures and their original inhabitants. He was also well versed in the mythology and rumors that circulated about he site.

223

Nick was surprised to learn that the structures were not all erected in the same time frame. Cuello was a simple farming settlement representative of Mayan infrastructure prevalent from 2500 BC to 1250AD. The original Mayan population lived off of a diet that consisted of armadillo, wild dogs, and maize. They consumed a large amount of deer as well, indicating that they were skilled hunters. Their dwellings were not the complex pyramids that are commonly associated with the Mayans but, in contrast, modest earthen mounds. Despite their humble lifestyle, the original settlement has at least one sweat bath, a structure used for therapeutic and ritual purposes by the elite. As numerous as the Cuello structures that remain, are the swaths of graves. Amyas postulated that the position of the remains indicates victims of human sacrifice. Suddenly, he stopped walking.

"I think this was her," Amyas said, pointing down to the grave in front of them.

"By her, do you mean . . .Ixchel?" Nick asked, astonished. "How do you know?"

"I not know for sure, but I know this grave fits the legend."

"What legend?" Nick and Roslyn both asked at the same time.

Amyas looked at them, dumbfounded. "Ixchel's legend. You know, about how she is killed?"

"You mean the one about Ixchel making girls smarter than boys?" Roslyn asked, recalling Lucia's story.

Amyas choked back a laugh. "What? I never hear that one. How could you make it here and not know full story?"

"Just tell us," Nick said, almost demanding.

"Some time near 1200 BC, the Mayans become very knowledgeable society. They start building ceremony centers and pyramids. They think of maths, look at stars and make a calendar. For thousands years they only farmers, and then, they learn building and maths. How do you think this possible?" Amyas challenged.

"I don't know," Nick said, perplexed.

"The legend says Ixchel and her husband, Itzamna start of the Mayans. Itzamna and Ixchel teach the Mayans all they know about stars, building, writing, government, maths, and medicine. Temple art say Ixchel and Itzamna first come to Cozumel after their homeland suffered a great flood. Mayans call them 'White Man' and 'White Lady.' With all their knowledge, wisdom, and powers, Mayans believe them to be God of the Sun and the Moon."

"So how does that relate to Cuello and us?" Nick questioned.

"Ixchel very beautiful," Amyas continued. "She loyal to husband, but he become jealous. One day Itzamna become angry because he thinks Ixchel is not loyal, so he banish her from the city. Ixchel wandered the lands for long time. Then, she settles in small village and teaches the locals medicine skills. After some time pass, Itzamna feels bad and goes looking for Ixchel. When he find her, she refuse to go with him. Itzamna become very angry again and decide that Ixchel only belong to him and orders her to be killed."

"That's terrible," Roslyn commented.

"I think this small village, Cuello, was where Ixchel settled. The bath dates back to when Ixchel would have arrived. To have a bath in very small village at that time period is never spoke of, and I think it built for Ixchel," Amyas said.

"This is all so incredible!" Nick said, excitedly. "Cuello definitely has meaning to Ixchel. Otherwise, why would she have chosen to bring us here? I think your theory is correct."

"That not the ending of story," Amyas smirked. "When Itzamna marry Ixchel, he give her a very special gift. He give her a magic stone. Ixchel always wear the stone around her neck. After she is killed, the stone never seen again. The legend say before she die, she very angry so Ixchel promise all children born after her death not receive knowledge that make Mayans great. She say future will need this knowledge or perish."

"So, what was the knowledge?" Roslyn asked, with heightened curiosity.

225

"I do not know. No one does," Amyas replied. "I hoping you know. Only clues to follow are pictographs and necklaces."

Nick took out his pictographs and necklace from his pocket. "Do you think that the 'salvation' mentioned in the pictograph is referring to some kind of enlightenment?" Nick asked.

"Yes. Whatever Ixchel's curse, she requests us to remove it. I think the necklaces are to help us!"

Nick put his pictographs back into his pocket and focused his attention on his necklace. As he did many times before, he rotated it in the palm of his hand. "Let me see your necklace," Nick requested. Amyas obliged. With both stones in his hand, Nick, Roslyn, and Amyas watched with astonishment as the stones gave off a slight glow, and then connected together as if magnetized.

"Oh my!" Amyas exclaimed. "How you knew this?"

"I didn't!" Nick replied, just as shocked as Amyas was. "I just wanted to see if the stones were identical. I noticed the grooves on my necklace a few days ago and wanted to see if your stone had the same ones. Based on the pictographs and the grooves, I thought my necklace was a key." Nick was about to continue with his thoughts when a noise startled them. All three of them turned around abruptly and saw two people that Nick and Roslyn hoped they would never see again.

* * * *

Crouching down behind one of the crumbling structures, Elliot and Walter could not believe their eyes and ears. After seeing Nick standing next to a nearly identical twin, Elliot suspected something more was going on than a sightseeing adventure. His suspicions were founded. Apparently, Nick had a brother who had a second necklace and pictograph! If that was not enough, it seemed that there were, indeed, higher powers at work. The speculations of Nick's twin were plausible. Perhaps Ixchel was a supernatural force, Elliot pondered. When he saw the two stones glow and come together, he could not control himself any

226

longer. *I want those necklaces!* Elliot sprang up from his hiding place and stomped toward the three teenagers with Walter scurrying behind. Nick's facial expression went from confusion to shock to fear in a matter of seconds. He grabbed Roslyn's hand and took off in one direction while his twin bolted the other way.

"You go after him!" Elliot shouted at Walter, pointing in the twin's direction. "I'll get Nick and the girl!" Elliot said, breaking into a run.

Elliot's running days were few and far between. He was not as out of shape as Walter but he could stand to lose fifteen pounds. Repeatedly, he cursed for wearing pants and inappropriate shoes, as he chased after Nick and Roslyn. They were about fifty feet in front of him, when they made a sudden right turn into one of Cuello's main plazas. He turned the bend, but he already lost track of them. He let out a monstrous scream of frustration. Panting, Elliot bent over to catch his breath and surveyed his surroundings. The same crumbling and overgrown structures that he was praising earlier for providing excellent cover were now an impossible labyrinth, lending Nick and Roslyn a plethora of hiding places. After a few minutes of searching, he noticed a passageway that was partially obstructed by vegetation. The layer of dirt covering the stone floor directly in front of the doorway appeared to be disturbed. Elliot pushed the weeds aside and walked carefully through the doorway.

* * * *

Amyas watched from his hiding place as the larger man waddled around looking for him. Amyas thought about his beloved mentor and caretaker, Madu. *What would Madu do?* While most of their time was spent fishing on the river, occasionally, Madu would take Amyas into the desert and show him how to hunt small game, such as jackal and wild boar. In the desert, there were few places to hide, so it was important to learn how to remain absolutely still, using whatever cover was available. Madu even stressed the importance of controlled breathing so as not to scare the prey. The large man stumbled around the rocky

227

terrain, continuously wiping the sweat pouring off his head. With his knowledge of the ruins, plus all the hunting skills Madu taught him, Amyas could stay concealed for days, though that was not his intention. At least one of the men had a gun; Nick and Roslyn were being chased through an unfamiliar place and were in immediate danger. Amyas did not think it would be difficult to overpower the larger man, but if the other man showed up, or if they both decided to use their weapons, Amyas would be outnumbered. He deliberated for a few moments and formed a plan. Drawing from his hunting experience, Amyas decided to trap the large man, like he would trap a wild boar.

Like a man, boars can be very intelligent. Certain procedures have to be taken to capture one. First, boars despise the heat. The trap must be set in the shade. This large man did not appear comfortable in the heat, either. Second, boars require a specific kind of bait, usually dried corn. In this case, Amyas would substitute the corn for an irresistible bucket of water. Judging by the amount of sweat pouring from the man's body and his increased stumbling, he was likely becoming dehydrated and was desperate for water. Next, came was the actual trap. For boars, an enclosure would be needed, but for this prey, Amyas needed to gather some vines from some nearby brush and rig a snare.

Amyas threw a large stone to divert the man's focus. While the man was distracted, Amyas crept into some brush and grabbed plenty of vines. In ten minutes Amyas managed to braid the vines to an adequate length and durability for setting his trap. He made the appropriate-sized loop with a few strong knots, and the snare was complete. Now, he needed the bait. The ancient ruins were once a thriving village which was used centuries after the Mayans abandoned it. Amyas remembered that the village water well was still useable and had been upgraded. The large man stopped searching and leaned against a pillar, trying to catch his breath. The well was conveniently located a sizeable distance behind the man. Amyas carefully crept over to the pump. Thankfully, the bucket he left there months earlier for the horses was right beside it. He quickly filled it, knowing the noise would alert the man to his presence. He placed the bucket on a nearby shaded rock and placed the looped end of the snare inconspicuously in the dirt. He took the other end of the snare and hid behind another ruin. Like the crocodiles of the Nile, soundlessly, he watched, as his victim walked right into his trap.

* * * *

Elliot entered a dimly lit tunnel that appeared to go straight through the structure and back outside. A foul odor hovered around him. If Nick and Roslyn ran straight through, he would have seen them exit on the other side. Three doorways lined the tunnel, two on the right and one on the left. He started with the door on the left. He peeked inside the doorway and was overwhelmed by the increasing stench that greeted him by the entrance. Other than rat remains, the room was empty. He proceeded through a door on the opposite side of the tunnel. A little bigger than the room with the rat carcasses, this room had large stone tables or altars throughout the room. He walked the perimeter to make sure Nick and Roslyn were not crouched behind one of them. Just as he was exiting the altar room, he saw Nick and Roslyn dart from the room he had not yet searched and run down the hall leading outside. Elliot immediately broke into a sprint, chasing after them. Attempting to find another hiding place outside, Nick made a sharp turn toward one of the pyramids, but Roslyn tripped and tumbled to the ground. Before she could recover, Elliot stood over her. Hot and irritated from having to chase two kids through ankle-breaking terrain, he yanked her up from the ground by her hair and grabbed both of her arms tightly. Trying to resist and break free from his grasp, she clawed and twisted. Watching her flail reminded Elliot of a helpless animal trying to escape from the slaughter. Her petite stature was no match for his size and strength. She winced in pain as he tightened his grip on her arms.

"Alright, Nick!" Elliot announced. "If you ever want to see your pretty little girlfriend again, I suggest you come out from wherever you are hiding."

"Tell me what you want!" Nick shouted from behind one of the ruins.

Elliot tried to determine which direction his voice came from but he could not tell. "Just come out, and we will discuss it," Elliot said.

Nick emerged from behind some large boulders to their right side. "Let her go!" He shouted.

"It doesn't work that way, Nick. I'll be making the demands here. I have the girl and a gun," Elliot said. "You have something that I want."

"And what is that?" Nick questioned, viciously.

"I want those necklaces. Hand them over," Elliot said, smugly.

"What do you want with the necklaces?" Nick demanded.

"Those necklaces are far more important than you realize. They are the key to the most important discovery of all time," Elliot replied.

"If I refuse, you'll kill her?" Nick tested him.

Honestly, Elliot never really thought about what he would do if Nick refused because he knew Nick would choose to save the girl. He decided to help Nick along with his decision.

"Roslyn is no use to me dead. Let me remind you that I am a scholar and a businessman. I have an acquaintance in Mexico that runs a very lucrative export business and is able to pay law enforcement to leave him alone. He can do what he wants, when he wants. I know you are thinking about drugs. No, no, no. Nothing as plebian as that. His business is far more," Elliot paused and smiled before concluding, "exotic." Pays a hefty finder's fee, too. Especially for such a young and beautiful girl." He stroked Roslyn's silky hair, making her squirm even more.

"You keep your hands off of her!" Nick shouted, clearly infuriated.

"Please help me, Nick! Just give him what he wants! We'll make do without the necklaces," Roslyn pleaded.

Elliot watched Nick, as he considered the choices he had. After a few minutes, Elliot grew impatient.

"Now, Nick! Bring me the necklaces or Roslyn goes to the highest bidder," Elliot demanded, waiving his gun around.

Reluctantly, Nick began walking toward him. Elliot pointed his gun at him.

"That's it. Nice and slow," Elliot said as Nick closed the gap between them.

Elliot extended his hand and Nick let both necklaces fall into his palm.

"There. You got what you wanted. Now let her go!" Nick enjoined.

"Of course," Elliot said. "But not before I ensure you two will not cause me any trouble on my way out. Let's go! This way!" He barked, directing them with his gun.

Elliot found a thick vine, forced them into the room with the multiple altars, bound them back-to-back, and shoved them to the floor.

"Now, you two make yourself comfortable. I'm not sure how long it will take you to break out of those restraints. If you are lucky, maybe someone will find you. I would hate for you to end up like the rat in the next room." Elliot exited the ruin in maniacal laughter.

Whistling as he walked back into the sunlight, Elliot was pleased with himself. He wondered if Walter was as successful with Nick's look-a-like. In order to decide their next course of action, he needed to know everything that the kid knew. If the kid proved useful, he could always take him hostage and bring him along to fulfill his mission. Somehow, the necklaces and the kid were going to lead him to Atlantis. He smiled greedily.

The heat was intensifying as Elliot trudged back through the ruins toward the entrance. There was no sign of Walter. He detoured through a few of the structures before deciding to continue in his original direction. *Maybe Walter took the kid back to the limo and restrained him there,* he thought. As he approached the gate, he found the answer to Walter's whereabouts. The scene that was unfolding before him made his stomach churn. He froze. Just beyond the gate, walking through the pasture back toward the distillery, was a hand-cuffed Walter. He was battered, bruised, and covered in dirt. A large, Belizean authority in uniform was escorting him. It was not the police but probably private security. Before Elliot could think of the best way to flee before being detected, a male voice yelled out from behind him.

"Don't move!" The voice barked. Elliot complied. "Now, put your hands up and slowly turn around," he ordered.

Elliot heard the gun cock. Obediently, he turned around. With a gun pointed at Elliot's head in one hand, the guard patted him down with the other. The guard found his gun, un-holstered it and flung it into a nearby bush. He threw Elliot to the ground and dug the heel of his boot into Elliot's back. As Elliot lay face down in the dirt, the handcuffs clicked onto his wrists. He was not as upset as one would expect. He was tranquil, pensive even. He took comfort knowing that he was armed with the confirmations of the day. Once he convinced security to release him, he would be on his way to discovering the greatest city that ever existed!

CHAPTER THIRTY-SEVEN

Nick and Roslyn were bound for what seemed like a half hour before Amyas came to their rescue. They spent most of that time trying to break free from their restraints and yelling for help. Roslyn kept apologizing for tripping. Nick kept telling her not to blame herself. When Amyas appeared in the doorway, Nick was elated.

"You are okay?!" Amyas asked them, rushing to untie their restraints.

"So good to see you! Besides a few scrapes, we are fine." Nick replied. What happened? Did they escape?"

"No. I stop the large man and security helped with other man." Amyas smiled. "Guards keep them until police arrive."

"Oh. I didn't know there were security guards. How did you stop the large man?" Nick asked, perplexed.

"Yes. Cuello family very serious about security after cows were stolen and the distillery vandalized. They patrol all property, but ruins only at night. The large man chasing me and I hid. I was scared for you and Roslyn's safety, so I make trap. When large man was trapped, I went for security."

Now free from his restraints, Nick embraced Amyas as he said, "Thank you!"

"I can't believe you made a trap!" Roslyn exclaimed. "Thank you, Amyas," she said, giving him a hug.

Amyas, Nick, and Roslyn exited the ruins together and trudged back to the distillery. Nick was astonished that Amyas put his own safety aside to come to their aid without hesitation, despite their short acquaintance. Indeed, Amyas was a true friend and brother. However, Nick could not get the image of Roslyn and Amyas's embrace out of his head. Of course the hug was completely normal under the circumstances but Nick remained perturbed. He fought to push the image from his mind.

They all watched as the two men were put into police cars and driven off the property back toward town. Professor Shelton's driver started the limo and followed behind them. Usually, the security guards would have just escorted trespassers off of the property, but Professor Shelton was apprehended with a gun. The security guards called the police and the simple trespassing situation turned into a firearms charge. Professor Shelton violated the Belize firearm code because he did not have a permit for his weapon.

"What do you think is going to happen to your history teacher and that professor?" Roslyn asked.

"I hope they rot in a horrible prison, but I have a suspicion that we have not seen the last of them. The professor has many connections throughout Central America. I don't think it will be too difficult for him to connive his way out," Nick speculated.

"Those two are very strange," said a security guard, approaching Nick, Roslyn, and Amyas. "Before I forget, one of them had these necklaces on him." He pulled out the two necklaces that Professor Shelton stole. "Amyas, they look like the necklace you wear," the guard said, handing Amyas the necklaces.

"Yes! Kórék, my friend," Amyas said, extending his hand. "Di ou mési! One is for me, and the other one is for Nick, my brother," Amyas said, smiling at Nick and tossing him the necklace."

"Your brother?! I didn't know you had a brother here in Belize," the guard said enthusiastically. "I'm happy for you. Take care; time to get back to work." The guard shook the boys' hands, kissed Roslyn on her hand, and retreated behind the building.

"Where you sleeping tonight?" Amyas asked Nick.

"There is a guesthouse a few miles up the road. Maria's Guesthouse, I think it's called. We stayed there last night after a very long trip from Cozumel," Nick said.

"I want to hear it all. You and Roslyn stay here tonight? We have many things to discuss," Amyas said.

"Where do you mean? Here, at Cuello?" Nick asked, confused.

"Yes, my apartment above the warehouse. I have spare room for you both. Maybe better than where you already staying.

Here, you have better company and tomorrow is New Year's Eve! Cuello family has huge fireworks. Here is best place to see them," Amyas enticed.

Nick looked to Roslyn to see if she was comfortable with the idea. She grinned ear-to-ear. "Let's do it!"

"All settled," Amyas concluded, laughing. "Pleased to have you. I have little work for finishing. You can help for short hour and then we go for dinner?" Amyas suggested.

"We are happy to help," Nick said.

They spent the rest of the daylight hours helping Amyas with the miscellaneous tasks he neglected. Amyas cleaned out the stalls in the morning, so they helped him put down fresh hay. They brought all the cattle and horses into the barn from the pasture, fed and watered all the animals, and groomed the horses. Amyas completed the last few, small chores, he locked up the barn, and they headed back to the main warehouse.

They followed Amyas to the backside of the warehouse and up a metal staircase that led to a door with a window.

"Home sweet home," Amyas said, holding the door for them.

Nick and Roslyn entered the doorway and stopped to take in their surroundings. Nick was impressed. He expected something like a college dorm room or studio apartment. He was surprised to find that the apartment seemed to span at least half the warehouse. There was a large open area that housed a full kitchen, living room, and small dining table. There were three doors on one wall, which Nick assumed led to the bedrooms. Two large windows were on the other wall. The modern décor was warm and inviting. Nick walked over to the windows to enjoy the view.

"Wow." The word escaped Nick's mouth, involuntarily. Roslyn and Amyas joined him at the window.

"I see why you live where you work," Nick said to Amyas. The picturesque view of the fading sunset over the ruins left Nick in awe.

"So beautiful, right?" Amyas said.

"Amazing," Roslyn whispered.

"So, how did you end up here all the way from Eygpt? How did you know to come to Cuello?" Nick asked Amyas. Amyas left the window and walked to the refrigerator.

"Please have seat and we tell life stories," Amyas suggested. "Is pizza from freezer good dinner? I can put in oven right now."

Nick and Roslyn giggled that they were having frozen pizzas in the midst of their adventure and agreed. Amyas put the pizzas in the oven and joined them on the couch with some bottles of water.

"You know already, I was left on Nile riverbed outside of Cairo," Amyas began. "I was found by old fishing man named Madu. His wife died many years before and he was very lonely. He had two sons. One died when young, and the other I never know. Madu never speak to him. Madu raised me like his son. He live only on money from selling fish we caught. He was very, very poor. We live in one-room hut by the river. We spend every day on river to catch fish. We save some to eat and sell rest at market."

"You never attended school?" Roslyn asked.

"No. Never," Amyas replied. "Madu was excellent teacher. He teach me to read, write, and maths. He teach me English and Arabic, but here I learn Kriol and little Spanish. Almost everything in life, I learn as boy from him. He was best teacher and father to me," Amyas recollected. "He never asked nothing from no one but he give you his own shirt. He gave but never took. That I loved most about him."

"It must have been tough to leave him in Egypt," Nick commented.

"If he were living, I could not leave. When I was eight years, sickness came to Madu. That time he talked about finding me on river and gave to me the pictograph and necklace. He called that night 'night the moon gave back his son.' Madu fought sickness for two years. Then, one day he fall down returning from river. I help him back to cottage and into bed. A short time later he was gone," Amyas said in a very sad tone.

236

"I'm so sorry," Roslyn said. "I can't imagine how you must have felt losing the only person you had in the world."

"It was very hard, but Madu made me ready for the world. I keep on fishing for some time after Madu died. Then, the dreams come. I gave them no thought first, but then it was hard to get them from my head. I find an expert for history to help me with pictograph reading. I study everything I find about Isis, ancient Egypt, Ixchel and Mayas.

"Wait," Nick stopped him. "Isis? Who is Isis?"

Amyas looked at him, puzzled. "Isis. Child of Isis, from pictograph. Isis is mother."

CHAPTER THIRTY-EIGHT

Nick, Amyas, and Roslyn all sat in the apartment with looks of bewilderment. Nick never heard of the name Isis in his life. All of Amyas' references to "her and "she" were apparently not in regards to Ixchel, but someone named Isis. "You mean Ixchel is our mother." Nick replied, confused.

"Let me see your pictographs," Amyas requested, pulling out his own pictograph for comparison. Nick complied and they laid all three pieces of paper out onto the table in front of the couch.

"Oh my!" Amyas exclaimed, staring at the papers. The differences were blaringly obvious. Amyas's paper was written with completely different pictographs.

"That's really strange," Nick commented. "Are those hieroglyphics? Ixchel was Mayan. How would she even know hieroglyphics?"

Amyas was silent. He got up from the couch, walked over to the window and stared out at the ruins. "Nick, what your pictographs say?"

Nick took out the translation report and read it aloud. "Savior Child of Ixchel. Leader at the end of time brings first key of salvation. Great altar brings isle of flame for peace."

"Mine almost same," Amyas said, reading his translation aloud from memory. "Savior Child of Isis. Son of harmony holds key of salvation at world's end. Seek Ixchel for primary key. Keys bring peace on island of fire from great altar."

"You speak of postcard that come in your mail? What that saying?" Amyas asked.

Again reading from the translation report, Nick said, "Time is ending. Union of five at great alter will give rise to salvation."

"Nothing new," Amyas commented.

"So what does this all mean? Isis is your mother, and Ixchel is mine?" Nick asked.

Amyas was silent again, still focused on the view of the ruins, contemplating the newest revelations.

"Isis was Egyptian goddess. I start studies with her, but then dreams start. They say study Ixchel. I stop Isis studies and start on Ixchel. All studies, dreams and pictographs bring me to Cuello. I take jobs on fishing boats to travel across the ocean. I arrive in Cuello after my twelfth year. Journey taking one year. I not know what I find here or what Isis want. I make deal with Cuello family. I tell him I am orphan. I promise him I work for free to live here in Cuello. I not tell him my true age."

"It was kind of true," Roslyn smiled.

"First, Cuello family say no. Then, they say yes! No security guards here yet, so family happy to have person at distillery all times. No apartment here, so I live in barn. Not long and they make apartment for me, and in future, they rent for other people.

When I arriving here, my mark look like yours, and dreams start with Isis saying 'Wait for Him.' Sometimes, I yell at Isis with anger and ask 'Who is Him?' Many times she show a reflection in mirror, but I think it is me. Now, I know it is your reflection," Amyas said to Nick.

"Are we really dealing with two different goddesses?" Nick asked.

"Before I see your pictographs, I think yes. Now, I not know."

"If it isn't both of them, which one is orchestrating everything?" Nick questioned.

"I not know. You tell me," Amyas yielded. "Now, I think Ixchel important. Isis important later."

"How did you find out about Ixchel's legend?" Roslyn asked.

"Many times I speak with local people in town about Mayan stories. I found very old woman selling fruit from street cart. One day, I sit down with her and ask about Ixchel. She tell me the story and say she think Ixchel is buried at Cuello."

239

"Truly astonishing," Nick said. "I'm glad I'm not the only one who receives messages from ancient goddesses."

"Dreams come to you?" Amyas questioned.

"I've had dreams, but, literally, Ixchel speaks to me. She is a voice in my head," Nick confessed.

"Oh. That very strange," Amyas said. "What she says? She always talking to you?"

"It's definitely strange. I've gotten used to it, though. Since I was a child, I could hear her. Only recently did she start giving demands and constantly repeating herself. Before, she was more of a guidance counselor, giving advice when she felt I needed it."

"Be careful who you tell. Many will think you to be crazy," Amyas joked.

"Ha!" Nick and Roslyn both laughed at the same time.

"It's actually too late for that. My parents have already written me off as a mental patient," Nick sighed.

"Really? I want to hear your story. How did you come to Cuello?" Amyas asked.

Nick recounted his entire life story starting with the night on the beach. He told them about all the psychiatrist therapies and that started lying to his parents and telling them the voice was gone. He explained how his parents told him he was adopted but never told him the full story until a few months ago. He went on through the story about how Mr. Ambrose led him to the Professor Shelton. He continued with his arrival in Cozumel and meeting Roslyn, who helped him understand the meaning of the pictographs. Finally, he told Amyas about being kidnapped by Mr. Ambrose and Professor Shelton on the way to Cuello.

"Wow, you both travel on great journey from Cozumel," Amyas said. "The men are more dangerous than I think!"

"Yes. The professor is very egocentric and knows something that I haven't put together yet. He was desperate to get his hands on the necklaces. I think they may be the key referred to in the pictographs." Nick said.

"Yes." Amyas said. "I am surprised by connection they make like magnets. They hold importance."

"What do you think it all means?" Roslyn asked. "Are you guys supposed to save the world from something horrible?"

"The legend says Ixchel put curse on all humans, denying us a type of knowledge. I think we must discover the knowledge or suffer bad future." Amyas speculated. "I know we are five. The dreams showing five necklaces. I think end of time is 21st December 2012 because is when Mayan calendar is ending. The island of fire is maybe volcanic island. I not know location or why it holds importance. The great altar could be anywhere. Many alters all over the world." Amyas observed.

The pizza was ready. They spent the rest of the evening sharing their uniquely different lives. Nick was immensely impressed with how far Amyas traveled at such a young age. At only fifteen, he already experienced so much of the world. Nick wondered why Ixchel did not elect Amyas as the leader. He was confident and fearless. His altruistic nature was also admirable. Nick lived in Georgia his whole life. The recent trip to Cozumel and Belize was the only time he left the United States. Nick went to sleep reflecting on the day. He arrived at Cuello disappointed that the ruins were disorganized. On the other hand, he was going to sleep happy that for the time being, Professor Shelton and Mr. Ambrose were restrained. He met a humble and benevolent new friend, who just so happened to be his brother! Per her request, Nick found Ixchel's resting place. He realized that the constant echoing of 'Find Him' stopped, and Ixchel was silent. Peacefully, he closed his eyes and drifted to sleep thinking about how Ixchel once roamed the exact place he slept.

CHAPTER THIRTY-NINE

The next morning was the last day of 2011. It was almost ten o'clock, before Nick and Roslyn were awakened by a wonderful aroma. Amyas woke up early and made everyone a traditional Belizean breakfast. Consisting of scrambled eggs, refried beans, and johnnycakes, Nick did not know where to start! Similar to a biscuit, the johnnycakes were stuffed with ham and cheese. Over breakfast, they discussed the activities Amyas planned for the day. Being that it was Saturday and also a holiday, the distillery was closed. Amyas decided that after breakfast would be the ideal time for a private tour. Later in the afternoon, Amyas had plans to help set up for the evening festival and fireworks show. He asked Nick and Roslyn if they would assist him and they happily agreed.

Everyone finished their breakfast and headed down to the pagoda building, which Amyas confirmed was the still. He began the tour by describing the distillation process. At Cuello, they used a column still. Comprised of several layers, each layer separated the alcohol from a fermented molasses mixture obtained from sugar cane juice. When Nick asked where they got the sugar cane juice, he was surprised to learn that there was a sugar cane factory on the property. The factory received deliveries of raw sugar cane and processed it into molasses. Once distilled, the spirits were aged in large barrels for a minimum of a year. They entered the first floor of the warehouse and saw the rows upon rows of barrels. Each barrel was labeled with batch numbers and dates. The other side of the warehouse was devoted to bottling, packing, and shipping. Amyas showed them all of the varied rums and liquors that Cuello produced. In addition to countless types of rum, they also produced gin, brandy, and vodka. Nick and Roslyn were thoroughly impressed with the entire operation and grateful for the private tour.

After the tour, they returned to the apartment and gathered in the living room. Amyas got everyone a drink from the refrigerator and they discussed plans for the rest of the day.

"Festival start at five o'clock. We start set up at three," Amyas said. "Now, is close to noon, but I full from breakfast. We sit and talk here for some time, and then, we go for lunch in town?" Amyas suggested.

"Okay. That sounds good," Nick said. "I need to call my parents at some point and figure out what I should tell them."

"Why you not tell them truth?" Amyas said, concerned.

"I tried that already. It didn't go well. They did not accept the idea of me being a son of Ixchel and having to save the world," Nick said.

"Maybe, now they see you are serious, they listen more. If parents love you, they supporting you, crazy or no crazy," Amyas offered.

"I hope you are right. Speaking of decisions, what exactly have we decided about the future?"

"You asking is reminding me about dreams that come last night," Amyas said. "Isis saying we go find others."

"Really? Did she mention how? Are they here in Belize somewhere?" Nick rapidly questioned.

"I not know. Dreams give clues to start, but place is very far."

"Great," Nick said, sarcastically. "Is it somewhere in South America?"

"No. Not in South America."

"Is it Egypt?" Nick asked, astonished.

"Little close than Egypt," Amyas laughed. "But not much."

Nick looked at Roslyn. "What do you think?" He asked.

"I have no clue. Somewhere in Africa?" She laughed.

"No. I thinking we go to Greece," Amyas revealed.

"Greece?!" Nick gasped. "Why would she send us to Greece? I don't understand."

244

"I not know, too, but I not know about Belize, also," Amyas reminded them.

"True," Nick conceded, overwhelmed by the thought of traveling across the world.

"No worry," Amyas said, seeing Nick's tensed face. "We figure out. My dreams and your voices, we get where we need to go."

"Okay," Nick said, forcing a smile. "I'm going to call my parents now. Wish me luck."

"Good luck!" Roslyn and Amyas chimed in unison.

Nick retrieved the phone from Roslyn and excused himself into the bedroom. He sat down on the bed and dialed the hotel phone number. It rang once, and his mom answered.

"Hi, Mom," Nick said

"Nick! How are you?! You haven't been answering my calls! I'm so worried!"

"I'm doing fine, Mom. Roslyn and I reached our destination, and I have some very interesting things to tell you."

"Ok." His mom replied.

"Just promise me you will keep an open mind. Listen to everything I'm telling you, and please, do not yell," Nick requested.

"Oh, Nick. I always listen to you. Please go ahead. I promise."

Nick proceeded. He relayed the story from the night he left, to the kidnapping, to meeting Amyas, to the subsequent arrest of Professor Shelton and Mr. Ambrose. He told her about the legend of Ixchel and that the voice in his head was not a mental problem but Ixchel's guidance. He purposely left out the recent development about Isis and Greece. Besides the occasional acknowledgement that she was still on the line, she was silent, as promised.

"Are you finished?" She asked.

"Yes," he replied.

"It's obvious that you are passionate about this and rather than fight you on it and push you away, I want you to know that your father and I love you no matter what. You have to understand that we are worried about your safety and overall well-being. We love you so much Nick and we would be crushed if anything devastating ever happened to you. The day you told us about this whole Ixchel thing, we were shocked and in a state of disbelief. Now, you're telling me that you have a brother, possibly more, and you all are expected to save the world before some supposed Mayan doomsday. It's all very hard to swallow, Nick," his mom said, before falling silent.

"So, you still don't believe me?" Nick accused.

"I didn't say that," His mom shot back. "I wasn't finished."

"Okay. Sorry," Nick said, as she continued.

"Despite the outrageous nature of your claims, I believe you should be free to explore this to seek out the truth," she said.

Nick had to make sure he heard her right. "So, you are ok with me pursuing this? He asked.

"Yes. We want you to be a young man that is sure of his convictions. Also, I remembered Mrs. Alvarez."

"Mrs. Alvarez? Who is she?" Nick questioned.

"I don't know if you remember, but right before your birthday, something particularly strange happened at the hospital with one of the comatose patients."

"Oh! Yes, I remember. She grabbed you and said something to you, didn't she?" Nick asked.

"Right. She grabbed my arm, looked right at me and said, 'Listen to him. He is the leader. Do not doubt him. He holds the key. Trust in him.' I think someone was speaking to me through Mrs. Alvarez. Whoever it was, he or she knew I would not believe you."

Nick was speechless. Never in a million years did he expect the conversation with his mother to go so well. "I'm not sure what to say. This is so unexpected," Nick said as tears welled in his eyes. He did not want his mom to know he was crying but a wave of emotions washed over him and he struggled to keep his composure.

"You don't have to say anything," she said after a brief silence. "Dad is in Belize City. Are you near there?"

After a deep breath in a desperate attempt to cease the waterworks, Nick finally mustered a response. "I'm in a town called Orange Walk. It's north of Belize City. We are staying at a distillery outside of town called Cuello."

"Okay. Please call your father and let him know you are all right. He should be able to pick you up tonight and you guys can drive back tomorrow. I have to warn you that your father has not fully come to terms with allowing you to pursue this. I'm working on him, but it will take some time."

Deep in his heart, Nick knew that it was unlikely he would be driving back to Cozumel the next day. He did not want to start another argument with his mom, so he simply promised to call his father. They said their goodbyes, and Nick hung up the phone with mixed emotions. He was extremely happy that he did not have to fight with his mom about Ixchel. Although, when his parents realized that he did not intend to return to school in January, they would go ballistic. He called his dad and had a terse conversation with him about where he was and his arrival time. Nick did not want to think about how irate his dad was going to be when Nick refused to go with him. Roslyn and Amyas would have to help break the news to him.

Nick left the bedroom and returned to the living room. He handed Roslyn her phone and she left to call her mom. Amyas went to take a shower. Nick walked over to the large window and gazed out over the ruins. He tried to imagine what life would have been like in Ixchel's time. He thought about the legend that Amyas recounted to him and the pictographs. He thought about Professor Shelton and the lengths to which he went to get the necklace. *What did the professor know that would drive him to such measures?* When Nick was examining the stones at the ruins, they emitted a magnetic connection and a soft glow. *Could their stones be pieces of the infamous power stone? Was that the driving force behind Professor Shelton's relentless pursuit?*

"Okay. I'm glad I got that out of the way," Roslyn said, emerging from the bedroom.

"That was quick," Nick commented.

"Yeah, I purposely called her when she would be busy. That way I didn't have to get into any details about what I'm doing. Basically, I told her I was fine and I would see her soon," Roslyn said.

"I was just thinking about the necklaces and why Professor Shelton was so desperate to get them," Nick shared.

"I know. He was almost salivating, like an animal," Roslyn giggled.

"What if our necklaces are pieces of the power stone? Nick proposed.

"According to the pictographs, the necklaces are keys, right?"

"Maybe they are both. Maybe the power stone is the key to something," Nick replied.

"That's very likely," Roslyn affirmed. "The key to what?"

"I'm still working on that part. I think Professor Shelton may know," Nick said.

"We go to lunch?" Amyas said, joining them at the window.

"Yes. Do you have a car?" Nick asked.

"Yes, but no," Amyas replied. "Cuello family keeps old truck for employees to use for working. I use on weekends."

They all walked down to the parking lot and crammed into the small pick-up truck. Thankfully, the small café that Amyas selected was not far away. Not many places were open on the holiday, so Nick was happy that there was a suitable place to eat nearby. Specializing in empanadas, the café was tiny with only three tables inside. It reminded Nick of a Chinese take-out place back in The States. Nick and Amyas each ordered two beef empanadas and Roslyn ordered one with chicken. In addition, Amyas ordered a large plate of plantain chips for them to share. Nick insisted on paying. They selected the farthest table from the door and sat down to eat. Amyas was curious about life in

America, so they discussed various topics about the people, food, and celebrities. When they finished eating and laughing at the hilarity of some of the United States culture and customs, they crammed back into the truck and headed back to the distillery to help with the New Year's Eve festivities.

For the past few years, the Cuello family hosted a large, evening festival followed by a fireworks display at midnight to ring in the New Year. Nick, Amyas, and Roslyn spent the rest of the afternoon setting up pony rides, two bounce houses, horseshoes, piñatas, face painting, rum tasting for the adults, and a large variety of food. They arranged a place for the disc jockey and created a dance floor. While Nick and Amyas worked together on building the dance floor, Roslyn helped organize the food and game tables. Around five o'clock, Nick saw a familiar face weaving through the tables. He took a deep breath and exhaled. *Here we go*, Nick thought.

"Hey! Dad!" Nick called out to him. They made eye contact, and Nick waved him over to where they were working on the dance floor. His dad looked disheveled, tired, and haggard. Before Nick could say anything, his dad had his arms around him in a tight embrace.

"Don't ever do that to me again, you hear me?" His dad whispered, still embracing him and choking back tears.

The words hit Nick like a dagger thrust in his side. Nick felt guilty. He pulled away from his dad and muttered a heartfelt apology. He never saw his dad look so defeated. Nick watched his dad quickly wipe the tears from his face.

"Wow. Nice work," his dad said, gesturing at the stage and abruptly ending the awkward moment.

"Yep. We are building this for the New Year's celebration tonight. I want to introduce you to someone," Nick said, motioning to Amyas to join them. "This is Ampheres, but he goes by Amyas. He's my brother."

Nick watched his dad's facial expression go from astonishment to deep sadness as he extended his hand to Amyas.

"Pleasure to meet you, sir," Amyas said, shaking Anthony's hand.

"Likewise," his dad replied. "The resemblance is unbelievable. You two could be twins."

"I know," Nick said. "I still cannot believe that I have a brother!"

"Please excuse me," Amyas interrupted. "I have to help on the field. I be back soon."

"Sure. No problem." Anthony and Nick both replied.

"Did mom tell you everything?" Nick asked Anthony after Amyas walked away.

"She gave me a brief synopsis. On the way home, you can fill me in on the details. Where's Roslyn?" Anthony asked.

"She's helping with one of the food tents," Nick said.

"Ok well go ahead and wrap things up so we can head back to Cozumel," Anthony requested. "I'm hoping we can make it back before morning," Anthony said.

"What are you talking about? You want to go back now? No way!" Nick argued. "If I'd known you were going to come here and demand that I leave, I never would have told you where I was!"

"Nick, I understand that you're upset, but this is not the proper way to handle things! You are alone in a foreign country! Let's go back to Cozumel, catch our flight back to Atlanta, and figure out the next course of action together," Anthony offered.

"No! No! No! I'm finally beginning to make some sense out of what happened that night on the beach and all you want to do is selfishly drag me back to The States, just like you did fifteen years ago!" Nick protested.

Anthony sat down, put his head in his hands and was silent for a brief moment before calmly saying, "Okay. What do you suggest, Nick?"

"I just found out I have a brother! I'd like to spend some time with him. We've spent all afternoon preparing for the New Year's celebration. I'd like to stay and enjoy it. Roslyn and I are completely safe at Amyas' apartment for the night. How about we leave in the morning?" Nick suggested.

Anthony took a deep breath and exhaled forcefully. "All right, fine. I can agree to that on one condition. You keep this phone with you at all times, and you answer when we call you," Anthony said, handing him a cell phone.

"I can do that," Nick concurred.

"Great. I see you are enjoying yourself, so I won't interrupt your fun," his dad said. "I haven't been getting much sleep the last few nights, so I think I'll go find a hotel and get some rest. I'll see you in the morning."

"Okay. Are you sure you don't want to stay for the fireworks?" Nick offered.

"Thanks, but I don't think I will be able to stay awake," his dad admitted.

"All right, see you in the morning," Nick said.

Nick watched his dad walk back toward the parking lot. He was mad at himself for not telling his dad about his intentions to stay in Belize. After seeing him in such a beaten and battered state, he was not sure how to tell him. It would be like kicking a man when he was already down.

"He look very tired," Amyas said, walking up behind him.

"Yeah. It's my fault. I've put him through a lot in the past few days. I don't know how I'm going to tell them that I'm not coming home," Nick said.

"Why you tell them that?" Amyas asked.

"I thought we were going to Greece?" Nick replied.

"Yes, but I needing a week or two for leaving here and find way to travel. You go home and be with family. Maybe long time before you come back," Amyas said.

Thinking about what Amyas said helped relieve the burden that plagued Nick. There was no reason why he should not go home. If he went home for a few weeks, he could help his parents understand what he needed to do and why. Hopefully, he would have their blessings when he left next time.

"And Roslyn? She come with us?" Amyas asked.

Roslyn was a very important factor. *Would Roslyn come with them to Greece or anywhere else that Ixchel led them?* He could not imagine continuing without her. "I don't know. I guess I will have to ask her. Ultimately, it is her choice," Nick said.

Nick and Amyas finished the dance floor at six o'clock. Nick never worked with wood and tools to build something functional. Amyas was a natural. He was physically strong and adroit with his hands. With the last bit in order, the disc jockey started the music. The smell of barbeque filled the air, and people arrived from near and far. Amyas introduced Nick and Roslyn to a few members of the Cuello family and some of the employees that volunteered for the event.

They ate delectable barbeque pork, laughed with one another on the dance floor, and soared in the bounce house. The festival was one of the best events Nick ever attended, not so much because of the venue, but because he shared an uncanny connection with Roslyn and Amyas. Amyas was everything Nick could have asked for in a brother. He never complained and did not care what the rest of the world thought of him. His level-headed nature was a perfect compliment to Nick's explosive temperament. Nick thought about what his other siblings would be like. Maybe, he had sisters! Hopefully, they could all find the 'isle of flame' and save the world from whatever doom Ixchel had cast upon it. At that exact moment, Ixchel began echoing, "FIND THEM." Now having his own confirmation, Nick smiled and whispered, "I will."

In preparation for the fireworks show, Amyas brought a few blankets for them to spread out on the field. Without the blazing sun, the temperature dropped considerably. Wearing only some short shorts and a tank top, Roslyn wrapped her blanket around herself and sat next to Nick on his blanket. Amyas excused himself to continue with his volunteer duties.

"You're not going to stay and watch the show?" Nick asked, disappointed.

"Sorry, I volunteer to clean up weeks before. I not know I having guests. I try to catch big ending," Amyas said, walking away.

Nick turned his attention to Roslyn as the fireworks began rocketing off in front of them. Having her accompany him was the biggest comfort of all. *Would she be willing and able to continue on this adventure?* While he knew she needed to finish school and had a bright future ahead of her, he selfishly wanted her to stay with him. She believed in him when no one else did and her unending, positive attitude uplifted him. Although he only knew her for a few days, he felt a connection to her that could have spanned a lifetime. He never had a connection like that with anyone. He trusted her implicitly. He put his arm around her and pulled her closer. The multi-colored flashes of light lit up her face; she was so gorgeous! Sensing his stare, she turned, and their eyes locked. People around them started counting down to midnight. He gently replaced a stray hair that fell over her face. He could not fight the urge that came over him! He leaned forward, and her lips met his. Nick could have paused that moment and lived it over and over again. When they finally pulled away from one another, the grand finale of fireworks shot off like gunfire. There was only one thing left to say.

"Happy New Year," Roslyn said with a smile.

"Happy New Year," Nick said, smiling back.

TO BE CONTINUED. . .